THE CH[...]

"Has precious gifts for all of us."
—The Washington Times

"A heartwarming story." *—Publishers Weekly*

"Heart-tugging . . . an inspiring Christmas story."
—BookPage

THE CHRISTMAS BLESSING

"A story of tragedy and, of course, ultimate triumph."
—New York Daily News

"Sweet and emotional . . . A perfect holiday gift."
—BookReporter

Also by Donna VanLiere

The Christmas Star
The Christmas Town
The Christmas Light
Christmas Keepsakes
The Good Dream
The Christmas Note
The Christmas Journey
The Christmas Secret
Finding Grace
The Christmas Promise
The Angels of Morgan Hill
The Christmas Shoes
The Christmas Blessing
The Christmas Hope

A True Christmas

Two Books in One

The Christmas Note & The Christmas Town

Donna VanLiere

St. Martin's Paperbacks

Published in the United States by St. Martin's Paperbacks, an imprint of St. Martin's Publishing Group.

A TRUE CHRISTMAS: THE CHRISTMAS NOTE copyright © 2011 by Donna VanLiere and THE CHRISTMAS TOWN copyright © 2016 by Donna VanLiere.

For information, address St. Martin's Publishing Group, 120 Broadway, New York, NY 10271.

www.stmartins.com

ISBN: 978-1-250-25871-7

Our books may be purchased in bulk for promotional, educational, or business use. Please contact your local bookseller or the Macmillan Corporate and Premium Sales Department at 1-800-221-7945, ext. 5442, or by email at MacmillanSpecialMarkets@macmillan.com.

Printed in the United States of America

St. Martin's Paperbacks edition / November 2019

10 9 8 7 6 5 4 3 2 1

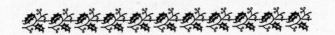

The
Christmas
Note

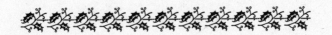

For my father, Archie,
who served in the navy

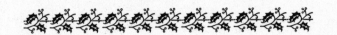

Acknowledgments

Special thanks to:

Troy, Gracie, Kate, and David for loving Christmas and keeping it crackling at our house.

Jen Gates and Esmond Harmsworth for your belief and passion.

Jen Enderlin, Matthew Baldacci, Michael Storrings, Rachel Ekstrom, and the St. Martin's sales staff for being outstanding in all that you do!

My longtime friend, Captain Bryan Ralls, United States Army, for guiding me through all things military. I appreciate your service to this country!

Mary Weekly for invaluable help and your gracious, sweet spirit.

Ann-Frances Barker, Carole Consiglio, Lynn Cook, Kim Cotton, Dawana Hunt, Dorothy Ley, Carri McPeek, Misty Riggs, Renee Sly, and Elizabeth Sweatt for your heart.

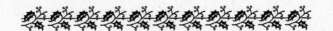

The family you come from isn't as important as the family you're going to have.
—RING LARDNER

One

All things must change to something new, to something strange.
—HENRY WADSWORTH LONGFELLOW

GRETCHEN
November 30

I look out the window and wait, wondering what will happen today. Life is weird. Just when I think I'm making heads or tails of it, when I'm getting used to today, along comes a new morning. The kids are running through the condo screaming, listening to their own voices echo off the naked walls. As Ethan checks out every closet and cupboard space, his face is fixed in a wide, transforming smile, just like his father's. Emma is like me, more cautious as she looks, envisioning where her things will go. Her eyes flame out fiery blue from her olive face as she swings her favorite stuffed animal, a bunny named Sugar, around her bedroom. When I was six, I had a stuffed dog named Henry. He's somewhere in the moving boxes. Ethan says that now that he's six he doesn't need a stuffed animal anymore, but I noticed he brought Friska the one-eared dog in the car with him. Seems all of us, no matter how old, have a hard time letting go sometimes.

The clouds look upset, puffing the sky up in a solid wall of gray. I hate moving when the trees have dropped their leaves. Everything's drab and bare and the feeling of emptiness chokes me. But that's today. Tomorrow will be different. "The truck is here!" I yell from the living-room window. My cell phone rings and I see that it's my mother. "It just pulled up," I say to her. "Bring your crew anytime."

I haven't lived near my mother since I left for college sixteen years ago, but Kyle and I always wanted to live closer to our parents; the trouble was always which one. Kyle's parents are still living in the small Oklahoma town where Kyle was raised, but I'd have to travel too far for work as a hygienist if we moved there. My parents are divorced. They decided when Jeff and I were teenagers that they couldn't live together anymore and it took me years to forgive them. I loved them always, but sometimes I couldn't stand to talk to either one of them because of what their decision did to our family. Dad lives in a town in Arizona near his children from his second failed marriage and enjoys his grandchildren there, but my mom doesn't live close to either Jeff or me. Not that she needed us; Miriam Lloyd-Davies stands just fine on her own, but I thought Emma and Ethan should be closer to her, three-blocks-away close, to be exact.

Ethan bolts past me and stands on the front stoop; it's not big enough to be called a porch. The builder planted some nondescript shrub in the spot by the door in a halfhearted attempt to make it feel homey. The garage door for the adjoining condo opens and I notice a car turning into the driveway. Ethan waves at the driver like he's been expecting her all day, and she pulls slowly up her drive, watching the moving men open the back of the truck, revealing all of our prized possessions. She stops her car and opens the door, staring at the movers without a hint of expression on her face. "Hi," I say, crossing my arms over my chest against the cold.

"We're moving in today," Ethan says, stepping closer to her. "What's your name?"

"Melissa." She's not heavy or thin, pretty or ugly. Her brown hair looks as if it was cut impatiently and her coat is too big for her. I can just see the tips of her fingers peeking from the sleeves.

"I'm Gretchen," I say, stepping next to Ethan. "My daughter Emma is in the house." She nods and I know she couldn't care less.

"Emma's eight," Ethan says. "Two years older than me. My dad was in the army. We have all sorts of medals that he won."

"Oh," Melissa says, dragging the *O* out and raising her shabby brown eyebrows and puckering her lips in that way people do when they don't approve of something: the soup, the new boyfriend, the performance of the car, the politician, or the way a new bra fits.

"All right," I say, turning Ethan toward the moving truck and away from Miss Personality. "Let's get busy." She doesn't offer to help or ask any questions of where we came from or how we ended up here, and from behind me I hear her garage door closing. I lead the men into the condo and point out where each box should go; in order to make today easier I had marked them with "kitchen," "bathroom," "bedroom 1," "bedroom 2," and "living room" as I packed up our former home.

Mom's car pulls in behind the truck, and she and her best friend Gloria step out. Mom is wearing black slacks and a soft green sweater. "Please tell me you're not unpacking boxes in angora, Mom," I say, walking toward the car. Ethan slams himself into her legs, and Gloria, although it's only been twelve weeks since I was here scoping out a place to live, greets me with one of her I-haven't-seen-you-in-twenty-years hugs. She's outfitted in what a normal person moves in: jeans and a lightweight cotton shirt.

"No matter what you're doing," Mom says, reaching for me, "there's never any reason to dress like a ruffian."

"That's what we are," Gloria says, looking at me. "Ruffians."

I'm still amazed that my mother and Gloria became best friends. Mom is all English with soft edges to her words and wardrobe, and Gloria is Georgia born and bred with fire in her soul and clothes from the thrift store, but they are good for each other. Gloria was widowed for more than a decade before marrying Marshall Wilson two years ago, but somehow she and Mom still find time to prowl around and work together at Glory's Place, Gloria's center for single moms and their children.

Another car comes to a stop behind Mom, and four young guys step to the curb. I greet each one of them but know I won't remember any of their names ten minutes from now. My mind is inside each of those boxes and where the contents of each one needs to go.

"Where'd you find all those guys?" I ask, watching them run up the ramp of the truck.

"Your mother still has a way with men," Mom says, kissing the top of Ethan's head.

Gloria laughs, walking to the house. "She put an ad in the university paper and said she'd pay for an hour's worth of work."

Mom trudges behind her, whispering through her teeth. "You make it sound so tawdry, Gloria!"

The truck is unloaded in less than ninety minutes with all the extra hands; the college guys even set up the beds for me and moved the furniture pieces into place. When they left at noon, they were carrying two pizzas Mom had ordered for them and a wad of cash. "I could have paid them, Mom," I say, unloading a box of glasses into a kitchen cupboard. If I can get the kitchen set up, the beds made, and some clothes put into drawers, I'll feel great about today.

"Nonsense. I told you. This was my gift. This," she says, from the living room, "and a new sofa."

I can't see her but imagine her face pinched up into slight disgust. "We don't need a new sofa. That one's comfortable."

"Well then, I'll help with schooling for Ethan and Emma."

"They'll go to the public school, Mom. Taxes pay for that." I can hear her sigh. "Hey, Mom! Why don't you load up the kids and go get lunch for all of us?" She's trying so hard to be positive and not step on my toes or say something that upsets the children that she's driving me crazy. I'm relieved to get her out of the house for a while.

"She's worried," Gloria says. "The explosion and—" She turns to look at me.

"I know," I say, not letting her finish. I'm worried, too, but not in the sick-to-my-stomach way. I'm cautious or anxious; I don't know. I stopped believing a long time ago that life fits together like a jigsaw puzzle. The pieces are there; it just takes years, a lifetime, or sometimes beyond that life before the pieces make sense. I'm just trying to put together the ones that fit today.

"For all her faults . . . and Lord knows she has a lot," Gloria says, making me smile, "deep down Miriam's a person."

I break down another box and lean against the counter. "I need to find a job, Gloria."

She stops and stands, grunting as she rises. "I know you do, babe, and I've already got the word out. The good news is people always need clean teeth."

"The bad news is the local dentists already have their hygienists. I'll have to look at the next town or two over."

Gloria wipes her forehead with her sleeve and small gray ringlets bob around her face. "Well, thankfully, people always get mad and quit or get fired or take a leave of absence to have a baby and then decide they don't want to work anymore. So let's hope somebody gets fired!"

I look around at everything that needs to be hooked together, like the TV and DVD player, the computer and printer, and all the stuff that goes with it to get Internet access. "I need my dad to come help me with a lot of this stuff that I don't know how to do."

Gloria snaps her head up to look at me. "When's the last time Miriam's seen him?"

"My college graduation."

She laughs and swipes the hair out of her eyes. "That'll be good!"

I hadn't really thought of Dad and Mom seeing each other again when we decided to move to Grandon, but Dad *will* come visit the kids and me and Mom and Dad will be forced to be civil or hostile to each other. I can't think about that right now. All I know is that I need my dad.

We work until seven and my body is sore. I can't imagine how Mom and Gloria feel. Gloria looks as if she walked through a car wash, and Mom's honey-colored bob has been shoved behind her ears and her black slacks are sagging, ready for the dry cleaner. The kitchen is organized and Mom has stocked our fridge and freezer with food for the upcoming week.

The kids give big hugs good-bye and I help them find their pajamas in the drawers. "How long do we have to share a room?" Ethan asks, picking out his red jammies with the big football on the front.

"Until I don't know," I say, looking through Emma's chest of drawers.

"This room is too crowded," Emma says, balling up her blue jeans.

"Don't wad those up, please. Lay them at the end of your bed so you can wear them tomorrow." I pull a purple nightie over Emma's head and pull her long hair out of the neck hole. "This room isn't too crowded. You've got room for your beds and you each have a chest of drawers."

"There's no room for us to play," Emma says.

I sit on the edge of her bed and look at them. I am exhausted. "I think we're all tired and it's easy to be negative when you're tired. Let's eat some soup and call it a day."

The kids are overtired and I calm Emma down from a long crying jag at dinner. "I miss Daddy," she says, tears streaking her face. I cry along with her and hold her on my lap while she finishes eating.

When I put them to bed I run my thumb back and forth over each of their foreheads, trying to rub out or smooth away any worrying thoughts that are crowding their minds. We say our prayers—well, I say them for the kids because I know they're beyond tired at this point—but I pray out loud as they snuggle deep into their blankets. I kiss them and fall into my own bed after a quick shower; it feels like my body is humming, still pulsing after a busy day. These plain-as-cracker walls are so empty. Kyle always helped hang pictures. If left to me, these walls might be for-ever barren. I see the box marked "bedroom photos" and sit on the edge of the bed, opening it. I remove the newspaper wrapped around two framed photos of Ethan and Emma's baby pictures and I set them on the dresser. I unwrap the next frame and it's a picture of Kyle and me at Niagara Falls before we had the kids. He's holding me from behind, resting his chin on my shoulder because I'm so short. I smile, look-ing at him: so handsome with his thick, brown hair and sharp green eyes. "I miss you," I say, tapping the picture.

Although it's late, I pick up my cell phone off the nightstand and check one final time for texts and e-mails. I need to call the phone company tomorrow to get us hooked up with Internet and phone service ASAP so I can set up the computer. I spend an hour writing an e-mail because it takes me forever on the tiny cell phone pad. The muffled sounds of yelling creep through my walls, and I set the phone on my nightstand, listening. Our neighbor is shouting, but it seems to be one-sided, into the phone no doubt. I lie down and stare up at the ceiling, holding Kyle's picture to my chest and waiting for her to hang up so I can get some sleep. The shouting ends and I wonder what she's doing over there now? Pacing the floor? Raiding the refrigerator? Breaking something? It's all part of the process. I know it well. Now I'm just tired and praying and thinking of Kyle and waiting for tomorrow.

Two

I've learned from experience that the greater part
of our happiness or misery depends on our disposi-
tions and not on our circumstances.
—MARTHA WASHINGTON

GRETCHEN

I wake up early and begin to unload boxes of clothes into my drawers and closet. I'll work in here as long as I can so I don't wake up the kids. They begin school on Monday and I want them to be rested. At eight o'clock, I'm inside my small bathroom organizing my cabinets when I hear the soft padding of feet across the carpeted floor. Emma stands in the doorway with Sugar in her arms and eyes half cracked from heavy sleep. Her hair is blond like mine and hangs at the side of her face, tangled like fishing line. "It smells kind of funny here," she says, stretching.

"That's a new smell," I say, emptying out the final

box and breaking it down. "New carpet, new glue, new paint."

"So it's fancy?" she says, trying to fit inside one of the bigger boxes.

I laugh and motion for her to get out of the box. I know full well the construction is cheap; the builder cut costs wherever he could, including these thin-as-cardboard cabinets, but it's home. When Kyle would come home after a tour of duty, he would hold his tongue when someone complained about their house, job, the heat, or potholes in the road. He would have just come from sleeping on a cot, brushing his teeth outside with sand beneath his feet, driving on a road that was more holes than dirt, with hidden bombs along the way, and holding his position in one-hundred-plus degrees of heat, wearing long sleeves and carrying a rifle. He didn't have much tolerance for someone when they complained that their coffee was cold.

"Sure! Let's think of it as fancy," I say. Emma leads us into the hallway, and I can see Ethan digging through a box in their bedroom.

"Whatcha looking for?" I ask, leaning my head inside the door.

"My connecting pieces I build stuff out of." He's so much like his dad. He loves to put things together: a model airplane, a Radio Flyer wagon, a block castle just for the challenge. He's in heaven if something can be dismantled and then put back together again, whereas I cringe at the thought of Lincoln Logs or LEGOs.

"Just empty out that box and I'll take it out to the curb along with these others, and then we'll eat breakfast." Ethan brings the box to me as I'm coming back in for another load. A gust of early winter wind blows in, and I hurry as I pick up several more of the boxes that I've flattened. Ethan grabs a few and stumbles out the door behind me. Emma chooses to watch us from the warmth of the entryway. My pajama bottoms and T-shirt are too flimsy for this wind and I hurry, stacking the boxes at the curb. A rolling sound makes me look up and I see our neighbor, Mary Sunshine, pulling her garbage can down the driveway. I attempt a half smile, embarrassed to be out here in my pajamas, and if she smiles, I don't recognize it. Perhaps people smile differently here; maybe their mouths look frozen in a perpetual scowl.

"We have garbage, too," Ethan says, dumping his boxes onto the stack. She bobs her head in what I guess is a nod. "Bet we'll end up having more garbage than anybody on the whole street today." The revelation sinks into the competitive part of his brain and he glances down the street. "Yep. Just look. Nobody has higher garbage."

"And we're not even done bringing it all out yet," I say, more to Ethan than to her, whatever she said her name was.

"Are you going to work?" Ethan asks.

"Yes," she says, slapping the garbage handle grime off her hands and walking up her driveway.

"My dad had a bad accident on his job. A bomb went off and he—"

I don't want to talk about this so early in the morning. I fold my arms against the winds and take quick steps toward Ethan. "Let's go get some more boxes and see how high that stack can get." I look at her. "Have a great day at work." The look on her face is a smile, frown, grimace—what in the world do you call that kind of expression? Ethan and I finish hauling out the boxes, and he gives me a high five when we discover that yes, we do have more garbage than anyone else on the street.

Emma is tilted back on her heels, holding on to the doors of an open cabinet, and I imagine the entire cupboard coming loose from the wall. "Don't swing on the cabinets, Em."

"Why not? I'm hungry."

I open one of the bottom cabinets, revealing the few boxes of cereal we have: Cheerios, Rice Krispies, and Frosted Mini-Wheats. "Ta-da!"

"Where's the fun cereal?"

"This is it," I say, reaching for the Rice Krispies. "Ta-da always means *whoo hoo!* Look at this! Nothing says fun like snap, crackle, and pop." I pick up the boxes of cereal and give each of them a shake. There's hardly any Frosted Mini-Wheats left, and I wonder why I packed the box in the first place. Kyle wouldn't have packed it. Army men pride themselves on their packing skills! "Kyle, you need to go through these cupboards," I say to myself, throwing away the empty box. I'm feeling sorry for myself again and I hear Kyle's voice telling me to push myself up out of the rubble.

He grew up in Oklahoma, and when he was ten a tornado swept through his small town in the early morning hours. Kyle and his parents and brother leaped from their beds, his mother in her nightgown and the men of the house in their underwear, and ran to the cellar as the twister tore off the roof of their home. When the winds died down and his father cracked open the cellar door, the sky was jagged with splintered trees and their truck was missing along with the living room and Kyle's bedroom. The henhouse was razed and the chickens stripped of feathers and lying dead, but the barn was standing so they walked toward it to check on the horses. Kyle heard a noise, something like scratching, and stepped toward the boards of the henhouse. He yelled for his family, and each of them stepped closer, listening for the sound. As the sun rose, the noise became more frantic and they watched as the featherless head of the rooster pushed his way through the boards. He lifted his naked body from the rubble and stumbled to the top of the boards, crowing with what strength he had left.

Kyle told that story several times in our marriage. "He had to crow," Kyle always said. "It was in his DNA."

One night during my senior year in high school, I was driving home from a waitressing job and was pulled over for speeding. The officer flashed his light in my face and the streetlight illuminated him. I tried not to smile but couldn't help it. He took my license and car registration to his vehicle and was gone for just a minute, not long enough to issue a ticket, when he walked back to the car and let me go. "Slow down, Gretchen," he said, making me smile.

Days later I was at a pancake house eating with a friend when a yummy-looking guy walked in wearing jeans and a short-sleeved shirt, and I thought he looked familiar but couldn't place him. He walked to the table, and when I looked up at him, just as I'd done out my car window a few nights earlier, I recognized him. "Taking it slower?" he asked. I laughed and felt so high schoolish but realized a guy his age (he looked twenty-something) wouldn't be interested in me. He sat with us and we all talked for two hours, but I still didn't think he liked me. He was seven years older than me, five years with the police department, and he'd just joined the army. Somehow, I knew that was in his DNA. He was born to help and protect. You just know that about some people. I never saw myself as an army wife, but when Kyle and I started dating, I suddenly couldn't see myself being anything else. We married after I graduated from college. My parents were adamant that I wait. I think they fully expected Kyle to lose interest, but he didn't. Kyle had been in the army four years when we married; he wore his dress blues at our wedding and we began hanging a sign outside the door of our home at each military post that said, HOME IS WHEREVER THE ARMY SENDS YOU! The sign is hanging in my new kitchen now. I just couldn't get rid of it.

Ethan and Em are chattering away over their bowls when I hear a knock at the door. A sweatshirt is crumpled on the sofa, and I slip it over my head before reaching for the door. A man's bald head is all I can see through the peephole and I open the door. He's fiftyish, I guess, with dark bags under his eyes and heavy lines on each side of his mouth. He looks cold and aggravated. "Hi," I say, making it sound more like a question than a greeting.

"Sorry to bother you so early," he says, pulling his coat collar up to cover his neck. "I'm looking for Ramona's daughter."

"Nope. I'm Miriam's daughter," I say, smiling.

His chest deflates, pushing a huge gust of air out of his mouth. "Do you know Ramona?"

"I've never heard of her. I'm brand-new here as of yesterday."

He looks behind him, at what I don't know. "Great!" He scratches his head and sighs again.

"I need to find Ramona's daughter. Another tenant in my building said she lives on this street, but he couldn't remember her name and I can't either."

I cross my arms to keep warm. "I have no idea. Did he say if she's married or has children? That could narrow it down."

"She's single."

"I think the woman who lives on the other side of me is single, but I'm not sure. I can't even remember her name."

"Her name's Melissa," Ethan says, wedging in next to me.

"That's her!" the man says. "Ramona's daughter is Melissa."

"Then that's her place," I say. He turns to step off the porch. "She's not home right now. I saw her leave a few minutes ago."

If it's even possible, his chest shrinks even more. "Do you know how to contact her?" I shake my head. "Okay, this has been a"—he sees Ethan and stops— "rotten morning. When she gets home, would you tell her that her mom died and I need her to come clean out her mom's place?"

Ethan snaps his head to look up at me, and I feel letters burbling up, but none of them are coming out as words. "What? No! I only met her for the first time yesterday. Don't the police make that sort of notification?"

"The police came late last night when Ramona wouldn't answer her phone. The old dame's hand turned the stereo up blasting loud when she keeled over and died. Had every tenant calling me to take care of it. She wouldn't answer the phone or the door so the police went in and found her."

"So why can't they notify her daughter?"

He popped a cigarette into his mouth like it was an M&M. "I told you," he says, lighting the cigarette and puffing. "Nobody knows Ramona's kid. Hard to contact next of kin when the dead woman never said she had kin. If I hadn't heard them screaming at each other a few times I wouldn't even know it." He turns to leave. "Tell her I'm giving her one week to go through her mother's things and then I'm dumping all of it."

"I'm not going to tell her," I say to his back.

He turns to look at me. "Tell her I'm being nice. I could just rummage through that junk and keep what I like."

I nudge Ethan to get back into the house and I stand out on the porch, closing the door. "I can't tell her that. You need to leave a note on her door."

He won't turn back to look at me. "I've been out here for an hour knocking on doors." He tosses his hand in the air. "I'm done."

Ethan is staring up at me when I step back inside. "Who was that guy, Mom?"

"A landlord," I say, busying myself by putting away the cereal.

He picks up his football and tosses it from hand to hand. "Who died?"

Emma looks up from her soggy bowl of cereal, frightened. "Somebody died? Who died?"

I cross to her and kiss her head. "Our neighbor's mom."

"Oh." Ethan tosses the ball up and down now, and I try to ignore it as I go back to work in the kitchen. I'm not in the mood for the whole football-in-the-house argument. "You don't like her very much, do you, Mom?"

Great! Caught not liking someone by my own child! I stop my work to look at him. "What makes you say that? She seems fine."

He tosses that confounded ball higher into the air. "You don't talk as much to her as you do other people."

"I just don't know her very well yet."

The ball goes up again. "You talk long with other strangers."

"Please take that ball out of the house, Ethan." He tosses it back and forth all the way to the front door before tossing it out into the yard.

All the big kitchen items have a cupboard to call their own, but the counter space is littered with things that will eventually wind up crammed into a drawer or shoe box: rubber bands, pens, old address book, two small picture frames, sticky pads, cow-shaped eraser, handful of magnets, Magic Markers, a whistle, two batteries, a tube of ChapStick, a purse-size package of tissues, a ruler, and a stack of cards we received after Kyle's accident. I fan them out in my hand, not knowing what to do with them. I see a small, empty box and stack them in a corner of it, pushing the rest of the stuff from the counter on top of them. I sigh, setting the box on the table. There's so much to do, but I know Kyle's accident and the move have been a lot to take in for the kids. I wander through the hall to their bedroom and peek inside. Emma is using one of her baby blankets to make a bed for Sugar, and Ethan is pulling children's books out of a box.

Whenever Kyle was home the kids would beg him to read to them every night at bedtime. I always read using inflection and different, even if sometimes weak, voices, but Kyle had a certain flair when he "read" *Charlotte's Web* or *Goldilocks and the Three Bears*. In Kyle's translation, Charlotte the spider spun the words *armpit, nose hair,* and *burp* into her web. Ethan and Emma especially liked *burp* because Wilbur the pig then walked through the barnyard belching. For *Goldilocks and the Three Bears*, I could hear Ethan's high-pitched belly laugh as Kyle read, "Then Mama Bear said, 'Somebody's been pooting on my chair,' and then little Baby Bear said, 'Somebody's been pooting on my chair and blew a hole right through it!'" It didn't matter how many times Kyle read that story, the kids would howl like it was a brand-new telling. I watch the kids and pray. I've never prayed so much in my life. I wash the dishes and pray. I fold laundry and pray. I shower and cook and scrub the floor and pray. It keeps me tethered, grounded, buoyed, or from going insane.

I hang on to their door as I stick my head into their room. "Hey! Do either of you know where the box of games is? We could play something."

"Right now?" Emma asks, pushing Sugar's head hard into the blanket.

"Sure."

"I thought you were busy," Ethan says.

I step into their room. "Why don't we get the books and games and everything put away in your room and then it will be totally done! That should only take a few minutes. Then let's play a game." I feel the crush of things to do, but know I need to spend time with them.

We finish their room and we celebrate by playing two games of Candy Land and then one of Sorry! and then Battleship with Emma before Mom picks them up to take to her house to eat lunch and spend the rest of the day. Hopefully, by the time they make it home tomorrow I'll have most everything in order. "Are you sure you don't want me to stay and help you?" Mom asks.

"You are helping by giving the kids a break from tripping over of all this stuff," I say, waving my arm into the living room. "Hopefully, I'll find a spot for all of it." I kiss Emma and Ethan and resist asking them to stay with me so I can see them, touch them, and hear their voices. My throat tightens as I wave to them from the front door.

I haul out the final empty boxes from the kids' room and feel good that their bedroom is organized. I make a quick trip to the school to take the kid's shot records and fill out the rest of the enrollment papers and then spend the rest of the day working in my bedroom and organizing the linen and laundry closets. I walk through the condo and know I need to put up some Christmas decorations soon. The sight of lights, evergreen swags, stars, bulbs, the tree, and nativity will make all of us feel better. The first Christmas after my parents divorced I hated putting up the tree and dragging out the nativity, but once they were up, my feelings changed. I search for the boxes filled with all things Christmas so the kids and I can start decorating in the next few days.

The stack of flattened boxes is growing at the front door, and I start to take them out when I see the neighbor's car pull into her driveway, so I close the door before she sees me. Through the window sheers I can see her walking to her mailbox. I set the boxes down. I'm not going to the curb now. If I see her, I'll wonder if anyone has told her about her mother and then be plagued with guilt that I didn't tell her. I shake my head. What a preposterous situation!

This place is too quiet without the kids. I fall into bed and dial Mom's number to say good night to them but discover they're too busy to come to the phone. "They're distracted," Mom says. I smile. She's always been very distracting, and right now that's a good thing. I hang up and stare at the ceiling, thinking of my neighbor. Kyle would have told her her mother had died. Even if his world had collapsed in on him, Kyle would have pushed his way up through the rubble and done what he was supposed to do.

"Someone has to tell her," he'd say. "If the landlord is a coward, then someone needs to step up." Kyle would get out of bed at this very moment and go knock on her door, but I turn the light off and pull the blankets up to my neck.

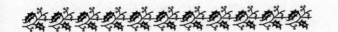

Three

It is dismal coming home, when there is nobody to welcome one!

—Ann Radcliffe

MELISSA

I never knew my father, but when one of Ramona's men traipsed through our apartment late at night, I'd tiptoe out to the living room, kitchen, or her bedroom where I could see them drinking, smoking, or dancing while each of them held on to a bottle of Jack. I'd imagine which, if any, of those nightly visitors was my father. I asked Ramona one time who my father was, and she slapped me across the face. "It's none of your business," she said, her rancid liquor breath burning my eyes. "The only thing he ever did was plant the seed of a fool." It took me years to realize that seed was me. She has gone out of her way to let people know she doesn't have children, least of all a daughter, the most worthless of seed. The fact that I live less than three miles from Ramona is ironic to the point of being absurd. We lived in Florida for as long as I could remember. Ten years ago, out of loyalty or extreme stupidity, I followed her here to Grandon, where the winds are as cold in winter as Ramona was on any given day. We talk when she needs money, and the sick, crippled part of me actually wants to help her, while the other part loathes her whiskey voice and the sight of her swollen, overliquored face. She called two nights ago and asked for a hundred bucks to "see her through," calling me "baby girl" and "lamby," the names she's always called me after she's cussed me or slapped my face until it welted in stripes. "Don't leave me, baby girl," she'd say when I was a child. "What would Mommy do without her lamby?" When I refused to give the money to her two nights ago, she called me every four-letter word in the book and I reciprocated. I learned how to do combat with her years ago.

This condo is as barren as I am: white, empty walls, cheap carpet, and tacky furniture. It's a reflection of me and I hate it. I groaned when I saw the moving truck next door and two small children running through the yard, their high-pitched voices slipping through the cracks in my windowsills. I work two jobs to pay my bills and I don't have the time or the interest in "learning more" about my neighbors. They've lived there two days and already the mother has a Christmas wreath on the front door. The condo on the other side of me, owned by an older husband and wife, is bloated with Christmas decorations: lights, wreaths, evergreen swags, nativity set, and two reindeer that move their heads as if they're eating. My condo is the thorn between two roses. I've never owned a Christmas wreath or put up a Christmas tree. What's the point when you live alone? I was married once; it lasted almost two years, an eternity really, considering neither of us was fit for marriage.

As I pull out of the garage I see my new neighbor draping Christmas lights over the miserly shrubs in front of her condo with the phone pressed to her ear. That's the second time I've seen her wandering in the cold, talking on the phone. From the corner of my eye I can tell she's watching me pull away, probably hoping for a moment of witty banter between us or to invite me in to their warm, smells-like-pumpkin-bread home that's already fully decorated for Christmas. I dislike her already, and I can't even remember her name.

I've worked in the mail room of Wilson's Department Store during the morning hours for two years now. It's only part-time work, so I transfer hard copy files on to the computer for Layton and Associates, a small law office, in the afternoon. In the same sense, I take the latest cases, which are on computer and make a hard copy file for each one. Feels like they're doubling up on their work, but hey, they're paying me to do it, so I don't complain. Both jobs are what Ramona calls "grunt work," perfect for grunts like me, she says. Before that, I worked on the assembly line at the pencil factory. You'd be surprised how many pencils don't make the cut and get pitched into a huge trash barrel. I do my jobs and go home. How I learned to work is beyond me because Ramona couldn't hold a thought in her head let alone a job. She'd been a cashier, gas station attendant, waitress, prep cook, night janitor, and Avon Lady all in the same year. "I change jobs like I change men," she said to me once, all boozed up and proud. I pay my bills. I stay out of the way. I probably drink too much, although I've always said

I'd never be like Ramona. I'd cut my right hand off before I turned into her.

Robert Layton is a good twenty-plus years older than me, but I think he's good-looking with the lines shooting out toward his temples and curving the sides of his mouth. He's not slobby; he hasn't let himself go like some older guys you see. I guess he's a good lawyer because his office is busy, with Jodi and Susan turning more people away than taking them on as clients. Robert's a grandfather and doesn't run, in his words, the hamster wheel anymore. I don't pal around with Jodi and Susan, the other women in the office, and when Robert invites the staff over to his house on the Fourth of July and for the annual Christmas dinner, I never go. The file room is at the back of the office and I'm always in there alone so I'd feel out of my skin if I was plopped down at a dinner party next to Jodi or Robert's wife, Kate.

I finish work earlier than usual because it always slows down around the holidays at Robert's office, and I sit in my car, letting it warm up. Snow is falling, but it looks like it's in slow motion, the flakes are so big and puffy. I watch a woman who looks like my mother—hunched shoulders, thick in the middle, and short legs—walk across the square. She's holding the hand of a small child and heading into Wilson's to buy a Christmas gift for the child's mother, no doubt. I've always felt as if there were two women inside me: one who is desperate, drowning, and clinging to anything that can float and the other woman who feels the depth of loss and the hope of beauty and is always searching for the marvelous to spring up out of the gray. That woman rarely shows up, it seems. There's no need to sift through my emotions right now; the image of the grandmother and child leaves me with a drowning feeling in my stomach, so I drive away.

The little boy next door is tossing a football into the air and catching it when I approach the condo. He waves and I ignore him, pretending not to see as my garage door opens and I pull inside, shutting the garage door behind me before he can run over and tell me all the inane parts of his day. I feel at some point that I should ask what happened to his father, but something inside me doesn't want to know. I prefer this in-between existence, where I know very little and have to give little in return.

I'm eating a bowl of canned soup and watching TV when someone knocks on the front door. I try to ignore it but realize the light from the TV shines out the front window, giving me away. I step to the door and see the mother from next door through the peephole. She probably wants to borrow something, like a screwdriver I'll never be able to find or a hammer I've never owned. I open the door a few inches and look out at her face. She's around my age, I suspect, but she looks younger. She's taken better care of herself. She's blond and petite to my blah-brown hair and lanky torso. "Hi," she says. "I'm Gretchen from next door. Remember?" I look at her as if that was a stupid thing to say and her face registers that she agrees. She's cold and wraps her arms around her. The little boy and girl come running up behind her, and she turns in a huff. "Go back home and stay inside like I asked."

"But what are you doing?" the little girl asks.

I feel myself getting irritated. It's cold and I want to close the door.

"I'll be right back," Gretchen says. "Go inside and

get your pajamas on like I asked. Take your brother back inside." The girl grabs the little boy's hand and jerks him toward her. "Sorry," the woman says, looking sheepishly at me. "I . . . a man knocked on my door yesterday morning looking for you and . . ." She pulls her sweater tighter around her and looks out toward the empty street. "I told him that you lived here, but he said he wasn't going to come back."

This is going to take forever. "Who was it?"

"I don't know his name. He didn't say. He's the landlord at the apartments where your mother—"

"What about him?" I'm abrupt and she looks startled.

"He said that he found your mother . . ."

Stand still. Don't react. Ramona did this to herself. It doesn't involve you.

"She died in her apartment, and he said he'd like you to clean out her place or else he will."

I nod. "Thanks."

She catches the door before I can close it. "I'm sorry about your mother."

"I'm not," I say, leaving her in the cold.

I walk back to the sofa and sit down, staring at the TV screen. What am I watching? Today's Friday. When did she say Ramona died? The landlord came yesterday morning. When did she die? Wasn't it just two days ago that I talked to her? She asked for money and called me a worthless pig. That's how sixty years ended. She yelled, she took, she misused, she swore, she badgered, she abused, and then her eyes closed and her mouth shut. I'm glad it's over. That sliver of me that always wanted something, anything from Ramona, will have to find something else to covet now. I turn off the TV and sit in the dark, waiting for morning.

Four

*We make our friends; we make our enemies; but
God makes our next-door neighbor.*
—G. K. CHESTERTON

GRETCHEN

Ethan's chatter wakes me up way too early. His
voice has always had a way of drilling through hard-
woods and mortar. It took me half the night to fall
asleep. I tossed and turned, thinking about the look
on Melissa's face when I told her her mother was
dead. Shouldn't there have been something—a short,
quick gasp, a sigh, a twitch, even a nervous laugh?
Who doesn't have some sort of emotion when a parent dies? I replay her closing the door on my face as
I make pancakes for the kids and feel the irritation
burrowing beneath my skin. But what's irritating
me? The fact that she doesn't care that her mother
died or that I took so long to tell her? Kyle was right.
I overthink things. While the kids are playing, I

check my e-mail and find myself getting teary-eyed reading them. There are several from Kyle's parents, Tom and Alice, who attach several pictures of Kyle to each e-mail with a detailed description of when the photo was taken. I dry my eyes before the kids can see me and send an e-mail, attaching a few photos of our new home and the kids before making breakfast.

Ethan is eating his pancakes before I have time to put syrup on them. "Are we going to that lady's funeral?" he asks.

"What lady?" I realize who he means as the question crosses the air between us. "Oh. No, we're not."

"Why not?"

I pour syrup over each of their pancakes and then my own. "Because we never knew her."

"We got lots of cards and flowers and stuff from people we don't know," Emma says.

"I know but . . ."

"That's what we should do, Mom," Ethan says, his mouth too full to talk. "We should make her a card and send her flowers."

I take a bite and realize that my kids are better people than I am. "You're right. That's what we need to do." I don't want to; I envision Melissa crushing the flowers in her hand like a cookie and torching the card by breathing on it.

They dig out a piece of blue construction paper and work on the card together after breakfast, and by the time I have cleaned the kitchen, the paper is covered in flowers with bloated, misshaped petals and a rainbow dripping glittery glue streaks. "We'll let it dry and a little later we'll go out for some flowers."

"Let's go now, and by the time we get back, the card will be dry," Emma says.

I don't want to go now. "Why don't we get some things done and then we'll make a trip out?"

"What's left to do?" Ethan asks. "We already unpacked everything."

"Yes, we did, didn't *we*?" I say. It's no use. They'll just keep asking and wear me down. "Get your clothes on and let's go."

As we back out of the driveway I'm already planning what to say to Melissa this time. Maybe when she opens the door she'll sock me in the eye or twist my arm behind my back or take the flowers out of my hand and clunk them over my head. None of the scenarios are looking good. I know I can't really afford a bouquet from the florist, so I pull into the grocery store for one there. "All I have to do is tie a ribbon around this and it will look just like we bought it from a florist," I say, picking up a small glass vase.

"Can she dry these?" Emma asks, holding a small bouquet.

I look at the flowers. "No, not really. These aren't good ones for drying."

"Then we need to get ones she can dry." She looks up at me. "Like you did with all our flowers."

"But those flowers were for your dad and . . . I don't think Melissa was very close to her mom, so I don't think these flowers are going to mean as much as—" They're both looking at me. I set the flowers back in the container and pull out a bunch with more roses in it. "These will dry much better."

The card is still tacky when we get home, and it takes me far too long to convince the kids that we really should wait for it to dry before we deliver it. Part of me just wants to get it over with, but the other part clearly wants to put this off until Emma's college graduation. I spend the greater part of the morning on the phone while the kids play, and when I'm finishing the last conversation with Kyle's parents, both Em and Ethan are staring at me and patting their bellies. We eat sandwiches and chips, and I dread one of them bringing up the card and flowers. To my surprise and delight they both forget and run back to their room to continue playing, when Ethan yells from the hall, "Hey! What about our card, Mom? When are we taking it over?"

"Right now," I say, as if I had it planned all along. I make the kids put on their coats or else we'll just stand out on Melissa's porch looking like those toy monkeys with the chattering teeth and clanging cymbals. Ethan is the first to her door and knocks on it, way too loud to be polite, and I stop his hand from knocking again. I groan when I hear footsteps and put on a pleasant, barely there smile when I know Melissa's looking at us through the peephole. The door opens and Ethan shoves the card through the slim opening.

"We made this for you," he says, propping his fisted hands onto his hips.

"Thanks," Melissa says, glancing at the card.

I work hard at a smile but feel awkward.

"We got these for you, too," Emma says, handing her the vase full of flowers.

"Thanks."

All four of us stand in gangly silence before she says thanks again. "Okay, come on, kids," I say, turning them back to our house. The door closes before I can even get the kids off the porch, and it takes all the willpower I have not to say something ugly. "There," I say, opening our door. "That was a nice thing to do, and the flowers and card will be just the things to make her home a little happier." I doubted this completely, but it sounded convincing enough so that the kids ran back to whatever they had been playing in their room.

When Mom drops by later in the afternoon she is carrying a big pot. Mom doesn't cook; she never did. My father did most of the cooking when they were married, but when it was up to Mom, we mostly ate a lot of canned soups, boxed rice dishes, and noodle dinners. Mom's third and final husband, Len, was a great cook. I still miss his sweet potato bread pudding he made every Thanksgiving. Len was a great fit for my mother, whereas she and Dad could rub each other the wrong way without even being in the same room. It wasn't always that way. I remember them being happy together. I don't know how things went south in their marriage.

"I didn't make this," Mom says, reading my face. "Gloria made a huge pot of chicken and dumplings for you and the children." I step forward to take it from her. "I did make a salad, though, along with a batch of chocolate chip cookies."

"You made cookies?"

She stops on the sidewalk and turns back to me. "I have learned to make some things over the years." Her red silk scarf blows in the wind as she reaches inside her car. "Since Gloria insists on serving cookies to the children at Glory's Place she also insisted that I learn how to make them." She steps inside and looks around. "Look at this! You are all put together."

"Still odds and ends that don't have a place, but most of it's put away," I say, taking the cookies and salad from her.

The kids tackle Mom when they hear her voice and drag her by the hand to their room. I lift the lid of the pot and breathe it in; I haven't had chicken and dumplings in ages. I yell for the kids and Mom to wash up as I gather some plates. Kyle always complained that I didn't make chicken and dumplings enough. "They take so much time," I always said to him. If he was here today I'd double the recipe so he'd have chicken and dumplings for days. As I scoop it onto the plates I wonder if I had ever made it for him at all?

"We bought flowers for the woman who died," Ethan says, taking a seat next to Mom.

"What woman who died?"

I shake my head, filling Ethan's plate with food. "A man showed up here and said the mother of the woman next to us died and that I had to break the news to her."

"I've never heard of such a thing."

I laugh. "Yeah. Neither did I, and I told him I wouldn't do it."

"So he told her and you bought her flowers?"

"No, he didn't tell her. Kyle told her." Mom glances up at me. "His voice kept nagging me . . . so I did it."

"What an awful way to break the ice. Was she just devastated?"

"I wouldn't say that," I say, choosing my words. "The guy has given her a few days to clean out her mom's place, but I don't think she's going to do it."

"I'd clean your house out if you died," Emma says. Mom and I both laugh. "And I'd take every single picture of you and Dad and Sugar and the toy box Dad made me."

"What about my stuff?" Ethan says. "What about my plastic soldiers and all my animals?"

"I don't want those things," Em says.

Ethan opens his mouth to fight about the soldiers and fluffy lambs when I stop them. "Hey! I'm not dead." They both look at me with fallen, flat faces. I laugh and point to their food. "This is delicious!"

Mom dips another helping of chicken and dumplings onto her plate. "Well, there must be something in her mother's place that she'd want. Surely, she doesn't want a complete stranger rifling through her memories."

"Yeah," Ethan says. "I wouldn't want some stranger touching my soldiers!"

"Nobody would want your soldiers!" Emma says.

"I want 'em! Dad gave them to me." Mom distracts the kids with the story of the time she took my brother and me to the zoo and I thought it'd be a good idea if we just left him there. Em thinks that is especially funny.

Mom plays a card game in the living room with the kids as I put our plates in the dishwasher and work at finding something for the leftovers. "There's enough food here for twenty," I say, looking for bowls I hope will be a good fit. I find two bowls and pour the chicken and dumplings inside them, thinking. Why was that blasted woman next door making me wrestle so much? I toss some cookies into a plastic bag, pick up one of the bowls, and walk over to the card game in the middle of the living-room floor. "Be right back," I say, before any of them can question me. I knock on Melissa's door and decide I'll just leave everything sitting here if she doesn't answer. It's dark on the porch and inside her home; her place doesn't even *feel* like Christmas! When she opens the door, I can see from the streetlight that her face is puffy and her eyes are small. "We had extra food," I say, keeping it short. "A friend made it. It's delicious."

She opens the door a bit and reaches for it. "Thanks."

I turn to leave but look at her over my shoulder. "I can go with you if you want." Her face is blank. I don't know why I suggested such a thing, but I'm still blabbing away. "I can help you clean out your mom's place."

"I'm not going to."

"I know. But . . . one day you might really regret that . . . letting a stranger go through her stuff." She opens her mouth and I plow ahead. "There may be something there that you didn't know about or had forgotten about or something you want to give to somebody." She is shaking her head, and the air is sitting on my cheeks, hurting them. "You can let me know. The kids start school on Monday and I can go then, or my mom can watch them if you want to go tomorrow."

"I don't want to go."

"All right," I say, stepping off the porch, relieved she doesn't want to do it. "If you change your mind, you know where I am."

I shiver going through the door and plop down on the sofa. "Where'd you go?" Mom asks, shuffling the cards.

"Tried to deliver some Christmas cheer."

"And how'd that go?"

"People make it hard," I say, picking up the cards Mom is dealing for Go Fish.

"Well, you know, I've always been a very good judge of people," Mom says, organizing the cards in her hand. "That's why I like so very few of them."

I laugh out loud and look at the kids. "She doesn't mean that."

"I wasn't even listening," Emma says.

Mom rears her head back and cackles. I organize my cards and realize I've been dealt a bum hand. That's how it goes sometimes.

Five

Grief can't be shared. Everyone carries it alone.
His own burden in his own way.

—ANNE MORROW LINDBERGH

MELISSA

I never went to bed but stayed on the couch watching mindless television. I wondered if Ramona died in her bed or while watching TV on the sofa, or was she about to leave her apartment when death came for her? I wondered if it was snowing out when she died and if she was standing at the window watching it fall? I wondered, too, if the man who was my father would even remember her or care that she was dead? He wouldn't, I say aloud to no one. I don't care, so why would he? I ate some of the chicken and dumplings at one in the morning. I can't remember the last time I've had something that good. When I was seven or eight, Ramona and I lived next to the Schweigers, a family whose apartment always smelled like a bakery. Mrs. Schweiger was Hungarian or something; I don't remember, but I loved her accent. She invited me over a lot for dinner, and years later I wondered if she suspected that I didn't eat much at my place. "Would your mother like to come, too?" she'd say, looking over my head for anyone who might be supervising me.

"She's not here," I said every time. Most of the time it was true, but sometimes Ramona would be inside the apartment, passed out on the sofa or sleeping with the man of the hour. The Schweigers ate every meal together: bacon and eggs, pancakes, meatloaf and mashed potatoes, baked chicken, scalloped potatoes, or spaghetti with meatballs, and there was always dessert. Karla was fifteen when I met them, Madden was twelve, and Louie was eight. I played with Louie every day. Sometimes I fell asleep on their couch and Mrs. Schweiger would leave me there. She'd knock on Ramona's door, and if Ramona wasn't there, she'd leave a note on the door, letting her know I was with them.

The Schweigers took me to church every Sunday. I remember the first time Mrs. Schweiger asked if I wanted to go with them. I shrugged and said sure. I'd never been inside a church before, but if it meant being with the Schweigers, I was all for it. There was nothing complicated about the Schweigers' faith; it was dirt plain and natural. When I remember Mrs. Schweiger I realize she never talked about religion. She talked about God and Jesus like they were part of the family. I spent three Christmases with the Schweigers. Ramona and some sidewalk Santa Claus spent one Christmas together at his apartment, and I don't remember where she was for the other two

Christmases I spent inside the Schweigers' apartment, opening presents, like a baby doll and a purse, that I never expected.

"I know what God is like, Mrs. Schweiger," I said on that Christmas Day, watching her peel potatoes.

"What is he like?" she asked, throwing the peels into the garbage.

"He's like you."

She stopped her work and looked at me. She knelt down and held my face, kissing my forehead: I could feel her wet potato hands on my cheeks. "Believe it or not, God loves you even more than I do, Melissy," she'd say. She always called me Melissy, and I was surprised at how much I liked that. I loved being loved by Mrs. Schweiger.

Louie and I played with Bruce Linton from upstairs, a kid four years younger than me who always had a snotty nose. Every day in the winter his sleeve was crusty with dried snot. If things didn't go Bruce's way, he'd slap or kick Louie and me, but we were both bigger and could pin him down until he stopped acting like a baby. Bruce also ate dinner a lot at the Schweigers' but not because his parents weren't around. Many times his parents ate with us, too. Playing with Louie and Bruce and being with the Schweigers was the best three years of my life, and I gushed like Niagara on the day we moved away.

"I've prayed for you, Melissy," Mrs. Schweiger said on that final day. "And I'll keep praying, okay?" I nodded, not really believing in it too much because I prayed that we wouldn't ever, ever move away from the Schweigers, but Ramona got a wild hair and loaded us into the station wagon. "Don't ever stop praying," Mrs. Schweiger said, her eyes wet and drippy. "Don't ever stop believing." Tears streaked my face as we pulled away, my arm flapping in the air. I think what little belief I had ended that day on those two hundred miles to Jacksonville.

To my knowledge, Ramona never really talked to Mrs. Schweiger beyond that occasional cracked apartment door. Ramona made it a point to never know anyone at any of the places we lived; it made running out in the middle of the night so much easier. She cheated landlords out of a lot of money but always waved it off, saying, "It will cost them more to track us down than what we owe them."

I warm up another plate of chicken and dumplings for lunch and hear someone talking outside the front window. Moving the blinds, I see Gretchen on the phone again. Talking to her boyfriend, no doubt, a man the kids don't necessarily like but someone she can't break things off with, not yet, anyway. I sit on the sofa and eat, watching her through the blinds. The conversation is serious. She hasn't smiled yet but keeps pushing her hair behind her ear and looking at the front door of her home. I finish eating and step to the window, watching. She takes the phone from her ear and crosses toward her door. I open mine and pretend to see her. "Oh. Hi."

"Hi," she says, waving at me with the phone.

"Those chicken and dumplings were really good."

"My mom's friend made them."

I step out and look at her. I'm just standing here, and she feels uncomfortable, I can tell. I clear my throat and take a breath. "I don't know how long it will take to clean out Ramona's apartment . . . so if you can't, it's no big deal. I thought it might go fast if two. . . . she had a lot of junk mostly, so it shouldn't take too long."

"Sure," she says, thumping the phone against her thigh. "When?"

"I work until five each day so . . ." I fade out and look at a passing car.

"Do you want to go today?"

I wasn't expecting this, to do it so soon. "Could you?"

"I'll call my mom and see if she can come over to be with the kids."

I close the door and feel my heart racing. Why was I doing this? Why do I even care what's in the middle of Ramona's pile of rubble? Anger at what I just did makes me flush with heat, and I fan my shirt to get cool. I feel so stupid asking for Gretchen's help. I didn't need help to walk into Ramona's apartment and kick at the garbage. I'm embarrassed and want to take it back when a knock on the door behind me makes me jump. Gretchen is on the porch, and I open the door, relieved to tell her I'm calling the whole stupid thing off. "Mom can be here in about an hour."

"But I was going to—"

"Do you want me to follow you there, or do you want to ride together?"

I never thought things would move this fast, and my heart beats double-time. "I need to go somewhere afterward," I say, making it up as I talk. "So it'd be best if you followed me." She looks as relieved as I feel.

"I'll knock when Mom gets here."

I close the door and wonder what I need at Ramona's? What would I find and what would I put it in?

A garbage bag? A box? Just an envelope? In the end, I leave the house with a box of garbage bags because I know where most of her stuff will go. Gretchen follows me the three miles to Ramona's, and my brain hurts trying to figure out what to say to her when we arrive.

The apartment house is a three-story, ugly light-brick building with shabby trees and cracked sidewalks. I can tell that Gretchen is sizing it up when she gets out of her car. This pit is as unkempt as Ramona always was. She follows me to the office door, and I realize for the first time that finding someone here on Sunday will be next to impossible. I ring the buzzer and hold my breath, feeling uncomfortable with this stranger who's about to schlep through Ramona's junk. "Maybe no one's here on Sunday," Gretchen says. I ring the buzzer again and wait, staring at the cheap wood grain on the door.

A man with a balding head and potbelly walks down the stairs and faces us, smoke from his cigarette filling the small vestibule. He looks at me while squinting in the smoke. "You looking for me?"

"My mother was Ramona" is all I say.

He turns to go back up the stairs. "I wondered if you'd come."

We follow him, and our shoes squeak on the shoddy linoleum steps. If it wasn't for tacky Christmas wreaths hung on two apartment doors, you'd have no idea Christmas was just weeks away by visiting this place. The bald man sticks his key in the door and pushes it open, leaving us without another word. I run my hand along the inside wall, looking for the light switch, and a bulb flickers on the ceiling of the entry. The light illuminates the filthy floor, and I smell the pent-up dirt and dust inside the apartment. "I'll go find other lights," I say, leading Gretchen inside. My shoes stick to the linoleum as I walk to the window and pull open the curtains. I turn to look at the place and feel something heavy on my chest, making my breath short. Papers, cans, liquor bottles, rotten food, fast-food wrappers, and cereal boxes—garbage is everywhere. I hold my hand under my nose. "I'm sorry I asked you to do this."

Gretchen's already rummaging through cabinets in the kitchen. "We just need some trash bags," she says.

"I brought some," I say, walking to the door. "I forgot them in the car."

"I'll get them," she says, holding her hand out for my keys. I reach into my coat pocket and pull them out.

Her eyes are big and soft. "This won't take long."

I hear her running down the stairs, and I feel nauseated. I crack open a window and a blast of cold air hits me in the face. I stick my head into the small bedroom and look at the mattress and box springs on the floor and wonder if that's where Ramona died or if it was over there on the sofa or just in front of the sofa on the filthy throw rug? I step through the garbage in the bedroom and peer into the closet—nothing in here but more garbage and a few pants and shirts on the floor. I imagine some people go through their parents' things with a swelling sense of grief from love and pride and gratefulness, but then there are people like me, who move things aside with their toe. This gulf of loss is different from grief. It's mostly dread and disappointment and regret.

"I'll take the kitchen," Gretchen says, startling me.

Donna VanLiere

She hands the box of garbage bags to me. "Should I ask you about what to save or—"

"If there's anything that can be used again, I'll take it to the secondhand store. From what I see, there's nothing here that I'll want." She nods and makes her way to the kitchen while I move to the living room.

The garbage feels sticky on my hand, and I use another garbage bag as a glove. I'm disgusted with every piece I throw away. "You lived like a pig, Ramona." I shove a hamburger wrapper and nearly empty bottle of booze into the bag along with a half-eaten can of Vienna sausages and a stack of magazines. "You never, ever, ever lived like a human being!" I sweep the garbage off the sofa into the bag and kick up the cushions, shaking my head. The couch is full of garbage and dried pieces of food. I throw the garbage away and stare at the stained sofa cushions that are destroyed. In an instant I pick one up and heave it out the window. Out of the corner of my eye, I can see Gretchen, frozen at the kitchen sink, watching me. I lunge for the other two cushions and hurl them after the first. They lie on the asphalt below, looking small and ruined.

"Are you okay?"

Gretchen hasn't moved from the kitchen, but I can't turn to look at her. I nod and push more garbage into bags. On top of the TV is a picture in a black frame of Ramona and me standing in front of an enormous plastic cow. We saw it in front of a roadside restaurant as we were moving from one apartment to the next. "What a sight!" Ramona said. "Let's get our picture." The sun was bright, so I'm squinting up at the camera and Ramona is holding her cigarette aloft, looking as if she'd just taken me to Disney

World. Propped up against that photo is a smaller shot of us taken in front of a stunted Christmas tree strung with popcorn next to an RCA television set on a metal stand. I glance around the room trying to spot any other photos or keepsakes, but there are none. The door closes and I turn behind me to see Gretchen putting two empty boxes on the counter.

"I ran down to the Dumpster to see if I could find a box for the plates and pots."

I didn't even know she had left. The dishes and pans clank as she fits them into the box, and she steps into the living room. "I threw away all the food. There wasn't much of anything but it was all open and stale or—"

"Ruined," I say.

"Everything she had is here in the boxes if you want to—"

I don't let her finish. "No. I don't want it."

We work in silence for the next hour or so. Gretchen hauls bags of trash down to the Dumpster, and a couple of times I hear her talking in the stairwell on her phone. Checking on her kids, I suppose. Three more trips are taken to the Dumpster, and on her return she walks beyond me to the bedroom and I hear her snap open a trash bag. I finish pawing through the garbage in the living room and then stand in the bedroom doorway. Gretchen has taken the sheets off the bed and is pushing the mattress off to see if there's anything under it. I help her lean it against the wall, and together we prop the box springs on it. The bed's metal railing looks like a picture frame around the trash that was under the bed. "Unbelievable," I say, snapping up a bag and pitching cans and bottles into it.

Gretchen works through a stack of magazines and papers on Ramona's nightstand as I reach for the garbage and clothes inside the closet. At one time, Ramona had nice skirts, dresses, and slacks that fell over her curves and long legs in soft lines. I pick up worn shirts, stretched-out sweaters, and holey pants and realize I can't give any of them to Goodwill.

"Melissa." I look up and see Gretchen standing by the nightstand holding a stack of papers in her hands. "This has your name on it."

She holds out a small envelope that has never been sealed, and I reach for it. I pull out a note-size piece of paper and read it. *Melissa, I know I haven't been much of a mother to you. You do have a brother and a sister you might like to . . .* I turn it over looking for more and laugh out loud. "You're kidding, right! This is it?" I keep laughing and lean against the wall, reading the note again. My eyes fill with hot liquid and I close them, pressing the note to my face. Thoughts and words buzz through my brain, but I can't pin them down. "All this time I was alone . . . with just her." I hold out the note and Gretchen walks over, taking it from me. "She never could give me anything that I needed. Not even now." A mixture of anger, resentment, and grief piles up in my throat and I want to run. "No, 'Sorry, Melissa I really blew it.' Even now she won't take responsibility for anything. She couldn't even finish the letter!"

"But she started it." I look at Gretchen. Her face is solemn and plain but kind. "She could have started this months ago and just couldn't figure out what else to say and left it here at her bedside hoping for the right words."

I laugh up at the ceiling. "Ramona never lacked for words, believe me! Apparently, her problem was remembering she had more children! Messy lives don't usually create good recall." I shake my head. "She kept them from me. This could have brought some chance of happiness, you know, having a brother and sister? She couldn't stand the thought of any glimmer of a normal life for me." The silence in the room is too loud, and I take a step to get away.

"I'll help you find them."

I look at her. "I don't want to know them."

"Yes, you do." I open my mouth, but she talks over me. "You do. You would have wanted to know them when you were a child. If then . . . then why not now?" The thought terrifies and cripples me. What if they're like me? Or Ramona? "You said she never gave you anything." She hands the note to me. "She did today."

It feels like my chest is in flames and I move past her, grabbing a bag of garbage from the bedroom and another from the living room on my way to the Dumpster. The air outside hits my lungs and I feel like screaming, crying, beating something. I don't know. The bags hit the side of the Dumpster with a thud, and I move to the couch cushions I had thrown out the window.

"How's it going?"

I look up to see the bald man; a cigarette is barely hanging on to his bottom lip. Smoke swirls into his eyes, making them slits in his face.

"Great," I say, heaving one of the cushions into the Dumpster. "Ramona's place is empty and ready for your next squatter. You or your tenants can take whatever furniture you want." I walk past him and open the door to my car.

"So that's that?" he yells after me.

"That's that," I say, sliding behind the wheel and closing the door. Sixty years of life. Done. Just like that.

Six

It is our relation to circumstances that determine
their influence over us. The same wind that blows
one ship into port may blow another offshore.
—CHRISTIAN NEVELL BOVEE

GRETCHEN

I take the kids to the new school and walk each of them to their classrooms, then cry all the way back to my car. Their little faces were wide-eyed and brave even as they squeezed my hands right up to the last second before letting go. New things are always so hard.

It takes a while, but I find the cemetery and pull into the parking lot, looking around. Two other cars are here and I get out, shoving my hands into my coat pockets. I haven't heard from Melissa since she ran from her mother's apartment. There was a part of me that felt so sorry for her as we worked together in that atrocious space. I could hear her mumbling and cursing and see her throwing things out of anger and rejection, and my chest felt so heavy thinking about her growing up with the woman who had lived there. Then there is another part of me who can barely stand to be with her. It's too much like work. So why in the world am I here? I see two people in the distance near the back of the cemetery grounds and walk on a path through the headstones toward them.

Melissa's back is to me, and I watch as the wind picks up her hair and she shifts her weight from one foot to the other. Wisps of snow seem to fall from the trees and swirl on top of the ground. The undertaker nods and I step next to Melissa; her eyes are dark and tired looking at me.

"How'd you know?" she asks.

"Ramona's landlord knew she was being buried today. He told me before I left the apartment."

Clear liquid leaks from her nose and Melissa swipes at it with her hand. "Big turnout, huh?"

I look inside the hole at the simple box and wonder if the state paid for this plot or how Ramona ended up here.

"Why are you here?" Melissa asks.

I pull my scarf tighter around my neck. "I've been to a lot of these. Men in my husband's unit."

"Heroes," she says, wiping the snot away from her nose again. "This is Ramona."

I look into the hole. "She was your mom, and everybody should have someone at their side when they bury their mom."

I sit behind the wheel of my car and watch as Melissa pulls away from the cemetery. The cold, the open grave, the memories of Kyle and his unit rattle my brain, and sobs from somewhere in my chest overtake me. I cry until my head hurts, my eyes are puffy, and my tissue is in soggy shreds.

I wipe my face with a napkin from the glove compartment before I step inside Mom's house. She's going crazy because she can't figure out how to fix this new life of ours, and if she sees that I've been crying, she'll worry the rest of the day.

Gloria is making her morning visit, and I smell freshly baked something or other. "Cinnamon rolls," she says, putting one oozing with icing on a plate for me. I stare at it and Mom laughs.

"You must eat that because if you don't, she'll leave it here for me and my trousers simply cannot take the pressure."

I take a bite and Gloria leans in, waiting for my response. I moan and she bangs the table with her hand. "See that, Miriam! We are going to *bake* a difference this Christmas!"

Mom rolls her eyes and I take another bite. "What's that mean?" I ask.

"Another one of her ideas," Mom says, filling a cup with coffee for me.

Gloria waves her hand in Mom's face to hush her. "Every year the chamber orchestra does a Christmas concert. This year all the funds from the admission tickets are going to Glory's Place to help the families we work with. And while that's a wonderful thing, the ticket price is only five dollars. It has always been five dollars and will always be five dollars, and that doesn't add up to much money at the end of the night. Well, I thought we could raise even more money by offering quality baked goods. You know, some people don't have time to bake a pie or a cake for Christmas get-togethers."

"And others can't . . . or don't want to," Mom adds, winking at me.

Gloria waves at her to shush again. "So this year I think we can bake a difference by gathering really nice baked goods and selling them at the concert." She bangs the table again and Mom jumps, grabbing her head. "No brownies are allowed! Everybody always makes brownies. Cakes, pies, candies, and Christmas cookies only. No chocolate chips!" She spins in her seat and looks around. "For heaven's sake, Miriam! Where do you keep your paper? I have to write all this down."

Mom jumps up and glides in her pink satin robe to the drawer under the coffeepot, and I smile watching her. She's owned a pink satin gown and robe set for as long as I can remember. "Cakes, pies, candies, and cookies," she says, handing a notepad and pen to Gloria. "What's so hard to remember?"

"Let's think of good bakers in town." She puts the pen to her mouth and begins to think aloud.

"Oh, Gloria, please! Can't your brainstorming wait? Gretchen just got here."

"Don't stop," I say. "I love the idea. Put me down for something. Mom and I can surely bake a difference together." Mom refills my coffee and groans at the idea, sitting down with a swish and a swirl.

"You could ask your neighbor if she'd like to help," Gloria says, tapping the notepad. "What's her name?"

"Melissa. But I don't think she's the baking a difference type." Although Mom heard all about the apartment cleaning trip, I give Gloria the 411 of what happened, ending with the note.

"It is just so sad to me," Mom says. "I can't imagine not being a part of my children's lives to the point that neither of them would even know that I was dead."

"Now don't get worked up," Gloria says. "I'll make sure that your kids know that you're dead."

I smile and pat Mom's hand. "You were a great mother, Mom. Don't worry. You weren't anything like Melissa's mom."

"I never made you things like chicken and dumplings or cinnamon rolls."

"No. But you made lots of mac and cheese."

She makes tiny circles with her finger in the air. "Big deal."

"You showed up at every choir concert and musical."

Mom shoves a bite into her mouth and leans her head down on her hand. "Oh, yes! Those concerts could be brutal."

Gloria holds her cup with both hands. "What's Melissa like?"

"I don't know," I say, pushing my plate away. "She's just so odd to pin down."

"I'd be a bit wacky too, if I had a mother like hers," Mom says. She points her finger at Gloria. "Don't say a word, big mouth!"

Gloria laughs out loud and writes something on the notepad. "Just for that, I'm putting you down for two cakes." She looks at me and cocks her head; salt-and-pepper ringlets bounce on her forehead. "Why'd you offer to help her find her siblings?"

I sigh. "Because she's so pitiful . . . and if I had siblings that I didn't know about, I'd want to find them."

"But it seems you have so much on your plate right now," Mom says.

"I'm alone right now, Mom. I'm going to go home and clunk around in that empty condo. Trust me, this will be a good distraction." She wants to say more but practices unbelievable restraint.

"She should call Robert Layton," Gloria says. "He's a lawyer in town and a longtime friend of mine. Miriam would latch onto him if he wasn't ten years younger than her."

Mom's cup hits the table with a thud. "Robert Layton is a married man, and if truth be known, he is a good five years *older* than I am." Gloria pretends to choke and Mom looks at me. "Do not encourage her, Gretchen. She is a child stuffed inside an old woman's body."

Gloria laughs out loud and takes another nibble of cinnamon roll. "Robert would know where to start in tracking down her siblings." She offers me another cinnamon roll. "Eat up, kiddo. These are so good you'll want to smack your mama. Which I'd love to see, by the way."

"You simply must eat another roll," Mom says. "Because if you don't Gloria will leave all of them here for me. This is what she does. She brings me fattening food and then gloats when I can't fit into my trousers."

Gloria smacks the table. "Ask Melissa to *bake a difference.*"

"No, Glor—" I begin.

She holds up her hand. "Just ask her if she'll bake something to help raise money for people who can't pay their electric bill or buy their little boy a puzzle at Christmas. People want to help other people. They really do. Ask her. You never know what she'll say." I try to say something but she holds up her hand. "Ask her!"

I look at Mom. "She'll never shut up until you say you'll ask her. Trust me. She'll never, ever, ever, ever shut up."

I laugh and give them each a quick hug before I make my way to the door. "All right! I'll ask her to bake a difference. I'm off to surf the Internet classifieds for a job!" Mom's face gets long and somber, and I hurry putting on my boots. "Gloria? When do you need the baked goods?"

"On the twentieth, babe."

"The twentieth?" She nods and I slap my forehead. "That's the day my dad gets in."

Mom rises like a majestic pink cloud. "What?"

"Didn't I tell you?" I know I hadn't. "I invited Dad to come for Christmas."

"Here?"

I zip up my coat and look at her. "I want him here, Mom. I want my dad and I want you." She is slack-jawed and clutching the fabric of her robe on her chest. "I haven't seen him since . . . I want him here, Mom." She nods and I slip out the door with what feels like a peach pit lodged in my throat. The crappy thing about divorce is that you rarely get to see *both* of your parents on holidays or birthdays or any other day, for that matter. The fact is, my parents are in their sixties and should be mature enough to be in the same room without killing each other. I don't think that's too much to ask at Christmas.

On my way home I drive around the square and notice someone at Wilson's Department Store putting up a sale sign in the front window. Gifts have been the furthest thing from my mind, and I pull into an empty spot. Gloria's husband, Marshall, has owned Wilson's for most of his adult life, and I keep my eye out for him as I enter the door. The store is lovely, with huge silvery snowflakes hanging from the ceiling and a giant Christmas tree made from enormous bulbs hovering over the jewelry counter. Employees are dressed in gold, silver, or red blouses and shirts and slacks. A sign for Santa's workshop leads down the stairs, and Vic Damone singing "It's a Marshmallow World" filters through the store.

After I browse the women's department for ideas for Mom I run downstairs to the children's department and Santa's workshop. As I reach the landing and make the turn for the final set of steps I run into someone carrying a large, plastic bin and packages tumble down the stairs. "I'm sorry," I say, reaching for two plain packages. "Melissa?" She picks up some envelopes at her feet and puts them into the bin. "Do you work here?"

"Did you think I was a doctor?"

There it is again. One of the reasons she's so hard to like. I ignore her question. "I was talking to a friend. Gloria. The woman who made the chicken and dumplings." I am amazed at how blank Melissa's eyes and face look when I talk to her. "She said her friend Robert Layton could begin tracking down your siblings." Something lights in her eyes.

"Are you kidding?"

It's not the response I was expecting. "No. She said he's a lawyer in town and could—"

"I work at his office in the afternoons."

I step aside so a customer can get down the stairs. "That's great! You could ask him if—"

She clutches the packages and heads downstairs. "I don't want to ask him."

I race after her. "Why not?"

She walks to a sales associate in toys and hands her a stack of mail. "I can't jeopardize my job there."

Melissa turns toward the shoe department, and I grab her arm. "Hold on. You'd pay him just like any other client." She starts to speak and I talk over her. "You want to do it." There's that blank look again. "You need to do it. The not knowing will drive you crazy."

Her face never changes expression. "I'll talk to Jodi about it."

She marches toward shoes again and I run in front of her. "One more thing. Do you bake?"

"Do I bake?"

"Gloria. My friend who—"

"Chicken and dumplings. I know."

"She has a place for families who need help. You know, like single moms and their kids, called Glory's Place. This year she's"—I make finger quotes in the air—"'baking a difference' to help raise money for them. You know, help them pay their electric bill or help with rent."

She shuffles the few pieces of mail in her hands. "I don't really bake, but . . ."

Kyle once said that the word *but* erases everything before it, so I rush ahead before she says anything else. "You can come over to my place. Mom will come, too. We can all bake together." She nods with that same vacant face. "Just let me know."

I watch her walk away and look at my watch. I've been here five days. I have a feeling that despite what I think of her, one of these days I may actually see Melissa push herself up out of the rubble and crow.

Seven

Call it a clan, call it a network, call it a tribe, call it a family: Whatever you call it, whoever you are, you need one.

—JANE HOWARD

MELISSA

Gretchen nags me. Not in a physical way of always being around or in my face, but she's always in my head prodding and nudging me. I sort through the mail at Wilson's and hear her in my head telling me I want to find my siblings or I need someone to be with me as I bury Ramona. Maybe I don't want to find my siblings and couldn't care less if anyone acknowledges Ramona's death. I rummage through the boxes and packages for each department and tell myself that I don't really want to know who my siblings are, but it's a lie and I know it. Gretchen knows it.

Ramona has a half sister, Kay. I've only seen her on a few occasions, but one time, when I was a teenager and she and Ramona had drunk too much one night, she asked Ramona if some girl named Louanne was my sister.

"You know, Louanne? Jake's girl. I *know* you remember Jake," Kay said, laughing. Ramona shot her a look that could have ripped out Kay's spleen. "My God, you look just like each other," Kay said, looking at me.

"Shut up, Kay!" Ramona hissed. Kay withered a bit in her chair, and I was too frightened to ask any questions. All these years later I never asked Ramona a thing about that night, but it was the last time I saw Kay.

"Hi." I jump and turn to see a young kid standing in the mail room doorway. He has dark hair and a tall, lanky body. "I'm Josh. I was told to be here at eleven today."

I throw packages for the office into a bin. "For what?"

"Melissa's supposed to train me for the mail room."

I sort the letters in my arms and toss each one into a slot on the wall. I look over my shoulder at a mail bin on the floor. "Well, I'm Melissa and that's the morning mail. We pick it up and put it into these slots. If it's a big package we put it into the bin with the department name." I kick at the bins on the floor with my foot. "If you have time you can deliver it right to the department. Otherwise, just leave it here and somebody will come get it. Every day we receive some sort of merchandise and we help unload it into the stockroom or take it directly to the floor." I toss a few more packages into bins for security, ladies' wear, and jewelry. "There. You've been trained."

Josh walks to the mail bin and lifts out a few packages. "This just has a person's name at it," he says, reading the top envelope.

"A list of employees and which department they work for is right there," I say, looking at the wall to the left of the mailboxes.

He steps close to the list and glances for the name, putting the envelope into the slot for the children's department. "How long have you worked here?"

I'm not interested in chitchat with this kid and I sigh. "A while."

"Do you think it will be a problem if I have to take off suddenly someday?" Already he's scamming for a way out of work. "My grandma is really sick, and my mom doesn't know if we'll just have to run out of town real quick."

I shrug. "Shouldn't be a problem. I'm sure there will be enough part-time help to cover you."

He reaches for more mail and is painstakingly slow finding the department name on each package. The buzzer rings in the mail room, and I sigh in relief. A shipment is at the loading dock, and that means I won't be alone with this kid anymore. "Come on. There's a truck that needs to be unloaded. Grab your coat."

Unloading the shipment and getting it on the floor or in the stockroom takes up the rest of my time before I leave for the law office. "Will you be working tomorrow?" Josh asks as I put on my coat.

"I'm here every day with bells on," I say, leaving.

I usually walk through the city square to get to the office but today I'm especially hungry and realize I didn't stop for lunch and left it in the fridge at Wilson's. I walk the few extra blocks to get to Betty's Bakery, thinking of my aunt Kay and the girl she said could be my sister. The place is decorated with those big, papery snowflakes that hang from the ceiling, and a tinsel swag with ornaments hanging from it is draped over the bakery case. I choose the empty booth in the corner and wait for a waitress. A couple of older women are sitting at the table next to my booth and chattering like magpies.

"I just want some soup and water," I say to the waitress when she hands me a menu.

"Vegetable beef or clam chowder?"

I hand the menu back to her. "I'll try the clam."

"Do the vegetable beef, babe," one of the older women says. "That clam chowder isn't fit for consumption."

The waitress turns to look at her. "Thanks for the rousing endorsement, Gloria. You're great for business."

"Sorry, Heather. I love Betty's stuff, but that chowder has got to go!"

"Vegetable beef," I say.

"Thatta girl," the older woman says.

I look at her, wondering, and then just come out with it. "Are you the Gloria who's friends with Gretchen?"

She smacks the table in front of her. "One and the same, and this old broad here is Gretchen's mother."

Her friend rolls her eyes and speaks through her teeth. "You have absolutely no tact when introducing people, Gloria!" She looks at me. "I'm Miriam, Gretchen's mother."

"I live next door to her. She gave me some chicken and dumplings you made," I say, looking at Gloria. "They were great."

Gloria jumps out of her seat and plops down on the bench across from me. "You're Melissa!" She reaches for my hand and puts her warm, soft palm on top of it, squeezing. "I am so sorry about your mother, babe." Something in her touch or in the way she said "babe" makes my throat quiver and I look down at the table, pulling my hand out from underneath hers. "Come on up here, Miriam, and let's eat with Melissa today." I don't have time to say no or tell them I'm in a rush. Miriam reaches for Gloria's coat and purse and hands them to her, taking her seat next to Gloria. "So, how are you, babe?"

It's the second time Gloria has called me babe, and I push a lump in my throat as far down as I can, trying to find my voice. "I'm fine."

She pats my hand again and smiles like she knows me. "Life is short. It's so, so short. Makes your head spin when you think about it." She squeezes her warm hand around mine and I don't pull away. "Were you close to your mother?"

I look at both their faces and wish to God that either one of them could have been my mother. I don't even know them but sense they are good and kind, decent, and soft. They were there when their kids wanted to play a game. They wiped runny noses and bundled up little bodies for playtime in the snow. They cooked meals and baked cookies, even if the meal was Hamburger Helper and refrigerated slice and bake cookies. "No," I say.

Gloria's eyes mist over, and I can't imagine why she's crying. "She never knew what she was missing. Isn't that right, Miriam?"

"Awfully tragic," Miriam says, nodding at me.

I bite the inside of my cheek and feel so stupid. Why am I so emotional? These women are strangers! Gloria pushes Miriam out of the booth and then slides in next to me, putting her hand on my arm and keeping her voice low. "It's harder to let go of a bad relationship than a good one. With a good one you've got sweet memories and kind words. With a bad one you just got a whole lot of unanswered questions and open wounds." I keep my eyes on the table. I can't speak and feel like a fool. "Don't ever think that tears are a bad thing," she says, somehow knowing that I feel like exploding. "Lord have mercy! I've cried buckets in my lifetime. But Miriam here doesn't cry much." She leans in and whispers. "Afraid it will melt the wax." I laugh and Miriam hisses through her teeth. "I buried my first husband and cried myself sick. My son ran away from home and was gone seven years. I can't begin to tell you how many tears I cried over that loss. Grief takes a while, but joy does come." She wraps her arm around me and she's as warm and soft and sweet-smelling as I imagined. She squeezes my shoulder and then smacks the table, the silverware bouncing in front of me. "I know! Why don't you come on over for Christmas dinner? Miriam and I will be cooking for the whole gang, although Miriam doesn't really cook. But she has always wanted to pretend to cook sweet potato casserole, so that's what she'll be doing this year." I smile and Miriam shakes her head, unaffected.

I begin to say, "I don't really know anyone and—"

"Now don't make a lot of ballyhoo out of nothing," Gloria says, "because you know Gretchen and now you know us. And you can plainly see that we're about as simple as people come."

"I wish you would speak for yourself, Gloria," Miriam says.

I twist the napkin in my hand, glancing at Gloria.

"Okay." I can't believe I've accepted an invitation to eat with strangers. "I'll be baking a difference, by the way."

She throws her arms in the air. "Gretchen asked you! Good girl!" She grabs her head as if a lightning bolt just struck her. "Did she tell you about Robert Layton?"

"I work for him, actually."

She bangs the table again, and Miriam grabs her head this time. "Would you please stop making that confounded noise, Gloria!"

"Well, this is just downright providential! Of all the people to work for in this town and you're working for somebody who can help you find your family."

Family. The word lodges in my throat and heat breaks out on my back. The search sounds so easy when Gloria talks about it, and she makes me smile. "It all still seems so crazy," I say. They're looking at me, waiting for more. "All these years I thought it was just Ramona and me. Now . . . someone else is out there who may not even want to know about me. It's a strange way to piece a family together."

"What?" Gloria says. "It means that your siblings were adopted, and that's the most powerful, beautiful story of love there is, isn't that right, Miriam?" Miriam smiles. "Both of Miriam's children are adopted, and they are two of the most loved kids I've ever met. Love is learned, you know, and your two siblings were loved long before they were even born and have grown up in families of love. I just know it. And that means they will only have love for you, too."

I look at Miriam. "It's true," she says.

"For all I know, it's going to be hard to track them down," I say.

Gloria leans close to me. "Just keep a little faith, babe." I don't even react to that because I've never had any faith to begin with, let alone even a little of it. I wanted faith; the kind that Mrs. Schweiger had that just spilled over and out of her as natural as a breath, but I've never known what that's like. Gloria seems to read my mind and moves her hand to mine, patting it. "When you say 'I believe,' it has the same power as letting a tiger out of its cage."

Sometimes you meet people, total strangers, who feel like home. Even if that home is filled with noise and dysfunction and silence that is beyond bearing, it's still home, with its secondhand furniture, worn comforters, and smiles from people who love you despite your lopsided personality and crooked moods. Gloria and Miriam make me feel like I'm home. "I'll talk to Jodi when I get to work in a few minutes."

Gloria lifts her fists into the air as if she just won a race. "How old are you?"

"Thirty-nine."

She nods, looking at me. "For thirty-nine years you never knew you had family out there. Now everything has changed just like that," she says, snapping her fingers.

The wind is sharp as I walk the few blocks to the law office, but I don't feel it against my face. My mind is crackling with what will happen in the days ahead. Somewhere there is a woman in this world who is my sister and a man who is my brother. I shake my head, still not believing that Ramona lived with that secret her entire life. My siblings could be wasting their days like Ramona did, living from bottle to bottle or they could be like Gretchen and Gloria and Miriam.

I know how my luck runs, and I hold little hope that my siblings won't be like Ramona.

When I walk into the office I notice that Jodi isn't in her office, and I wave at Susan at the front desk as I walk to the room at the back, where I work. I sit at the computer and type in the name Kay Hart. It's a long shot, but I'm hoping to find Ramona's sister still alive so she can tell me if I have a sister. A two-year-old obituary for a Gene Riggins in San Antonio pops up and I read through it, spotting Kay's name, "survived by his wife, Kay Hart Riggins." I have no idea if it's her. I never knew she was married, and Ramona never said anything. I do a search of the white pages in San Antonio for Gene Riggins and find a number. My cell phone is in my backpack, and I reach for it but realize that if Kay has caller ID, she'll recognize my name. I decide to use the office phone and dial the number. It rings, but I can barely hear it over the sound my heart is making in my ears.

"Hello." Sweat sits on my lip. Is that Kay's voice? "Hello?"

I'm hoping that Ramona shared secrets with her sister and that Kay can tell me whether Louanne, whoever Louanne is, is my sister.

"Hello," she says again, sounding like Ramona.

I try to find my voice. Kay could be the key to letting the tiger out of its cage.

Eight

*Sometimes a neighbor whom we have disliked a
lifetime for his arrogance and conceit lets fall a
single commonplace remark that shows us another
side, another man, really; a man uncertain, and
puzzled, and in the dark like ourselves.*

—WILLA CATHER

GRETCHEN

I like distractions. Some people can't handle them. If
something distracts them from their already planned
day, it drives them bonkers. Not me. I like busyness
because it keeps my mind from slipping here or there.
Gloria's Bake a Difference project and helping Melissa find her siblings are great mind occupiers for me.
Since Mom and Melissa met on Monday, I decided
to strike while that iron was hot and invited them to
come over Friday afternoon to start baking. Mom insisted we come to her house since she has the bigger

kitchen. I spent Tuesday and Wednesday looking for a job and recipes online and found great ones for turtle candies, German chocolate cake, hummingbird cake, chocolate raspberry cake, and caramel candy. (I didn't find any job postings.) I don't know which ones we'll end up making, but all the recipes were supposed to freeze well and Mom said we could store whatever we made in her freezer until the bake sale.

I haven't seen Melissa this week. She's worked late the last three days at the law office, but at eight twenty, as I finish packing the kids' lunches for tomorrow, I notice her car pull into her driveway. I creep down the hall to check on Ethan and Em and see that they're asleep. This first week of school has worn them out. I pull their door closed and walk to the sofa, falling into it. This is always the worst part of my day. Just sitting alone with everything quiet except my thoughts that make a tremendous racket. A knock startles me and I jump to my feet, peering through the peephole in the door. Melissa is standing on my dark stoop, and I flick on the outside light, opening the door.

"Your mail was put in my box today," she says.

I take it and step aside. "Thanks. Come on in." I'm not sure if I'm inviting her because it's the neighborly thing to do or if I want to drown out the noise inside my head. She stands as if glued to the front stoop, and I motion with the mail. "Come in! Have you eaten?"

"I was going to have some cereal."

I lead her to the kitchen. "I have spaghetti." I open the fridge and take out the bowls of noodles and sauce I'd put in there a couple of hours ago. "It seems like I always have spaghetti because my kids love it." She looks uncomfortable just standing there, and I look at the table. "Have a seat. Would you like iced tea or water? Those are my only choices right now."

"Water's fine," she says, looking around. "Looks like you're all moved in."

I cover the plate of spaghetti and put it in the microwave. "For the most part. Still need to hang things, but my dad's coming to help with them." I reach for a glass and fill it with ice and water and set it in front of Melissa.

"Thanks." She moves the glass back and forth in front of her, watching the ice. I don't know if something's on her mind or if she's tired or doesn't want to be here or a combination of all three. The microwave dings, and I set the spaghetti on the table. She stares down at it. "I haven't eaten spaghetti in years."

Her voice always sounds so tired or uninterested. "Years!" I say, getting a cup of hot tea ready.

"The fast-food restaurants I eat at don't serve it, and I never go out at night and I can't make it so, yeah, it's been years."

When the water's hot, I sit across from her and dunk the tea bag up and down in my cup. "You can make it. It's easy."

She takes a bite and I can tell she enjoys it. "No, I can't. I can't make anything, really. If it doesn't come in a box, I can't make it."

"Did your mom cook from a box?"

She makes a noise in the back of her throat. "Ramona cooked from a can and ate out of a box. Growing up, I thought my dad must have worked for either Campbell's or Kellogg's." She's quiet, but I can tell she's angry.

"You never knew him?"

Melissa laughs while taking another bite. "I doubt

Ramona knew him!" She moves the meatballs around on her plate and talks into one. "Your mom is great."

I reach for the Tupperware container of cookies behind me on the counter and open it, pulling one out for my tea. "My mom can't cook, either!"

"But she was there, wasn't she?" Melissa asks, wiping her mouth with a napkin. "She looked at your homework and sat across from you at the dinner table and showed up when you had a part in the sixth-grade play and searched the house for your stuffed bunny at bedtime. She did that, right?"

"Yeah, she did."

She's cutting a meatball into tiny pieces with her fork. "When I met her and Gloria, it was like being with a family I knew when I was a kid. That mom held on to my hand the same way that Gloria did. Like I meant something. That's the way your mom looked at me, and I knew that she and Gloria were great moms."

"Oh, Mom has her quirks, believe me," I say.

"And the only reason you know her quirks is because she was there," she says, sounding tired.

We use the silence to eat. My mother never could cook and she was terrible at crafts and spent way too much time thinking about what to wear or how she looked, but she has been a great mom. I can't look at her and think any of the things that Melissa must think of her mother. I finish the cookie and look at her. "When I was a teenager my mom and dad divorced. We went from all of us under one roof to three of us and Dad across town in an apartment. He eventually met another woman and moved to Arizona and became part of her family. Her kids called him Dad because they were so young when he married Liz. I'd sit in tenth grade math class and think about those snotty-nosed kids calling my father Dad while I went home to a house without him in it." Melissa is quiet, awkward is more like it. It seems she doesn't know how to carry on a conversation so I carry on without her. "I blamed Mom for everything. She was married briefly before Dad, when she was young. I brought that up and told her she didn't know how to be married. It just seemed to me that she could have done more to keep Dad in our lives. I hated her, I think. I wouldn't talk to her for months. It was awful. I loved my dad. I loved them together. I thought they were good, that everything was fine. I didn't know what was wrong about them. I still don't know."

"Your mom never remarried?"

Finally, she speaks! I wasn't sure if she was even listening. I reach for another cookie. "She did. After divorcing Dad, she married a college professor named Len and he was a good man. They were great together, but . . ." I think about it. "But I missed her with Dad. I wanted my kids to know them as grandparents together, not apart. Dad's marriage failed several years ago but he still lives in Arizona. He has grandchildren there. His life is there and Mom's was with Len. Len was good to Mom and he was good for her. He kept her grounded. Maybe that was Dad's problem. Maybe he let Mom get the best of him. I don't know."

Melissa finishes and twists the napkin around her index finger. "What happened to Len?"

"He died a few years ago, and then Mom and Gloria became best friends. She's done more for Mom than anybody in this world," I say, laughing.

"Ramona never had anybody." She says it with such gavel-rap finality.

"No one?"

She untwists the napkin and starts wrapping it around another finger. "She had lots of men—good-looking men, some of them married, and she'd use them for money and booze, something to eat, you know. They were after one thing but she didn't care. She played that game for a long time. Sometimes a guy would wise up and leave her alone but she could always find another idiot and string him along. Even when her looks started to fade she could still find some desperate fool. She never had one of them who stayed. Not one staying man or one staying friend."

"Do you hate her?" I'm surprised I asked that but watch her.

She drums her fingers on the table, the napkin looking like a poorly wrapped bandage around her middle finger. "I can't hate her. I hate everything she did and everything she didn't do. I hate everything she was, but I can't hate her. It doesn't make sense."

"Sure it does."

She slides her plate away from her and pushes her chair back. I can tell that Melissa thinks she's uncovered too much.

"Thanks for this."

I reach for the plate. "Hey!" I say, remembering. "Did you talk to your boss about finding your siblings?"

She looks small and sunken now. "He and Jodi weren't in on Friday when I wanted to talk to them." She twists her mouth and rattles the bottom of the glass on the table. "And then I lost my nerve after that."

"Why?"

She looks exhausted and defeated. "I don't know.

I've been trying to call my aunt and ask her about a girl she told me about years ago . . . a girl she said looked so much like me she could be my sister."

"Have you called her?"

"I did, but I hung up."

I'm not good at pep talks or encouraging people to buck up, but I give it my best shot. "So there's a chance your aunt knows something?" She nods. "Then that's a simple call. If the trail stops with your aunt, then what?"

Melissa looks at me with a look that says I know the answer as well as she does. "I look at Ramona's Social Security number every day," she says. "And I know she wrote that number down at each hospital she gave birth in. Those numbers are the key."

"So if it's that easy then . . . you know what? I'll do it." She looks at me. "Get the papers, fill them out, and I'll turn them in for you."

She looks shocked and confused. "No, no. I'll do it."

"When?"

"I don't know. I'll . . ."

"I'll do it tomorrow."

Her eyes begin to twinkle and her mouth turns up. "I will do it myself."

"No, you won't. Let me have the papers."

"I am not going to give you the papers. I will do it."

I cross my arms over my chest. "When?" She starts to open her mouth. "If I call the law office tomorrow and ask Robert Lawton if you turned the papers in, what will he say?"

"First of all, he won't take your call because you will have called him Robert Lawton and not Layton."

"He'll take my call. I can sound very convincing on the phone."

"Second of all, you don't even know Ramona's full name. Thirdly—"

"Three strikes. You're out! I'm calling and getting the papers tomorrow."

She stands and walks to the door. "No, you're not. I am getting the papers."

"So when I call and ask—"

She opens the door and walks to the stoop. "You are *not* calling."

"You just watch me, sister! I will call so fast it'll make your head spin."

I can tell she's laughing as she walks on the sidewalk to her condo. "You are a nosy neighbor," she says, her back to me.

"You're still baking a difference tomorrow, right?" I yell into the blackness.

"I don't bake!"

"Okay! Be at my mom's right after work. I left her address in an envelope in your mailbox."

Maybe it's because she's a good distraction or that my life doesn't seem so sad compared to hers or maybe it's because she's so different from me, but for whatever reason, I think I'm really starting to like that woman.

Nine

Friendship improves happiness, and abates misery, by doubling our joys, and dividing our grief.
—JOSEPH ADDISON

MELISSA

I sink into the sofa and stare at the phone. Before I talk with Jodi at the office I really want to clear up this Kay thing. If I don't get this over with, I really believe that Gretchen will show up at the law office and ask for the papers. I dig through my backpack for the number and dial Kay's number again. The phone clicks on the other end. "Hello."

I'm nervous and my breath is short. "Kay?"

"Yes."

"This is Melissa." She's quiet. "Ramona's daughter."

"Sure. Oh!" She's surprised and doesn't know what to say. That makes two of us.

"I saw on the Internet that your husband died two

years ago. Sorry. I never knew you were married, but that's . . . sorry."

"We were married twenty-three years. I have two children. How are you, Melissa? Where do you live and—"

I don't let her finish. "I thought you should know that Ramona died a few days ago."

There's no noise on her end. "It's been a lot of years since I've seen her. I sent her Christmas cards, but a few years ago they started to come back to me and I knew she had moved again and didn't tell me. She always was such an odd—" She stops. "How'd she die?"

"Heart." She makes a sound in her throat. "Kay? Years ago . . . years ago you said I looked like a girl named Louanne. Do you remember that?"

"Louanne Delgado. Sure. You looked like sisters."

My heart speeds up when she says that. "Is she my sister?"

There's no sound. "What?"

"Is Louanne my sister? Is she Ramona's daughter?"

"Louanne is Jake and Adele's girl."

I'm not convinced. "Jake was one of Ramona's men, right?"

She laughs. "No! They worked together at the factory and Ramona tried every which way to get to him, but that man was married for keeps. Drove your mom nuts."

"How do you know nothing happened? Why do Louanne and I look so much alike?"

"I don't know! It's just one of them weird things when strangers look alike."

I'm getting angry, disappointed, or frustrated; I

can't tell. "You know Ramona had two other kids, right?"

"No, I never knew that. How do you know?"

"She left a note, telling me. I thought maybe Louanne was my sister because you said something years ago and Ramona got angry."

"Bit my head off. I remember. She always was short-tempered. Wouldn't talk to me for a year or more after that."

"Maybe she thought you found her out. Louanne could be my sister."

"No." Her voice is soft. "It was a stupid thing of me to say. I was just teasing Ramona because I knew how much she wanted to get at Jake, and I thought it was so strange that Louanne and you looked so much alike, but she's not your sister."

"She could be. She—"

Kay cuts me off. "Jake and Adele moved to Florida when Louanne was ten. He never even met Ramona until Louanne was twelve or so and he started working at the factory."

Air is squeezed out of my lungs and I hold the phone limp in my hand, hoping for something to say. In a desperate way, I was hoping Louanne would be the end of my search.

"I stay in touch with Jake and Adele," Kay says. "I've seen pictures of Louanne over the years and now you don't look anything alike. Isn't that funny?" I don't respond. "I'm sorry about your mom. There'll never be another Ramona."

"Let's hope," I say.

"Will you let me know if you find your siblings?"

I tell her I will and hang up, worn-out from it all.

Donna VanLiere

* * *

Josh is clocking in at Wilson's as I'm getting off work. He's so different from the other teenagers Wilson's has hired every year around this time. He shows up several minutes before his scheduled time, and if he owns a cell phone, I've never seen it. One teenage girl texted as she sorted the mail until Mr. Wilson saw her one afternoon. Her mail room career ended that day. She was crushed.

"Hi, Melissa," he says, hanging his coat.

"You're in time for the shipment," I say, grabbing the shipping manifest.

"My grandma's better, so I won't be bolting out of here one day after all." I'm ready to go but can tell he wants to tell me more so I wait. "She got out of the hospital, and my mom flew to New Mexico to bring her and Gramps to stay with us for a while."

I open the door so he doesn't draw this conversation out. "That's great. What was wrong with her?"

"She had a mild heart attack. She blames all the German food she's eaten all her life." He sees that I'm ready to go and reaches for the shipment manifest. "See you around."

There's something about the way his jaw clenches or his face turns solemn as he sets to work that is oddly familiar and I stop, looking at him. "Have a good one," I say, letting the door close behind me. Something has always bugged me about Josh, but I can't figure it out. In the end, he'll put in his four weeks of holiday work and will have been just another kid who earned "i-something" money at Wilson's.

I take the stairs up to the break room to clock out and grab my coat and backpack out of my locker when a man stops me on the landing. "Excuse me," he says. "I'm trying to find something for my wife without her knowing it." He's holding a navy blue sweater in one hand and a yellow one in the other. "She's right over there with her mother." He lifts one of the sweaters toward two women in the jewelry department. "Which color do you think would be best on my wife?" All I can see is the profiles of the women, one is a brunette and the other has silvery white hair.

"I don't know," I say. "I'm not good at that sort of thing. You should ask one of the ladies on the floor."

He looks disappointed, but he shouldn't have asked a total stranger for shopping advice! "My son Josh works here. Do you know where I could find him? He'd have an opinion."

I glance at the two women and realize one of them must be Josh's grandmother that he told me about. "He's down these stairs," I say. "Just knock on the door." He heads toward the mail room, and for a second I watch Josh's mom and grandmother, trying to see their faces. I catch a small glimpse of his mother's face and think Josh looks like her. Navy blue, I say to myself, stepping into the break room.

The skies are bright for my short walk to the law office. I'm skipping lunch today so I can get out early and head to Miriam's to help her and Gretchen bake. I don't know why, but I find myself looking forward to being with them and baking something, anything for the first time. Once when I was around ten or so I begged Ramona to buy some of those slice-and-bake cookies at the grocery store. She wouldn't do it, and I noticed two other shoppers nearby so I got louder. "Please, Ramona! We never have cookies. I'll bake them myself." The other women looked at Ramona and smiled in an isn't-she-cute way, and I saw they were on my side. "Please! Please! We never bake cookies. I'll clean up the mess, I promise."

"All right, lamby," Ramona said, smiling at the other women and tossing the roll of cookies into the cart.

When we walked to the parking lot, Ramona set the bag of groceries in the trunk and pulled out the roll of cookies, bringing them into the car. I got excited when I saw her using her nail file to open the roll, thinking we'd get to enjoy some cookie dough on the ride home. She managed to open the roll and scooped out a large handful. "Here," she said, hitting me in the mouth with it. "Open up." I started to push her hand away, but she yanked my hand down, pushing the dough into my face. "Eat it! You made a fool out of me over it so you open your big mouth again and eat this." I opened my mouth and Ramona shoved the dough inside. "Swallow it." I gagged trying to chew the sweet, gooey mound but Ramona shoved another handful into my mouth. The dough hung from my nose and off my chin and tears filled my eyes but I willed them not to fall. I vowed at that moment to never shed another tear because of her and dried up then and there like Arizona. One handful after another was pushed into my mouth and when the roll was nearly empty Ramona threw what was left out the window and started the car. My face and shirt were a sticky mess and I wanted to throw up but I acted like I wasn't sick. Ramona looked over at me. "Do you still want to go home and bake cookies with your mommy?"

Ramona was on the phone when I threw up the first time. I didn't make any noise; I didn't want her to know that I was sick. I kept a bag by my bed so I wouldn't have to go to the bathroom and I threw up two more times. I threw the bag out the apartment window so she'd never have the satisfaction of knowing what she had done to me.

I bring the chill of outside with me as I open the door to Layton & Associates. Jodi is at her desk when I walk into the office, and I see she has the phone to her ear. I take my time hanging up my coat and scarf and untie and then retie my sneakers. When she hangs up, she waves at me behind the glass and I walk to her door, indicating I'd like to step inside. "Come on in," she says. I open the door as Jodi opens a file drawer at the side of her desk. Jodi is about my age, maybe older, for all I know. She runs several times a week, though, and is probably older than she looks. Her hair is light brown and hangs at her shoulders. She's married, but I don't know how many children she has, and I feel bad about not knowing. "How are you, Melissa?" This is as far as Jodi and I ever get, and I know she's curious why I'm standing in front of her.

"I was wondering if I could hire Mr. Layton's services?"

She shuts the file drawer and faces me. "Really?"

"I'd like to find a brother and sister I never knew about."

She smiles and walks around her desk. "Come on." I follow her to Robert's door, and she steps inside. Robert is typing on his computer and looks at us over his glasses.

"Hello, ladies." He stops typing and takes off his glasses. Jodi's smiling and my face is blank. I didn't think she'd tell him so quickly! I thought she'd get the ball rolling herself.

"Melissa would like to hire your services, Robert."

He leans back in his chair and crosses his arms, watching me. "What's happened, Melissa?"

I know I'm red in the face . . . from the wind, the cold, the heat in this office, or the fact that I've rarely spoken to this man who gave me my job. "I just discovered that I have a brother and sister that I never knew about." He waits for me to finish before he says anything. "I'd like to find them if you do that kind of work. If not, I'll—"

Robert smiles and puts up his hand. "You never knew about them?" I shake my head. "Isn't that something?" He smacks his hands together. "Let's find them!" He looks at Jodi. "Have her fill out Kate's papers."

I follow Jodi to her office and she opens a file drawer, pulling out a file. "What are Kate's papers?" I ask.

She pulls a stack of papers from the file and raps them on her desk to straighten them. "Cases that Robert knows his wife would want him to work on." I don't know what she really means. "Pro bono." She hands the papers to me. "He'll do it for free."

"I didn't mean for him to—"

"I know that. Fill out the papers and let's get working on your case."

My case! It feels too sudden. "How long do these things usually take?"

She puts the file back into the drawer. "Depends. We found a biological mother about six months ago and it took one day. One day! Over a year ago we tracked down a father, and that took a few months. You never know." She opens another drawer and pulls papers out of a file and checks to make sure she's handing me the right ones. "These papers will help us get started. They ask for your biological parents' names, if you know them, along with their Socials, if you have that info. Some people don't even have a name. Just a hospital or a town. We'll take what you have and get started."

"Thanks, Jodi." I walk to the back room, where I close the door and slump to the floor, reading the papers. One line asks for my mother's name. Another line asks for her Social Security number. I stare at them for what seems like an eternity before I reach for my backpack. I had written Ramona's Social Security number down years ago and carried it in my wallet. I hold the tattered note in my hand and read the number over and over. I print RAMONA JUNE MC-CREARY on one line and write down her Social Security number on the other. I run my finger over the words and numbers, and somehow I feel it. I've just opened the tiger's cage.

When I finish up at three thirty I walk to the front of the office where Susan is on the phone. I pull on my coat and hat and put the papers in Jodi's in-box. Susan taps on the box, gives me a thumbs-up, and then waggles her fingers 'bye in my direction. I take a breath and wave, opening the door.

I don't know if I'm excited or scared to death. I want to be excited, I say to myself. I want to pray like Mrs. Schweiger always did and have her kind of belief. I want to believe that my brother and sister would want to meet me and that they're good people. I want to meet them and tell them that they were the lucky ones; they got away. They never helped their boozy mother into bed or had cookie dough crammed down their mouths. They were the favored ones, the chosen ones. The blessed ones.

It's a little before four when I arrive at Miriam's house. Her home is decorated with simple Christmas lights draped over the shrubs and wrapped around the porch railing and posts. That must be Gloria's house next door with a Noel sign hanging on the door and evergreen and lights wrapped around the porch columns. I knock on Miriam's door and Gretchen's son opens it a crack, staring at me. What is his name? I can't remember.

"You're Melissa from next door," he says, opening the door wider.

"How are *you*?" I ask.

"My nana says you can't bake either, so this whole baking deal will be over with toot sweet."

"Now don't tell her such things," Miriam says, coming up behind him and putting her hand over his mouth.

He pulls her hand away and throws his arms in the air. "That is exactly what you said, Nana!"

"I know, but don't tell her such things."

He walks away, shaking his head. Gretchen steps into the entryway and holds her hands out at her side. "Well?"

"Well, what?" I ask, slipping off my shoes.

"Do I need to make a call?"

I hand my coat and backpack to Miriam and roll my eyes. "Your daughter can be very pushy."

"Don't I know it," Miriam says, whispering.

"I am not, Mother! Go put her coat away!" I follow Gretchen to the kitchen, where my nose goes into overdrive. Gretchen picks up a spoon and stirs something in a pot on the stove. "Well? How about it?"

"Leave her alone, Gretchen," Miriam says, motioning for me to sit at the table. "She'll tell us when she's ready." She sits across from me and slaps her hand on the table. "So, are you ready?"

I laugh and nod. "Yes. I turned them in today."

"Oh, that's splendid!" Miriam says.

"I don't know," I say. "I have this feeling in my gut that my siblings are going to be more like Ramona and not in the least like you two." It comes out faster than I realize and Gretchen smiles.

"Wow. That was pretty close to a compliment. Give her something hard to drink, Mom, and let's see what else she gives up."

"I didn't mean it as a compliment," I say.

Gretchen bangs the lid of the pot down. "Too late. Caught you being nice." She washes her hands and looks at me over her shoulder. "All right. Up on your feet, you two. Let's get a move on. Wash up."

The front door bangs closed and Miriam jumps, clutching her chest. "Gloria!"

Gloria peeks her head into the kitchen. "Aha! I was at home but had this creepy feeling, as if something was wrong over here. Now I see. Miriam's in the kitchen!"

Gretchen laughs and pulls out two big mixing bowls from a cupboard. Gloria rears back and opens her arms. "How are you, babe?" She hugs me to her, and I find myself hugging back. "Has it been a hard week?" I feel everyone's eyes on me and don't answer. Gloria wraps an arm around my shoulder. "Good days are on the way. Starting today! What are we baking, Gretchen?"

"Hummingbird cake and a chocolate raspberry cake."

Gloria pounds the countertop and makes yummy noises. She pushes up her sleeves and moves to the sink. "Tell me what you need, doll."

"Okay," Gretchen says. "You help Mom make the raspberry one, and Melissa and I will take care of the hummingbird."

Gloria shakes her head. "I knew you'd stick me with your mother."

Miriam laughs out loud, and I find myself smiling, listening to them. Gretchen puts me in charge of measuring out the flour, sugar, baking soda, and salt while she gets the pans ready. "I haven't helped bake a cake since I was a kid and helped Mrs. Schweiger from next door," I say, remembering Mrs. Schweiger and I crammed into her tiny apartment kitchen making a mess with flour and sugar.

"So you have baked something!" Gretchen says.

"Not really. Mrs. Schweiger did everything. I was just there to lick the beaters and eat the frosting."

When I'm done with the dry stuff Gretchen asks me to mash some bananas with a fork. I've eaten plenty of bananas but have never mashed one before. I press the fork into it and Gretchen laughs. "You don't have to be nice to it. Just mash it down." I mash away, and Gretchen opens a can of pineapple and chops up some nuts.

"These ingredients don't sound like they'll be good together."

"You'll be amazed," Gretchen says, chopping the pecans.

I am fascinated by the simplest act of pouring oil, breaking eggs, and using the mixer. I'd never had reason to use one before and find myself grinning.

"For crying out loud, Miriam," Gloria says on the

other side of the counter. "Grate the chocolate, not my nerves."

Miriam sighs. "I am trying my best, Gloria!"

"Are you trying to lull that chocolate to sleep? Grab a hold of it like you mean business and start working it over the grater."

"I want to switch teams," Miriam says, holding the grater in the air.

I laugh and read aloud the instructions of how to blend the rest of the ingredients. The bowl is awkward in my hands as I pour the batter into a pan. A huge glob of batter slides down the outside of the bowl and Gretchen swipes at it with a spatula. I'm leaning over the next pan when Gretchen's cell phone rings. She excuses herself to the living room, and Gloria and Miriam exchange glances.

"He's not just standing today! He's walking!" Gretchen says, running into the kitchen. The phone is still next to her ear. "They're sending him to Texas." She dashes back to the living room, and Gloria hugs Miriam, whose eyes are filling.

"Who's walking?" I ask, setting my sloppy bowl down.

"Kyle," Gloria says.

"Who's Kyle?"

"Her husband," Miriam says, laughing and crying at the same time.

"But I thought her . . ."

Gretchen hangs up the phone and flings herself into Miriam. Gloria wraps her arms around them, and they are a mass of arms, hair, and tears. Gretchen breaks away, laughing, dabbing at her eyes with her sleeve. She looks at me and I'm frozen in place. "I thought your husband was . . . you never told me he was alive," I say, feeling stupid as soon as the words slip past my teeth.

Gretchen reaches for a tissue. "You never asked."

"Was that Kyle or the doctor?" Miriam asks.

"Dr. Larimer," Gretchen says, her eyes pooling again. "He said Kyle tried to move his legs to the side of the bed again today and asked the nurse to help him stand. Dr. Larimer said it took all his strength but he put his feet down and lifted off the bed. Kyle wouldn't sit back on the bed like they asked but stood there for ninety whole seconds before he took some steps!" She lifts her arms in the air and waves them around.

"I thought he—" I stop. I never asked. Gretchen's words keep firing into my ears and my head feels hot. I never asked Gretchen one thing about her husband. Ethan had said he had gotten hurt but I never asked what that meant; I assumed he was dead. Since I have met Gretchen I have done nothing but ramble on and on about Ramona; I've never asked about what I presumed was her dead husband or her marriage to him. I sat in her home and ate spaghetti and didn't ask the questions that I thought would make me uncomfortable. I didn't even ask about her children, who were sound asleep down the hall. She looks at me and I know this is my one shot at a friend, but even now I don't know what to say. "I thought he was . . ."

Gretchen hands a tissue to her mom. "It's okay. I thought he was, too, for a while there."

A flash of anger balls inside my chest. "No! I met you and Ethan and he told me about his dad and a bomb but I didn't say anything. I just stood there." I step past them and head to the entryway, where my coat is hanging. I can't be here right now. This moment doesn't include me.

Gretchen follows. "Where are you going?"

I reach for my coat and put my arm in a sleeve. "You need to be with your family and friends right now."

She pulls the coat off my arm and holds it to her chest. "I am." Her face is soft, and Miriam and Gloria peek around the kitchen door, looking at me.

"I'm not a friend," I say, keeping my voice low.

"Then what are you?"

I feel like an idiot. "I should have asked."

Gretchen hands my coat to me and raises her eyebrows. "We're not finished baking, so come back in here and ask whatever you want."

I fumble with the coat in my hands. I've blown so many things in my life. I've never had this, whatever this new thing is that I have with these women, and I don't know how to act with them. Half the time I don't know what to say, but I do know I don't want to ruin it. I hang up my coat and walk back to the kitchen to finish our cake.

Ten

Every morning I wake up saying, I'm still alive; a miracle. And so I keep on pushing.
—Jacques Cousteau

GRETCHEN

The Eighty-second Airborne Division had been deployed to the southern region of Afghanistan in August of last year. Kyle's MOS (military occupational specialty) was infantryman, and he had risen to the rank of Sergeant First Class. His fifteen-month tour (his second in Afghanistan) would be over in November, twenty years in the army would be complete, and he'd be home for good. No more moving around. No more shipping out.

On Kyle's first day in the province he found a small circle of children to kick a ball with outside the base. He and several men in his unit always found time for the kids in Afghanistan. He said they were always sweet and loving and ready to play. On that morning, September fifteenth, he had gone out to the kids and kicked the ball around with them. They had things like cans or empty food sacks that they used for bases, and on that morning Kyle noticed that one of the food sacks looked fuller, but he thought it was nothing more than the wind that puffed it out. The children threw the ball here and there, not really playing any sort of real game when Kyle suggested they kick it like they had in days past and run the bases. Some of the little ones wanted Kyle to kick it hard, as he had done the day before, and he kicked it so the kids would have to run for it and he took off running. Two other guys from the division were cheering on the kids to get the ball before Kyle made it home, and he pretended to be out of breath running the bases. He ran to first and a little guy around six tried to hold him there, and then Kyle took second with the little guy still hanging on to him. Kyle ran on with the little boy dangling from his waist, not knowing that third base was a bomb.

The report says it blew Kyle thirty feet. It took his arm, part of his head and left him unconscious. Rocks and metal pierced his face, neck, jaw, and chest. The mother of the little boy who had been clinging to Kyle bent over the tiny broken body and clung to what was left of her son. A medic pinned a tag with the word *expected* on it to Kyle's chest, meaning he was expected to die as they transported him to the army hospital in Landstuhl, Germany.

The kids and I were going to move from our home in the little town of Spring Lake (near Fort Bragg) into our new house in Grandon that weekend, but then the phone rang. "Is this Mrs. Daniels?" I just knew the call was about Kyle, and I knew that something had gone horribly wrong. He told me who he was, but I couldn't tell you his name today if I tried. "A bomb exploded, and your husband . . ." I don't remember my knees buckling but recall the feel of the floor on my forehead as I pressed the phone to my ear to drown out *Go, Diego, Go!* on TV. My arms shook as I picked up the remote to turn it off. I hung up the phone and called upstairs to Emma, but my voice was gone.

When Kyle shipped off to Afghanistan the first time, he said, "It's nothing like it was when my grandfather fought," he said, referring to World War II. "They stormed the beaches, and thousands of men died a day." I wasn't sure how that was supposed to reassure me. He hugged me close. "It's not like that anymore, Gretch. We haven't lost as many during this entire conflict as we lost on one day at Iwo Jima." But the thought of receiving a phone call was always there in the back of my brain, and now it was real.

Ethan whined, begging me to let him finish *Go, Diego, Go!* I knelt down and clutched him to me, burying my face in his neck. Emma knew something had happened to her dad when she stood on the landing at the top of the stairs. She saw me clinging to Ethan and wouldn't come down, waiting for me to say something.

"Dad's been hurt," I said. She burst into tears and ran down the stairs, falling into Ethan and me.

Mom flew to North Carolina and stayed with the kids, and I flew to Germany. That was the longest flight of my life. I didn't eat; I didn't sleep; I couldn't read. I just prayed. I wasn't angry; I was frozen by the thought of what we are capable of doing to each other. Someone, an unknown face and name, left a bomb where children play in the hopes of killing one of us. It didn't matter that a child or several children could die as well. They were collateral damage and nothing more. Tears fell to my hands when I thought of the mother who still had to live there, passing her son's killer in the street or haggling with him over the price of fruit in the marketplace. There would never be any answers for her, just an empty place at her table. Kyle was alive, if even barely, he was alive. He didn't come home with a military escort. The mother wasn't even afforded the dignity of an escort for her son.

When I landed I learned that a small piece of metal had been lodged near Kyle's jugular vein and that he had nearly died during the surgery. My heart pounded in my head as the doctor explained all that *almost* went wrong with the brain surgery and all that could still go wrong. They had placed him in a medically induced coma, and they would keep him in a coma to give his brain time to heal and rest. "For how long?" I asked.

"It varies," the doctor told me. "But with his injuries I think it can be expected that his brain will need at least a month." I couldn't breathe or feel my legs. How could I explain this to the kids? The doctor tried to prep me for how Kyle looked, and even though I said I was ready, I wasn't. His right arm was missing below the elbow and his head was swollen to twice its size on one side with a hollowed-out part on top. Dark red scars with black thread were laid out like tracks over his head, neck, face, and chest and his face looked battered, but it was his eyes that were so unnerving. They were half opened when I walked into the room. They made me jump because I expected them to be closed, but they'd follow me around the room. I kept talking to him, expecting him to pick up a finger or wiggle his foot or something, but nothing happened. He just kept following me with his eyes. I could see him, I could touch him, but it didn't feel like it was Kyle in the bed.

"Does he know it's me?"

"Maybe," the doctor said. He said it in such a way that made me feel he was saying that for my benefit but that Kyle was still somewhere far off inside his brain.

I sat on the bed next to him and held his face, staring into those half-opened eyes. "Come out, Kyle. Come out of there," I begged. "Oh, God! Tell Kyle to come out. Please." I kissed his head. "Please."

Tom and Alice, Kyle's mom and dad, arrived the next day, and I couldn't imagine what they were seeing. What if that was Ethan in that bed? My mind couldn't comprehend what they were feeling. For the next few weeks I held Kyle's hand and held up pictures of the kids for him to see through those half-opened eyes. I told him I loved him and would take his broken, shelled body home with me as soon as I could. Doctors had no idea the extent of Kyle's brain damage but always prepped me for the worst: he may never talk like he once did; he may not be able to walk without assistance; he may never drive or be able to brush his teeth. They showed me the X-rays of his brain, and it looked like someone had scooped out a part of it and tiny pieces of rock floated in midair around his head and face. I put my lips up to his head and prayed as I've never prayed before. I prayed for

Donna VanLiere

a miracle, a sign, a new brain for Kyle. The week I
arrived I didn't eat for five straight days. I never left
his side.

On day thirty-two, doctors began pulling him out
of the coma. In the wee hours of the thirty-fourth day
his hand began to quiver. My heart drummed in my
ears and I jumped out of my chair and leaned closer
to him, squeezing his hand. He squeezed back and I
touched his face. "Kyle, it's me. Can you open your
eyes? Can you see me?" His lids must have weighed
fifty pounds; it took him so long to lift them. When
he did, he tried to grin.

I crawled into bed with him and yelled for the doctor. Kyle was shocked to see them. He thought we
were alone somewhere but didn't have a clue where
that was! He tried to speak, but the words were gar-
bled and I could see in his eyes that that confused
him. Doctors tried to explain what had happened to
him, and when they did, his eyes glistened. "None of
the other men were hurt, Kyle," I said. "Just minor
wounds. That's all." It would be more than a week
before I told him about the little boy.

"He's trying to talk," the doctor said, smiling at
me. "That's a good sign."

When we were alone I leaned close to Kyle and
kissed him. "I know you're going to fight this out,
Kyle! I know you're going to push yourself up out
of the rubble and crow." His eyes were still, but I
could see him in there. "Remember? Remember the
rooster? That's you! You are getting out of this bed,
and you are going to talk and walk and drive a car.
Do you hear me?" He babbled something unintelli-
gible, and I wiped my eyes. "Oh, yeah? Well, you've
never listened to me before. Why start now?" His

mouth tried to turn up, and I kissed the caved-in part of his head. "Remember the green SUV? I told you not to buy that truck and what happened?" His eyes were dull, looking at me. "It left us stranded on the highway . . . twice! That orange shirt? I told you orange was a horrible color on you and what happened? People always mistook you for a traffic cone." He attempted a grin again, and I squeezed his hand. "But this time you're going to listen to me. I'm giving you eight weeks to get home, Sergeant Daniels!" He closed his eyes, and I knew he was in there somewhere with fragmented pieces of the kids and me and of an orange shirt that could stop traffic.

"Max!" I jumped in my chair beside Kyle's bed and looked at him. It was the middle of the night and his eyes were closed. "Max! Maxey!" Max was our first dog, a big, lovable Lab mix. It was two days after he came out of the coma and the first words he spoke plain as day. I laughed out loud and told him we'd have a chat later about him saying a dog's name before mine.

I never went back to sleep but watched him throughout the morning, praying he'd wake up talking and wanting to take charge. I was staring at him when his eyes opened. "Bug," he said.

I bent over laughing. First a dog and now a bug! The word sounded thick, medicated and slurred, but I understood him.

"Apple," he said.

I couldn't stop laughing as I called the doctor.

"General."

Kyle always called me "General" when he was at home, indicating that I outranked him. "Now you're talking," I said, lying down next to him and kissing his face.

When he was able to string together clumps of three or more words over the next several days, Kyle began to ask about our life together. It took him ten minutes to remember Emma's name and he never remembered Ethan's; actually, he didn't remember Ethan at all. He could say Emma, but Ethan caused him trouble; he couldn't say the *th* without struggling. I spent much of the day pointing to things and saying the names of them so he could repeat after me: cup, water, ice, lamp, blanket, pillow, socks, underwear, nose, arm, hair, coffee, eggs. We went over the same words again and again because so many of them weren't understandable. He scrambled the letters the first few times he said the alphabet, but after several tries he made it from *A* to *Z* in less than ten minutes.

Each day a physical therapist worked his limbs to help him regain strength, and Kyle grew more deter-mined to get out of bed on his own. On Thanks-giving Day, I sat on the bed beside him and we called Mom to check on the kids. It was more than two months after the bomb exploded and the first time Kyle attempted to talk to the kids, and in his head he thought he was talking fine but they struggled to understand him. He was quiet when we said our final good-byes to the kids, and I knew what he was think-ing. "It's hard to understand over the phone," I said.

He was still the rest of the day, and I knew the phone call had taken a lot out of him. The next day he woke up, looked at me, and said, "You need to go home."

I put my hand on the little sprouts of hair on top of his head. "What?"

His eyes were liquid blue. "The longer you're here—" He stopped, reaching inside his brain for the next words. "They'll think I'm dying." I knew he meant the kids, and I started to say that Mom would assure them that he was getting stronger every day but he stopped me. "My mom and dad are here. Go move. Get them in school."

I swung my legs off the side of the bed, looking at him. "No, Kyle!"

"They'll be rushing—" He stopped, thinking. "Working—" He looked at me. "When you do a lot?"

"Busy?"

"They'll be busy and won't think I'm dead. Now they're home thinking the worst."

In a way, I knew he was right. The kids and I were always nervous when he returned home after being away for months at a time. We got into a rhythm of how things worked without Kyle and worried that he'd feel left out or that we didn't need him on a daily basis. I couldn't imagine how Emma and Ethan felt about his coming home now with so many injuries. They weren't even sure what those injuries were or what Kyle could or couldn't do. I dreaded leaving Kyle, but he was right. After the kids heard his voice they needed to know that he was okay.

He moved his hand to my leg and squeezed. "They need you. Go move and then—"

I put up my hand to stop him. "Hey! I'm the General, remember? I'll get us moved, but then I'm coming back."

He smiled. "I'll be walking for you."

"You mean you'll be walking *to* me!"

I had been e-mailing pictures of Kyle all along, but before I left, his mom took several of Kyle and me together to show the children that we were still a team and he was doing okay. Although I didn't really know what okay would look like for us now, I could tell Em and Ethan that he was alive and getting stronger every day. What more can any of us ask?

Eleven

In faith there is enough light for those who want to believe and enough shadows to blind those who don't.

—Blaise Pascal

MELISSA

The ringing makes me jump and I stumble out of bed, racing to the kitchen. "Hello," I say into the receiver.

"Melissa, it's Pat." My supervisor at Wilson's. I squint to see the clock on the microwave. It's five in the morning. "Josh has been in an accident." My brain struggles to remember who Josh is. "He was on his way to work." Josh in the mail room! "Can you come in this morning?"

I haven't worked on a Saturday in ages and try to recall what I have to do today but come up blank. "Sure. Yeah. I'll shower and be right in." Images of Kyle fill my mind. "Wait! How bad was he hurt?"

"All I know is he's at University Park Hospital."

At least four inches of new snow lie on the ground, and my tires slide when I back out of the garage. The roads are icy as I make my way slow and sure through the town square. For the first time in my life I can say I love it here. I love the sleepy streets and the three fir trees that are decorated for Christmas next to the gazebo. I love the dorky plastic Santa in the drugstore window and the evergreen wreaths that hang on each window of the fire station. Ramona died and I finally feel at home. I hope someday someone can explain that to me. Snow falls as if it's sluggish, taking its time, and I think of Kyle, his legs no stronger than these puffs of snow and I realize I've never known anyone who has served in the military, let alone someone who has fought in a war. I'm embarrassed because I've never thought about what they do or the families they leave behind, who try to maintain some sort of normal without them.

I enter Wilson's through the loading dock doors and make my way to the mail room. The shipping manifest shows a shipment is due at six this morning. I prep the shelves in the stockroom, although I know the shipment will be late due to the roads. When I finish, I walk to the office to see if by chance anyone is in yet. The office is dark and I check the door. It's open. I walk inside and flip on the lights, looking around. I know if I call the hospital that they'll never give me any information about Josh. Several file cabinets sit behind Judy's desk, and I wonder if one of them contains phone numbers for Josh or if his information would be on the computer.

I move to one of the file cabinets and try my luck there. I pull open a drawer, and it contains names of others businesses—vendors, I assume. I pull open each drawer and scan the files, looking for names I recognize. The third file drawer contains some names I recognize as employees, and I search for Josh, realizing I don't know his last name. A file for Joshua Dumont catches my eye and I pull it out, reaching for a sticky note and a pen off Judy's desk. I scan the file for phone numbers and write down his cell. For some reason, I take down the number for one of his emergency contacts, his parents, Mike and Karla Dumont, and jot down his home address. I slip the file back into the drawer and turn the lights off as I leave the office. Somewhere, the night security guard is either watching the cameras or walking through the store, so I act as if I was supposed to be in the office at this hour in the morning.

It's six fifteen when I make it back to the mail room, and I take my cell phone out of my coat pocket. I set the sticky note on the countertop and call Josh's cell. I don't know if I'm thinking he'll answer or someone else will pick up his phone, but for some reason I need to know what happened to him. His phone rings one time and goes directly to voice mail. I hang up and look at the other number on the paper. I can't call his parents. I'm not his supervisor calling to check on him. I'm not anybody.

It's one o'clock when the shipment is unpacked and the mail is distributed, and I clock out for the day. I'm heading toward home when I find myself sitting in the parking lot of University Park Hospital. I kept telling myself that I wouldn't come, that I'd drive straight home and watch something on TV, but I wandered onto the highway and ended up here. I've never visited anyone in a hospital before and am not sure how to find Josh. Two women sit behind a huge

C-shaped desk in the entryway, and I walk toward them, hesitating, ready to go back to the car because I'm not sure what to say to Josh. "Can I help you?" the younger of the two women asks.

"I'm here to visit Josh Dumont. He was in a car accident this morning."

"Are you a family member?"

My palms feel sweaty, and in a stupid way I feel as if I've done something wrong. "No. I'm a fr—I work with him."

She holds a pencil with both hands and lifts it right in front of her face. "We can't give out that information. A family member would have to let you know if he's here."

I turn to leave, feeling embarrassed and ridiculous. Deep down, I knew it was a dumb idea to come.

"Do you know Josh?"

A middle-aged man holding a small white sack is standing beside the desk. He looks familiar, and then it hits me. I blew him off when he asked which sweater would look better on his wife. "I work with him at Wilson's," I say, hoping he won't remember me.

"I'm Mike. Josh's dad."

He doesn't remember me. I don't shake his hand or hug him or do anything but stand here. "Our supervisor said Josh was in an accident this morning and I wanted to . . ."

"Come on up," he says, walking toward the row of elevators. "He had surgery first thing, but he's out of recovery and in his room now." The elevator doors close and Mike pushes the number eight.

"What happened?"

"Icy roads. A van lost control, slamming into Josh on the passenger side. He stepped on the brake when he saw the van sliding toward him and because his leg was braced for impact"—he straightens his leg to demonstrate—"when the van hit him, the force broke the low part of his tibia. They got him right into surgery, and it took a couple of hours. They put a pin in. They're keeping him for two or three days."

The doors open and I follow Mike down a bright hallway. "He probably doesn't want any visitors," I say, dragging behind him.

He stops and looks at me. "Who wouldn't want to see a friend after coming out of surgery? He'll love it. My wife went home to pick up Lyda, Josh's grandmother."

Josh's leg is raised in some sort of sling, and he's propped up on pillows when his dad and I walk into the room. "Melissa!"

I stand at the foot of the bed and lift my hand to wave. "I heard what happened and just wanted to see that you're . . . come say hi." Mike hands Josh the sack, and Josh pulls out some fries. A tray with traces of something brown and bland sits at his bedside.

"They made me eat that," Josh says, grinning. "But I had to have some fries to chase it down."

"I'm sorry about your leg."

He takes a bite of a fry and smiles. "I'm hoping I'll have years of fun setting off airport security."

"How long do you have to be off it?"

His mouth is full and ketchup sits on his upper lip. "Six weeks."

"So I guess your days are done at Wilson's?" He shrugs, eating. I swing my arms, looking around. "I should have brought you something, like a magazine or a bag of chips or something." I shove my hands in

my coat pockets to keep them from moving and realize I must look as awkward as I feel. "Well, I need to
get going. I just wanted to check on you and make
sure you're okay."

"Come back anytime," Josh says. "I like jalapeño
kettle chips."

He grins while eating, and I wave good-bye to
Mike. I wait for the elevator and stand aside when
it opens. Four people step out and I watch as two of
them, a middle-aged woman carrying a suitcase and
a white-haired elderly woman, make their way as
quickly as they can down the hall. Josh's mom and
grandma. I let the elevator doors close without getting on and strain to hear them in Josh's room. I can't
make out any words but I hear laughing and the rise
and fall of voices. My eyes fill and I press the button
for the elevator.

I knock on Gretchen's door when I get home because,
well, just because. I've been alone so much of my life
that I'm sick of it. "Did you have to work today?" she
asks, opening the door. It smells like something choc-
olaty in her house, and I hear the kids down the hall;
it sounds like they're dismantling their room.

"I was called in this morning because a kid was in
an accident."

She leads me to the kitchen. It's a mess of dirty bowls
and lunch plates. "What happened? Was he hurt?"

"Broke his leg. I saw him in the hospital."

"Did he have to have surgery? Is he okay?" I sit
down at the table and look at her. "Is he okay?" she
asks again.

"How many times have you asked that in your
life?"

She looks at me like I'm crazy. "What are you talking about?"

"Do you know how many times I've asked that?"

She leans against the counter and crosses her arms. "I don't know what you're talking about."

"I don't think I've ever asked if someone was okay."

"Sure you have."

"No! I haven't. I've never visited anyone in the hospital, shown up at anyone's funeral, baked a cake for a fund-raiser, or batted an eye when I heard someone in the military had died."

Gretchen turns on the light in the oven and mumbles as she peers inside at what I know is another cake for the Bake a Difference fund-raiser. She sits down across from me. "You just said you went to the hospital, so you *have* visited someone in the hospital."

"First time."

"And you *have* baked a cake for a fund-raiser."

"One time."

She gets up and crosses to a cabinet, pulling out two glasses. "There's a first time for everything." Her voice sounds strained as she puts ice in each glass and fills them with water.

I watch her and know that Gretchen is my friend. She is my friend for no particular reason other than she moved next door and cleaned out a crappy apartment and showed up at the graveside of a stranger, invited me in for spaghetti, and asked me to bake a cake. "Ramona never . . ."

She hands me the glass of water. "Ramona's dead." She is blunt and seems frustrated. "I don't know what you're going to say . . . that she didn't make you be a caring person because she was so self-absorbed or whatever. It doesn't matter. Whatever she did or didn't do . . . you can't change your past. Not even God can change your past."

She stops short of telling me to shut up and grow up. Two weeks ago I would have gotten up and walked out, but today I feel relieved. Gretchen is my friend for no particular reason at all and most particularly because she puts up with me.

I awaken at three, thinking of Josh. I roll over, rearranging the blankets, and see his mother and grandmother scurrying down the hall toward his room. "What's happening? Show me," I say aloud in what I realize is a prayer. It's three fifteen when I look at the clock again and I roll over to my other side, the image of Josh's grandmother running through my mind. What did his dad say her name was? At three thirty I'm frustrated because I can't sleep. What was his mom's name? The grandma's name? At four thirty I sit bolt upright in bed. Mike said her name was Lyda!

My heart is racing as I lie back down. I smile in the night and feel like a kid again. I'll never get back to sleep now.

Twelve

*Christmas waves a magic wand over this world,
and behold, everything is softer and more beautiful.*

—NORMAN VINCENT PEALE

GRETCHEN

I didn't hear anything in church today. I sat beside
Mom and Gloria and Marshall and thought of Kyle,
prayed for Kyle, hoped for Kyle, and cried, feeling
sorry for myself. I want him home. In one breath it
scares me to death that he'll never be able to walk as
he once did, but then in the next breath I'm grateful
he's alive. In another breath I worry that he won't be
able to do the work he loves, but as I exhale, I cry because he'll be able to hug Emma and Ethan each day.

I feel bad because I snapped at Melissa yesterday and never apologized. I just couldn't hear about
Ramona again. I couldn't take one more story about
why Melissa's life is pathetic and how Ramona is to

blame. The fact is, Melissa's life isn't pathetic. She not only works, but is able to keep a job and pay a mortgage, something her mother never did. Melissa's much smarter and brighter than she thinks she is; she could easily get a job in an office or even run her own business. I believe that. I need to apologize for snapping at her, but when we get home from church, I'm exhausted and just want to take a nap. Some days are like that. For days and months on end I am mother, father, nurse, cook, maid, teacher, taxi driver, laundress, and referee. Every now and then I want to climb into bed without any responsibility and pull the covers over my head.

I throw on a pair of jeans and am putting on a sweatshirt when the doorbell rings. I groan because I don't want to see anyone. I open the door without looking through the peephole and scream. "Dad!"

"Hi, sweet pea." Tears pour over my cheeks as I throw my arms around his neck. He smells like shaving cream and cigars. "I'm here nine days early. Is that okay?" I nod and sob into the whiskers on his neck. The tears I hide from the kids so I won't scare them pour over my father. "It'll be all right, Gretchen. Everything will be all right."

"I miss him so much, Dad."

He squeezes me tighter, and I'm eight years old again. "I know you do."

I try to hold it together but I can't; I'm a drippy mess. "Why are you here so early?"

"Because I thought you could use a break and maybe your old dad could give you one."

I laugh and cry at the same time. He's always known who I was. He's always known when I need to be quiet and when he needs to be quiet with me.

He's always known when to pick me up and when I need to pick myself up. He's always known when I need a wink, a hug, a shoulder, or a time-out. My dad has his own brand of problems, but he still knows me. I pick up one of his bags and yell as I set it down in the entryway, shouting for the kids.

Dad is playing his fourth game with the kids (this time it's Battleship with Ethan) when the doorbell rings. I nearly laugh crossing to the door because I called Mom from my bedroom and asked her to come over for coffee. I didn't tell her Dad was here. Sure, it was sneaky and maybe even a bit cruel, but I just had to do it. I swing the door open and smile. Her hair is perfect, and she's wearing a periwinkle scarf around her neck. She steps inside, and her eyes are the size of full moons when she screams. "Phillip!" She puts her hand on her forehead and I laugh, watching her. "I had no idea that you . . ." Her hand moves to her cheek and I laugh harder.

Dad is handsome as he smiles, standing to his feet. He is tall and his arms are well defined for a man his age. His hair is much thinner and grayer now, but his eyes are still as blue. "Look at you, Miriam," he says, crossing to her.

He kisses her cheek and Ethan laughs, slapping his forehead. "They can't kiss anymore. They're not married!"

Dad laughs and hugs Mom. She is stiff and gives me a dirty look. "You are an awful child, Gretchen Elizabeth."

Dad helps Mom take off her coat and he hangs it on the hall tree. "Relax, Miriam. She needs a good laugh."

"At the expense of her mother?!"

I take her gloves and purse. "I'm sorry, Mom. I just had to."

Mom straightens her hair and tries to peek at herself in the hall tree mirror. "I thought you were coming much later," she says, wiping something imaginary from her sweater.

Dad takes her hand and leads her to the sofa. "Sit down, Miriam. As I finish my game with Ethan I will tell you all about it."

"He came to surprise Mom," Ethan says.

Mom sits and straightens her slacks. "Well, good. We've all gotten a grand surprise today."

"D seven," Ethan says.

Dad makes the sound of an explosion and Ethan laughs. "You sank my battleship!" He looks at Mom and smiles. "You are a vision, Miriam."

Mom's face turns red and she swats at something in the air. "Oh, pish-posh applesauce. Be quiet, you!"

I laugh out loud from the kitchen because I've never heard my mother get flustered, but she doesn't know what to do with her hands and is grappling with the pillows on the sofa.

"No, no, you are," Dad says, sitting next to her. "It's like time forgot to march on with you."

I strain to hear them as I pour the coffee. "You look well, Phillip. It's good to see that you still have your hair and haven't gotten fat. You were quite portly at Gretchen's graduation. You're not stooped over, your fingers aren't gnarled, and you're not gasping for breath so that's something, too."

I put some cookies on a plate and laugh out loud. She's dying out there. I walk to the living room with two cups of coffee in one hand and put them in front of

Mom and Dad. That sounds so weird in my head. Mom and Dad. They each take a cup from me while Emma takes the cookies. I go back for my coffee and bring some cream and sugar. Something sweeps through my chest that feels like sadness or joy or maybe both. I don't know. I learned to live with the fact that my parents were no longer together, but here they are, sitting together and looking as I always imagined in my mind. Yet they're not together. I know that.

"Gretchen," Dad says. "Feel free to take off anytime to be with Kyle. Your mother and I can take care of the kids." I glance at Mom, waiting for her to protest the two of them working together, but she nods. "When are they moving Kyle to Texas?"

"On Tuesday."

He leans close to me on the couch and squeezes my leg. "Then why don't you book a plane ticket?" Tears fill my eyes and I nod. Dad wraps his arms around me and kisses my cheek. "Why don't you give me a list of things you need done around here, okay?" He looks around the living room. "I'll start with hanging the pictures."

I cry, blowing my nose, and laugh. "I can't hang them like Kyle."

"I know, Gretch. Your mother never could hang a picture, either."

Mom groans and shakes her head. "She picked up all my horrible traits and all of your glorious ones!"

Dad wraps one arm around Mom and her back stiffens. "She clearly picked up on all of your beauty, Miriam."

"It is getting ever so deep in here," Mom says. "Where are my green Wellies when I need them most?"

"Maybe you can work on hooking up the DVD player, too, Dad. I hooked it up, but a line divides the screen somehow so the kids only see part of the picture."

He pulls my head onto his shoulder. "I will check all electronics, and I will even plant some shrubs and a small tree out front. Now's the best time of year for that. It's the best time of year for so many things."

Thirteen

Each of us is here for a brief sojourn; for what purpose he knows not, though he senses it. But without deeper reflection one knows from daily life that one exists for other people.

—ALBERT EINSTEIN

MELISSA

It's a cute two-story house with an enclosed porch on the side. The smaller trees have Christmas lights, and strands are wrapped around the shrubs in front of the porch and outline the roof. I knock on the door and feel my pulse knocking hard. A teenage boy answers wearing a white T-shirt and flannel pajama pants. "Hi, is Karla home?"

"She and Dad and Gramps went to the hospital already. Were you the lady who was bringing food?"

Crap. I didn't even think to bring anything. "No. I work with Josh at Wilson's. I just wanted to talk to your mom about your grandma."

"Grandma's here. Do you want to talk to her your-self?"

I feel the pulse on the side of my head. "Yeah. If she's up and doing okay. Josh told me she was sick."

He tips his head back and says, "Come on."

I follow him through a living room decorated in warm browns, plums, and gold, through a hallway, and then step down into a family room with a plush sofa and big, comfy chairs. There, in one of the chairs by the window is Josh's grandmother. "Grandma, this lady works with Josh." I hadn't told him my name, and he doesn't ask as he bolts from the room.

She turns to look at me and my eyes fill. Her hair is white and her full face is lined with wrinkles, but her eyes are as brown and openhearted as I remem-ber. "Mrs. Schweiger," I say, choking on her name.

Her face opens in recognition and she puts some-thing from her lap into a box on the table beside her. "Melissy!" She tries to stand and I move to her side, sitting down. She puts her hands on each side of my face and water covers her eyes. "Look at you! Look at what a beautiful woman you grew up to be!" It feels like my throat is cracking, and streams of tears spill over my face. It's been close to thirty years since I've seen her, but all my life I've loved this woman as if she were my mother. She puts her arms around me and I crumble, remembering her hugging me as a child.

"I heard you were sick," I say, swiping at the tears on my face.

"I was sick, but now I'm much better."

"But you didn't go to the hospital this morning."

She shrugs her shoulders. "So this morning I'm not as better as I was yesterday." She sticks her finger up as if popping a balloon. "But tomorrow I'll be better than today. Eight years ago Albert and I moved to Albuquerque; the weather was supposed to be better for this and that ailment but look what happened. I got sick anyway." I love hearing her voice again and watching her gestures. "You are here." She makes it sound like she'd been expecting me. "Look at you. So beautiful. So smart. You were always so smart in school, bringing home those As in spelling and math. What do you do?"

"I just work in the mail room at Wilson's."

"What do you mean 'just'?" She looks at me and her face is solemn. "My Al just worked in the stockroom at the supermarket until he managed the place one day. *Just* is nothing but a phony-baloney word. You're good enough to work in the mail room and smart enough to work your way out of it." She believes that, too. She reaches for the box on the end table and smiles. "I never stopped praying for you, Melissy." She takes the top off the box and pulls out a stack of photos. "I pick up each of these pictures in here every day and I pray." She puts down a picture and names the person in the photo. "Josh, Eric, Taylor, Arianah, Drew, Taj, and Asia—my grandchildren. Karla, Mike, Madden, Grace, Louie, and Jen—my children and their spouses." She smiles at me. "And then all of my adopted children." She hands a photo to me, a picture of a kid about six or so standing in front of the old apartments where Ramona and I lived next door to the Schweigers. "Do you remember him? Bruce Linton from upstairs? Always had a runny nose?"

"Of course! He played with me and Louie every day! Mean little kid."

She laughs. "He was spirited! He's the fire chief now somewhere in California. These . . ." She rummages through the photos until she finds one. "These were Bruce's parents. Remember?" I nod. "Such nice people. His father died of a heart attack a couple of years ago, but his mother lives near Bruce." She puts another picture on my lap. "That's Rachel. She was Karla's age, so you might not remember her."

"She always wore her hair in a thick braid," I say, studying the picture.

"This was taken the day she got her hair cut. She's in Florida and is a fourth grade teacher." She flips through one picture after another. "That's Tommy. I don't know where he is. Garland lived next door to us after we moved away from the apartments. He works with computers. Ronnie is a policeman in Wyoming." On and on she went through a pile of worn photos of kids who wouldn't know her if they passed her on the street, but she prays for them anyway. She hands another picture to me, one of me when I was around nine, wearing green shorts and a striped yellow shirt and standing next to Karla, Madden, and Louie in front of a Ferris wheel at the county fair. "I saw your face every day. And I prayed for you." I look down at the photo and shake my head. "I prayed that God would protect you and guide you and your mother."

I look at her. "You remember what my mother was like, Mrs. Schweiger, so I'm not sure if praying worked."

She lays her hand on top of mine, and her voice gets quiet. "I know life was hard for you at that time in the apartments, and I always prayed that you would be strong and that you wouldn't give up. I know that you haven't, because look at you! You're here and your heart pops right out of your eyes." She squeezes my hand and leans in close. "I know your mother must be proud of who you are."

"Ramona died less than two weeks ago."

The sound of air escaping her lungs fills the room, and she wraps her arm around the small of my back. "I'm so sorry, love." A single tear sneaks down my cheek and I brush it away with my finger. "How did she die?"

I search the floor for answers. "Alone in her apartment. Her heart stopped." I laugh. "I could have told the coroner that years ago!"

She rubs my back and leans over to the end table for the tissues, handing me two. "How was she at the end?"

I shake my head, trying to put it into words. "The same." It's all I can say about Ramona. "I feel awful—"

"Of course you do," she says, cutting me off.

I look at her. "No." My throat feels like it's closing but I force the words through it. "I feel horrible because Ramona died and I feel free."

Her eyes are watery as she smiles, patting my hand. We sit in silence, and I know Mrs. Schweiger is trying to say something nice about Ramona but she's coming up blank. There is nothing to say about her. "You will have a place in your heart for your mother." I look at her. "You will. One day, someday, you will remember things and will store them away. You will love her in your own way." She squeezes my hand. "You always had so much love, Melissy."

Words clot together and form a ball in my throat. "You don't know me."

"I knew you as a child and I'm looking at you

now." I feel a tear leak from my eye and snake down my cheek. Mrs. Schweiger dabs it with a tissue and pulls my head onto her shoulder. "I loved you like one of my own, Melissy." That makes me cry more, and I hold a tissue under my nose. "You were always such a special child." I haven't heard anything like this since I was a child inside her apartment, and I press the tissue into one eye and then the other. Mrs. Schweiger sits with me in the quiet and lets me cry, rubbing my arm and patting my leg. "It is okay to feel free." I look up at her and she works at a smile. "You are not horrible. You're human."

I cover my eyes with the tissue. "This is the first time I've cried since she died."

She hands me two more tissues and pats my leg. "There will be more to come." She leans back and looks at me. "How did you know I was here?"

"I don't know," I say, wiping my face. "Josh works at Wilson's with me, and I don't think I ever paid attention when he was talking, but it all came together and made sense early this morning. I saw you and Karla yesterday as you got out of the elevator at the hospital, and this great sadness or something pushed down on me. I don't know what it was other than a great coincidence that I was leaving as you were getting there."

She smiles and lifts my picture from the top of the stack. "Or was it a finger snap from heaven letting you know to be aware and open your eyes?" I smile at her and she waves her hand in the air. "We pass everything off as coincidence. 'Eh, I needed more money to pay the rent and lo and behold I got paid more than I thought this week.' Or, 'I haven't worked in ten months. What a coincidence to run into an old friend who needs help!' Or, 'I think I'll stop by Josh's house and ask if his old grandma is Mrs. Schweiger from the apartment days in Florida but what's this? It *is* her and she's actually sitting here talking to me.' Is it all coincidence or is it God's way of letting us know that we are heard and seen?"

I throw both hands in the air. "I give up!" She laughs and touches her head to my shoulder. I lean down and lift Ramona's note out of my backpack. "I suppose you'll say that my finding this in Ramona's apartment wasn't a coincidence, either?"

She puts on a pair of glasses that were sitting on the end table and reads the note, her eyes widening as she smiles. "This isn't a coincidence," she says, her voice getting louder. "This is destiny!"

It's midafternoon by the time I make it home. Mrs. Schweiger wanted me to stay and talk with Karla, Mike, and Mr. Schweiger when they got home from the hospital, but I could tell she was tired and needed to rest. I discovered that Karla and her husband moved to Grandon two years ago, when Mike got transferred and Mr. and Mrs. Schweiger visited them for a week last summer. I wonder if I passed them in the car or saw them strolling through downtown? I'm smiling as I pull into my driveway and see Miriam's car at Gretchen's. It feels like I'm leaping as I run the length of sidewalk between our homes. I rap on the door to the rhythm of "Shave and a Haircut" and surprise myself. I've never done that before. Gretchen opens the door and I nearly burst inside. "You'll never believe what happened." I expect to see

Miriam and I do, but she's sitting next to a man I don't know.

"This is my dad, Phillip," Gretchen says.

He stands and makes his way to me with his hand extended, but I take everyone off guard and hug him.

Gretchen laughs at the sight. "Are you drunk?"

"I'm so sorry," I say to Phillip. "I didn't mean to burst in but I just had to!"

"This is Melissa from next door. And she's never like this."

"I thought you were coming later," I say to Phillip.

"He was," Gretchen says. "But he came to help Mom with the kids so I can go to Texas." She looks at me with a wary eye. "Why are you acting weird?"

I tell them everything as we eat pizza for dinner, and I remember Mrs. Schweiger said she would call about getting together with Karla tomorrow. I walk to my backpack and discover my phone is still on vibrate from my visit with her. There is a voice mail, and I hold the phone to my ear to listen. I feel the blood draining from my head and my legs turn to Jell-O as I walk back to the kitchen table. "Listen," I say, pressing the speakerphone button on my cell and holding it out at arm's length.

"Hey, Melissa, this is Jodi. I know it's Sunday and a weird day to call, but I really wanted to share this information with you. If you get this in the next hour, call me. If not, I'll be out of pocket the rest of the day. If I don't talk to you . . . well, I know you work at Wilson's in the morning, but if there's any time to come in in the morning, I think you should. We have some information on one of your siblings that Robert just discovered. A hospital called him back. I don't want to take up all your voice mail. Just drop in tomorrow morning if you're dying to know, or you can wait till you come in in the afternoon."

She left the message three hours ago while I was with Mrs. Schweiger, so I can't call her back.

Miriam is beaming, Phillip looks confused, and Emma says, "What's all that mean?"

"It means," Gretchen says, "that Melissa is about to meet one of her siblings."

I slept, but barely. It seems I woke up on the hour staring at the clock, anticipating and dreading the morning. Gretchen offered to go in with me when I talked to Robert and Jodi, but I didn't want to take her away from her dad, and I knew she needed to pack for her trip to Texas. I talked with my supervisor at Wilson's after I received the message from Jodi yesterday and told him I'd be in just as soon as I left the law office. My hands feel slippery on the wheel as I drive to the law office, and my chest feels like it's buzzing. I open the door and Jodi looks up from her desk, smiling. "You got my message," she says, coming into the entryway. I don't have time to respond. "Come on. Robert's here."

I follow her to Robert's office and feel nauseated or headachy, I'm not sure which. "I can't believe you already found one of them," I say.

"I told you that sometimes all it takes is one phone call." She uses the file in her hand to wave me into Robert's office and I walk past her. "The second sibling is proving problematic, but we're keeping at it."

Robert is at his computer and takes off his glasses when Jodi sets the file on his desk. He rubs his hands together and smiles. "So a sibling has been discovered! Are you ready to know?"

A sibling has been discovered. Never in my life did I think anyone would say those words to me. He bounces the file in the palm of his hand, a tiger pacing in its cage waiting for the door to open, waiting to be let go. I nod and he opens the cage.

Fourteen

*Miracles are a retelling in small letters of the very
same story which is written across the whole world
in letters too large for some of us to see.*
                                        –C. S. Lewis

GRETCHEN

I'm doing laundry when the phone rings. Dad took
Emma and Ethan to school and then said he was going to drop by the grocery store to stock up while I
was out of town. I don't even know what kind of junk
he's going to bring in for the kids. I can tell by the
connection on the other end that it's someone calling
from Germany.

"Mrs. Daniels?" He doesn't need to tell me who he
is; I recognize that Texas drawl as Dr. Larimer. Although he works at the Army Hospital and is a career
army doctor, I always found his accent to be so out
of place in Germany. "Kyle needs another surgery,"
he says with a tone like "My buddy here needs more

chips!" I try to figure in my mind how many surgeries Kyle's had already. Was it three or four?

"Do you remember the X-rays of Kyle's shoulder and face? The ones that looked like pieces of metal and rock were floating in midair?" I remember them as if I were staring at them now. "That area in the shoulder is called the brachial plexus." I imagine him using the tip of his pen and circling it above the X-ray as we talk. "It's basically a huge system of nerves that run from the spine to the arm. The shrapnel is floating. Over time, the shrapnel that is in Kyle's face will surface and make its way out." I want to ask how; wondering if it would swell to the surface like a pimple and eventually be squeezed out, but he continues to talk. "The shrapnel in his shoulder is getting dangerously close to this system of nerves, and our concern is that it will continue its way to the brachial artery, which could cause irreparable damage, even death. However, the surgery will slow his physical therapy because that arm will need to heal, but without it he could potentially lose feeling or use of his arms if those nerves and arteries are compromised."

"So will they do that surgery when Kyle gets to San Antonio?"

"We won't move him until we remove the shrapnel. We'll take him in today."

It registers what he's saying and it feels like he has knocked the wind out of my lungs. "He's not coming to the States?"

"Not at this time. In a few days. We'll keep you up-to-speed."

It's shocking how your mind and emotions can skyrocket and then plummet in seconds. When I heard the connection on the phone and knew it was someone in Germany calling, my thoughts were soaring as I imagined Kyle coming home and the two of us sitting together on the couch, watching the kids open their presents before I moved to the kitchen to cook my portion of Christmas dinner. Then all of us: the kids, Mom, Dad, Melissa, and Kyle and me would settle in at Gloria and Marshall's for Christmas dinner. Apparently, Dr. Larimer didn't receive my memo.

He hangs up before I can ask anything else and I sit on the couch. Hot liquid sits on top of my eyes and my chest tightens. My heart was set on seeing Kyle tomorrow. I thought all his surgeries were behind him and all he had to do was focus on rehabilitation. I want him home! I'm so tired of not having him here with us. I pound the phone into the couch, yelling at no one and nothing or someone and everything. I am so angry and frustrated and tired. I dial Kyle's dad's cell number. He and Kyle's mom have been with him the entire time in Germany. They'll have more to say than the doctor, but the phone goes to voice mail. Do I fly to Germany again or wait for Kyle to get to Texas? How long will that be? I throw my head back on the couch and stew in the disappointment, tears, and unanswered questions.

When the doorbell rings I ignore it. Someone starts to knock and I remain still. I don't want to see anybody. The doorknob jiggles and I jump up, wondering if I locked the door. I see Melissa's head through the peephole and I feel like a louse pretending I'm not here. I open the door and see that she's holding a piece of paper and I know she must have the information about her sibling. She looks tired and pale, and I can only assume that she didn't sleep much last night. "Come on in."

"Are you okay?" she asks, crossing to the couch.

I shrug. "Kyle's not being moved to Texas tomorrow. He needs another surgery."

"For what?"

I slump down on the other end of the couch, not wanting to talk about it. "His arm. There's lots of shrapnel that's moving too close to the nerves and arteries."

"When *will* he fly to Texas?"

I shake my head, sighing. "A few days." We're both quiet and I know I've put a damper on her good news. If she has good news, that is. I'm hoping I can act thrilled for her when she tells me. "Well! Do you know the name of your sibling?"

She nods, the piece of paper quivering in her hand. She hands it to me and I strain to hear her. "I hoped it was you."

I stare at the names on the adoption document. Birth mother: Ramona McCreary. Adoptive father and mother: Phillip and Miriam Branch. I am shaking and can't breathe enough to find my voice. Ever since I was a teenager my parents told me I could find the woman who gave me up for adoption, but I never wanted to; I genuinely never *wanted* to. As far as I was concerned I had my parents. "I . . ." I look at Melissa and she's as shaken as I am. Her pale, perplexed face makes me laugh out loud and I fall back into the couch cushions. "You look like I feel!"

She watches me laugh, and her baffled look makes me laugh harder. "This is how you respond?" She picks up one of the throw pillows and whacks me with it several times. "And I thought I was the one who got the socially backward gene. Obviously, it was you!"

I howl louder with a sense of relief and excitement

and look at Melissa, my eyes filling. It's one thing to get a package in the mail that you didn't expect or to hear the voice of an old high school friend on the phone who happens to be in town and wants to catch up over coffee. Those are nice, make-your-day surprises. Getting a sister you never knew existed is a bolt from the blue bombshell. It's a voice from the wings telling you to take your mark because the next act is going to be a doozy. Somewhere along the way I went from barely tolerating Melissa to missing her when she wasn't around. Maybe that's how it is for sisters. I throw my arms around her; it's the first time I've hugged her, and I laugh again because I'm hugging my sister.

I'm not sure if we're laughing or crying, but we stay tangled together until I sniff so loud that she pulls away, holding her ear. The weight of what has happened fills my living room, and we stare at the names on the paper that were typed by some unnamed secretary thirty-seven years ago. Did she know then, as she pecked each letter on her typewriter that lives would collide someday? Did Ramona ever think about it? Probably not, given what I know about her. "Why did you say you hoped it was me? Did you know I was adopted?"

Melissa nods. "Gloria told me the first day I met her and your mom. Yesterday when I heard Jodi's voice mail I immediately hoped that they found my sister and that she was you. It was a stupid, crazy thing to hope for because the chances of that happening were zero."

"Or one hundred percent!"

Melissa and I run to Mom's door and burst through without knocking. I called Dad and told him to go to her house right away, and Mom called Gloria. All I said was that I had news for them.

Mom and Dad never met the woman who gave birth to me, never even caught a glimpse of her; that's the story they always told me. They took me home the day I was born, and when the time was right, they told me I was adopted. I know Mom worried that somehow I'd be scarred, left with this big birth mother wound in my heart, but it never worked that way with me. Ramona was a woman who carried me to delivery and "handed me over," so to speak, to my parents. She wasn't my mom.

Mom is handing Dad a cup of coffee when Melissa and I stampede into her kitchen. "Sit down!" I say. "You have to sit down."

Gloria moves to a chair. "Lord have mercy. The last time I heard that, the doctor told me I was pregnant again!"

Mom, Dad, and Gloria are sitting at the table looking at us, their faces wondering and open and beautiful with age. "Kyle needs another surgery and won't be flying to Texas tomorrow, which means I won't be flying to Texas, either."

Mom looks confused. "And you're excited about this?"

"I can't even tell you how angry and disappointed and sad I am about this."

Gloria crosses her arms. "In Georgia we always had a different way of expressing those emotions."

"I know!" I say, my voice lifting like fireworks. "I am *sooo* disappointed!" The looks on their faces make Melissa and me laugh out loud, and Mom shakes her head. "You always told me to find the woman who gave birth to me, right?"

Mom nods. "And now you're going to?"

"I don't have to. Her oldest daughter found me."

The three of them sit for a moment, letting it sink in. Mom's hands attack each side of her face and she lets out a little squeak, her eyes shifting from me to Melissa. We're both grinning like cats and she rises, dazed, to her feet. "Melissa . . ."

Gloria's hands flap in front of her. "Are you kidding us?"

Melissa shakes her head and Dad pounds the table. Melissa lays the adoption document on the table, and Gloria, Mom, and Dad read it out loud, their voices mounting together as each name is read. "Where are those Action News people when you need them?" Gloria asks, hugging Melissa.

Mom holds the document and studies it closer. "So you have the same mother, but do they know . . ."

"We don't have the same mother, Miriam," Melissa says. "My mother was Ramona, and Gretchen's gestational carrier was Ramona. She had a different mother. A good mother." Mom purses her lips together and puts a hand on the side of her face. "I never knew the man involved in my entry, and given the fact that Gretchen and I are two years apart and Ramona never stayed with a man for longer than a week . . . the odds are low the same man was involved. That would be out of character for Ramona."

Mom looks dazed and seems to be taking this harder than I imagined.

"Marshall hasn't left for the store yet," Gloria says. "Would you come tell him, Melissa?"

"I told my supervisor that I'd be at work after I left the law office. Now look where I am!"

Gloria puts her hand on Melissa's elbow. "This is

the perfect excuse for your supervisor. Tell him you were at the owner's house!"

There are some things I know about Gloria, and one is that there's no way she'd ever leave a good party unless there was an urgent need, like she was about to throw up or saw that her best friend was about to throw up. I know she saw Mom's face, and because she knows Mom so well she wanted to give her room. The door closes behind them, and I sit down at the table, tapping it so Mom and Dad will sit back down, too. "So, what do you think, Mom?"

She holds the paper and shakes her head. Miriam Lloyd-Davies is stumped and stupefied. "I . . ." Her voice is searching for the words. "I . . . just never imagined such a thing happ—" She puts her hand on her head and looks at Dad.

"It's unbelievable," he says. "You have a sister! The kids have a new aunt! Kyle has a sister-in-law, and the way I see it, we have another daughter!"

Mom doesn't react and I get out of my chair, squatting down next to her. I haven't had much time to think about what has just happened, but in a fleeting moment I realize I stood at the graveside of the woman who gave birth to me, a woman who I would most likely never want to invite over for dinner or even chat with in line at the grocery. I'm sad that Ramona never appreciated Melissa or the trees and sky, the bright, hollow beak of a toucan or a patch of wildflowers. I'm sad that her life is over before she ever lived it. "You know, sometimes you just have to point out the obvious." Mom looks at me and waits. "No doubt about it. I got the better end of that deal."

       ❈   ❈   ❈

I finally get through to Kyle's dad, and he gives the phone to Kyle. "Hi, Gretch." I laugh out loud, crying, so excited to hear his voice and to tell him what has happened. His voice sounds stronger, but the words still take longer to come out. We'll talk about his surgery coming up in two hours and whether I should come to Germany or wait until he flies to Texas. I know we'll get to all that, but I'm about to pop. "Are you laughing or crying?" he asks.

"Both!" I yell into the phone. "Something amazing has happened!"

"Really? On a scale of one to ten, how amazing is it?"

"A thousand and twenty!"

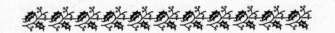

Fifteen

Small deeds done are better than great deeds planned.

—PETER MARSHALL

MELISSA

I picked up Mrs. Schweiger yesterday afternoon and took a bag of jalapeño chips to Josh in the hospital. Mr. Schweiger answered the door looking bald and much shorter than I remembered. His eyes nearly disappeared when he smiled and latched on to me with the strength of someone years younger. They were always so good together, these two with their fine German stock and sensible ways.

Before we left for the hospital I relived Jodi's voice mail for them about finding my sibling, and they sat on the edge of their chairs as if I was the most interesting storyteller they'd ever heard. When I told them my sibling turned out to be the woman next door to me, Mrs. Schweiger threw her hands in the air and yelled something in German. "It was destiny!" she says, holding both my hands. "I told you it was destiny!" Her eyes are watery as she looks at me. "You could have gone your whole life and never known your sister, but your mother wanted you to know that."

"Not really. If we hadn't found the note in her apartment, I would have never known."

She pats my hand too hard. "You don't know that. She wrote the note. She wanted you to know. She was trying to do the right thing for you." She is nodding, waiting for me to believe. Although she and my mother said very little to each other the three years we lived next to them and Mrs. Schweiger would have no reason to defend her, I know that she saw something in Ramona that only another mother can see.

"I know," I say, believing her.

I don't have to be at Wilson's until ten this morning and decide to do some laundry when I hear voices outside. I move the blinds and see Phillip and Miriam standing in the yard, so I open the door, folding my arms against the cold. Miriam is wearing a long camel-colored coat with black leather gloves and a furry hat, and Phillip wears a red-and-black-checked coat with a Pittsburgh Steelers hat. "Morning!" I yell, waving.

Phillip gestures for me to come closer. "Melissa! Come decide for us." I reach for my coat out of the closet and close the door. Five shrubs sit in black plastic tubs near the front of the condo. "I was trying to plant these this morning, but Miriam dropped in to boss me around and tells me I have them all wrong."

"I did not say that Phillip. I said if that's how you want to order them, then fine, but I wouldn't do it that way."

"I apologize. My translation was way off," he says, looking at her. "Melissa? What will look good? Those three are heather laurels and these two are azaleas. I thought the azaleas would be a good background for the laurels."

Miriam is shaking her head, and the way the fur on her hat moves around it looks like something alive is on her head. "You don't put a flowering shrub behind a big green thing, Phillip. You put the green and then the shorter flower bush in front of it."

"Azalea," he says.

"Whatever! You don't put the thing of beauty behind a wall of green."

Phillip looks at me for help. "She's right," I say, sheepish.

Miriam gives Phillip a smug eye roll. "When you told me you were going to do this, I just knew that I must come here to see that this is done properly."

"Where's Gretchen?" I ask.

"She dropped the kids off at school and was going to two different dental offices that are looking for hygienists," Phillip says. "One is thirty minutes away. I told her to eat lunch out and enjoy the day. I'm hoping I can get this done while she's gone."

Miriam marches to the door. "I'm going to find some proper clothes. I'm sure Gretchen has several grubby things I can wear."

Phillip is digging out the old shrubbery, which is so small and dead that it can practically be pulled up rather than dug, while I prepare the empty holes for the new plants when Miriam opens the front door. Even in Gretchen's "grubby" clothes she looks like a million bucks. "Besides his poor design judgment, Phillip has always had a green thumb. We had yard of the year one year. When was that, Phillip?"

"In '72," he says. "Miriam picked out all the plants and flowers. She's always had an eye for beauty. Beauty attracts beauty, though."

Gretchen would laugh watching Miriam's face turn flame red. I keep my head down as I help pull out another dead shrub so they won't see me grinning.

"People slowed down just to see our yard," Miriam says, pouring some bagged soil and fertilizer into a hole.

"Half the time they were slowing down to look at Miriam," Phillip says, serious as a news report.

Miriam laughs and reaches for some peat moss. "Oh, Phillip, really!"

"I can see that, Miriam," I say, loosening a heather laurel from the plastic container.

She laughs again and Phillip leans on his shovel. "People are still slowing down to look at her. Just look there."

Miriam and I turn behind us to see the mailman in his car. "The mail carrier!" Miriam says. "Do be quiet, Phillip."

"Look at him! He can't take his eyes off you."

Miriam laughs harder than I've ever seen her, and she uses her trowel to swipe at Phillip's leg. If I didn't know better, I would say they're getting along. I would say they're teasing each other, flirting even!

By the time I leave for Wilson's, Phillip and Miriam are heading inside Gretchen's for a coffee break, and something tells me the shrub planting might take them all day.

For the first time in years I look forward to going to work. The streets and storefronts seem to have their own energy. They're pulsing or buzzing or ringing out some melody that I've never been able to hear before, and thoughts rush through my mind. Ramona. Gretchen. Josh. Mrs. Schweiger. Layton and Associates. "We pass everything off as coincidence," Mrs. Schweiger had said. I stop at the square and look at the gazebo and the three decorated fir trees. Why would anyone take such effort to make those trees beautiful? Why would anyone go to so much trouble? Something in my chest catches and I swear I hear a finger snap from heaven.

Before I clock out at Wilson's, Jodi calls from the law office and says the computers are down. Since that's the bulk of my work there, she tells me to take the day off, which I'm happy to oblige! I race home and smile at the sight. Phillip and Miriam are in my yard planting what looks like the last of some new shrubs. For the first time since I've known her, Miriam looks worn and ruffled. I get out of the car, grinning. "What are you two doing?"

"One condo couldn't look that good and this one look horrible," Phillip says. "So we went and bought some matching shrubs."

"But I . . ."

Phillip puts his arm around my shoulder. "Just so you know. This is my gift to our newest family member."

"I never know what to say," I say, frustrated with

myself. "This is so great!" I hug them both and stand looking at them. "Will you both help me with something?" Honest to goodness, I've never had a brainstorm before. Seriously, I haven't. But this is a good one and it's bigger than me.

Sixteen

Out of difficulties grow miracles.
—JEAN DE LA BRUYÈRE

GRETCHEN

I never thought I'd see the day that my parents were actually working side by side together again, but Melissa swore to me that they planted the shrubs together Tuesday, and on Wednesday Mom and Dad came for the kids and me and we went shopping for a Christmas tree after school. The kids stayed up too late decorating it, but I didn't mind. I found myself standing back and watching Mom and Dad with Ethan and Emma. Dad's always had the ability to be so silly with children, and Mom would laugh out loud at his lousy jokes and poor impersonations. When the tree was decorated, we took pictures in front of it: just the kids, the kids with Mom, the kids with Dad, the kids with Mom and Dad, the kids with me, and me with Melissa. It felt so strange to pose for a picture with her because in a way it felt as if we'd always done it.

Kyle called on Thursday and said that doctors still hadn't told him when they'd move him to Texas. His surgery was successful on Monday, so I couldn't figure out why they just didn't move him. I wanted to come to Germany but Kyle wouldn't hear of it. "You'll just get here and they'll transfer me. Just wait until they decide to move me and then come to Texas." Although my parents are here and I have the kids and Melissa, this faraway feeling is getting worse as Christmas gets closer.

The kids got out of school for Christmas break on Friday, and since then they've managed to tear through our house and Mom's like crazy people. Tonight is the chamber orchestra concert and benefit for Glory's Place. Gloria has been in the newspaper and on the local radio station soliciting anyone and everyone to help Bake a Difference for Glory's Place. Melissa even baked in her own oven! She brought over a chocolate cake yesterday and was beaming as she set it on the table. "That actually looks good enough to eat," I said.

I haven't seen much of her in the past few days because of her work schedule, but we've spent time in the evening trying to find similar toes or hands, ears or kneecaps, but have come up with few resemblances. She's tall and I'm short. Her face is angular and mine is round. Her fingers are long with soft fingernails and mine are short with hard fingernails. Dark hair sits on her head and blond strands cover mine. She is abrupt and I am deliberate, but hopefully I'll teach her how to be more measured and she'll teach me how to speak freely.

Dad and Melissa went to church with us this morning. Dad's never been a church man, but he's always open to it at Christmas, especially when he's with his grandkids. Melissa's been to church a few times when she was a kid, with the Schweigers but never with Ramona or on her own. She was still as she listened to the reading from Luke and wiped her eyes when all the children sang "O Holy Night" and "Hark! The Herald Angels Sing." I cried, too, and I caught Dad rubbing his eyes. For Kyle's first tour of Afghanistan the soldiers sang "Silent Night" together on Christmas Day, and Kyle said nobody dared look at one another because there wasn't a dry eye in the whole bunch. Seems like the songs of Christmas have the same effect no matter where you are in the world. I cried through the entire service again.

Two days ago, Gloria asked Melissa and me if we'd help set up for Bake a Difference at the community center. We eat a quick lunch with Dad and the kids before driving across town to the civic center. The chamber orchestra is already in place practicing on stage as Mom, Gloria, Melissa, and I set up tables in the lobby. Gloria hands me a tightly rolled banner. "Could you figure a way to hang this, babe?"

"What does it say?" I ask.

"Bake a Difference. And right under that in letters that look like gingerbread it says, 'To Benefit Glory's Place.'"

"Don't you think if people see all these baked goods, that they're going to know it's a bake sale, Gloria?" Mom asks, flapping a tablecloth out in front of her.

Gloria helps her smooth out the tablecloth. "This is not just a bake sale, Miriam! People all over this community have been baking a difference! Do you see Rice Krispies treats here? Brownies? Overbaked cookies? Saran Wrap, for crying out loud?" Mom hangs her head, waiting for Gloria to finish. "No. That's because this is not your run-of-the-mill bake sale. We have boxes and ribbons and bows! This is an event!"

Mom looks down at herself. She's wearing black slacks with a red chenille sweater and a strand of pearls. "I don't know what I was thinking. I always wear an evening gown to an event."

"I was hoping you'd go home and change," Gloria says, winking at me.

Mom's eyes are ablaze. "You are wearing a sweatshirt with a mouse dressed like Santa Claus, Gloria!"

"Don't worry. I got you one for Christmas."

Mom flaps her hand in the air as if brushing Gloria away, and Melissa and I work on figuring a way to hang the banner. A steady stream of women and men come into the lobby throughout the afternoon, delivering their baked goods, and as they do, Gloria makes a beautifully handwritten card for each one stating what it is. There is every imaginable cake: coconut, pistachio, chocolate rum, red velvet, white chocolate, cranapple, banana pecan, lemon, spice, apple, German chocolate, and more! There are yule logs, truffles, caramels, a chocolate hazelnut soufflé, pecan torts, pumpkin cream and cranberry tarts, a tower of cupcakes, countless cheesecakes that could be on the cover of *Bon Appétit*—pumpkin, toffee, gingerbread, eggnog, persimmon, turtle, and cherry amaretto—and a string of pies that could be displayed in any bakery: sweet potato, chocolate pecan, sour cream raisin, apple cheddar, orange meringue, lemon meringue, mincemeat, coconut custard, cherry crumble, caramel, and pear. But Gloria didn't just write "apple" or "coconut" on each card. She wrote, "Apple Bliss Cake" or "Coconut Dream Pie." Mom ripped up the card that said "Banana Bonzo Cake" because she said that anything with the word *bonzo* in it should not be taken seriously. She wanted Gloria to call it Banana Surprise Cake, but Gloria said she wouldn't want to be surprised by a banana. They settled on Decadent Banana Cake.

An older woman holds on to the arm of a middle-aged woman and delivers a cake. Melissa sees them and grabs my arm, pulling me toward them. "Mrs. Schweiger! You baked a cake!"

"When has she not baked?" the other woman says.

So this is Mrs. Schweiger? She wraps her arms around me and then holds me out by the shoulders, looking at me. "I know who you are," she says. "You're Gretchen."

"This is Mrs. Schweiger and Karla," Melissa says.

"I figured that out."

Mrs. Schweiger continues to eyeball me, and then she hugs me to her again. "I need your picture," she says.

"Okay. What kind of picture?"

"A family picture."

"It's been a while since we've taken a family picture, but I'll get one to you. I could e-mail one when we have one taken again."

She holds on to my hand and squeezes. "I don't do the e-mail. I need a picture for my box."

"Her box of prayers," Melissa says. "You're going

in the box." I don't know exactly what that means but have a feeling that Melissa's picture spent more time out of Mrs. Schweiger's box than in it.

When Dalton and Heddy arrive from Glory's Place, we all work together placing each cake and confection into a box donated by Betty's Bakery and then wrapping it with a ribbon and bow.

Everything is in place at five o'clock, and we stand back and look at the tables. I have to admit that when Gloria first talked about baking a difference, I never thought of it turning out looking this good. She runs to her bag and pulls out prices she has slipped inside picture frames.

Mom bends her head to read one sign. "Beginning donation of fifty dollars per baked good! Are you crazy, Gloria? Who's going to pay fifty dollars for a pie?"

"They're not paying fifty dollars for a pie, Miriam. If they wanted a pie they'd go buy one at Betty's for twelve bucks. They're donating to a cause."

Mom shakes her head. "What in the world are we going to do with all these cakes and pies?"

Dad drops the kids off an hour before the doors are supposed to open. Emma and Ethan take their place behind the tables to help Mom sell, and I know they'll be doing more playing than working, but Mom gives me a look that says she has it all under control.

I am in front of the tables and arranging a stack of cakes when the audience begins to fill the lobby. Dalton and Heddy take charge as Gloria and Mom have disappeared, and I realize Melissa isn't nearby, either. A man writes a check to Glory's Place for one hundred dollars for the Captivating Cherry Cream

Cheese Cake, and I hand the box to him when I hear a voice somewhere behind me.

"Do you have any Snickers bars?"

Did he say a candy bar?

"How about popcorn?"

Can't he see we aren't a concession stand? I want to laugh, but the voice pounds at my heart and I turn around, screaming. The kids fly out from behind the table and slam into Kyle. I can't move because I can't feel my legs. Is it really him? Is he here? He's wearing Kyle's fatigues, so it looks like him, but I can't think straight. Kyle is in Germany. A man and woman in front of me step aside, and I see Emma crying and gripping her dad around his waist. Ethan is jumping up and down, and I don't think I'm breathing. Kyle uses some sort of crutch and walks toward me with Emma attached to him, and I fall into his shoulder. It is him. I reach my arms around him and try to say something, but it's all lodged in the back of my throat. If people are around us, I don't hear them. I don't even know where I'm at anymore.

Mom is a mess as she reaches for Kyle. "Welcome home, Kyle," she says. "We are all so grateful to have you back. You just have no idea."

Melissa is videotaping the whole thing, and I signal for her to come closer. "This is . . ." I say, but it comes out in squeaks.

"This is Melissa," Kyle says, looking at her. "The brand-new sister and event coordinator."

Melissa's eyes are smiling and she hugs Kyle; this part of the video is going to look like a train wreck. "Welcome home," she says.

Mom smiles, with her arm looped through Kyle's. "It was Melissa's idea to call the doctors in Germany

Donna VanLiere

to see if there was any way Kyle could come home for Christmas." I look at Melissa and she shrugs, barely smiling. "Your dad called Tom and Alice." She points to the side, and I see Kyle's parents, stepping toward us. "They talked to the doctors. And here is Kyle."

"You mean everyone knew about this?"

"Not everybody," Kyle says, pulling me into his side. "The hard part was keeping you from booking a plane ticket to Germany or Texas!"

I'm still so confused. "When do you have to go to San Antonio?"

"I don't. The doc says I can do physical therapy right here."

I can't keep the tears off my face, and someone finally hands me a tissue. Gloria and Marshall sweep in next to us and introduce themselves to Kyle, then Robert and Kate Layton and Betty Grimshaw from Betty's Bakery. Word buzzes through the lobby of what happened and people I've never met in Grandon take the time to welcome Kyle home and thank him for his service. Mrs. Schweiger pulls a small camera out of her purse and holds it to her eye. "Smile," she says. Several of us are clumped together for the photo, but I don't think it matters to her. The picture's going straight into the box. On and on people come to clap Kyle on the shoulder or shake his hand. Parents look at their children and say, "This man just got back from serving our country," hoping they'll understand, and some do, but most don't know what that means.

A woman from the chamber of commerce leads us to seats at the front that have been reserved for our family. Ethan sits on Kyle's lap and Emma leans over onto his chest, wrapping her arms around him while I hold his hand. We're just one big pile of flesh waiting for the concert to begin. Mom and Dad and Kyle's parents are with us, along with Gloria, Marshall, Melissa, and the Schweigers. I try my best to capture their faces in my mind, hoping I'll always remember, but I'm afraid much of this night will be a blur.

Adam Clark, the chamber president walks to the front of the stage and greets the audience and tells a little about the Bake a Difference fund-raiser for Glory's Place. In the next breath he looks at Kyle and welcomes him home. "He was wounded in September in Afghanistan and just got here today." The place erupts in applause and whoops, and everybody is on their feet cheering. Kyle lifts his hand to wave, but I know he is embarrassed. I've never met a man or woman yet in the military who serves for this sort of thing; it's just not in them. "Kyle and Gretchen and their two children chose Grandon as their new home for when Kyle finished his service in the army." More applause and I feel Kyle's hand clamping harder on mine. "So the welcome wagon has been busy. Well, Melissa has been busy," he says, looking through the crowd of faces for her. Melissa's not looking at me, afraid of what that will mean to her emotions, I suppose. The same woman from the chamber who showed us to our seats hands me a basket of cards. "Businesses in the community responded to your coming home, Kyle, and you'll find discounts to Wilson's, free meals at Betty's Bakery, oil changes and tire rotation and balance at City Auto Service, passes to Jump World for the kids, a new deck that will be built onto your home courtesy of James Lumber, painting the interior of your home donated by Three

Donna VanLiere

Guys and a Paintbrush, and lots of other things to say thank you and welcome!" The music begins with "Sleigh Ride" and Kyle's grip on my hand finally relaxes.

Gloria waves me away from the tables when I come back at intermission to help. Mom, Melissa, Dalton, and Heddy work alongside her, and Dad gives me a thumbs-up. The fund-raiser for Glory's Place is going to be a success. Money adds up fast when someone pays one thousand dollars for Wonderland White Chocolate Cake or Visions of Sugar Plum Pie.

Kyle and the kids and I leave after intermission. Kyle is exhausted, and in truth, he just wants to be home, to see it for the first time, and tuck the kids in bed, our bed. We all pile in it together and look through the gift cards and certificates to businesses I wasn't even familiar with yet, strangers who are blessing us. Melissa solicited Mom and Dad, and they spread out across town, visiting businesses and telling them about Kyle. We open haircut certificates and free movie passes, massages and lawn mowing, weekend trips to a bed-and-breakfast and a vacation package to Florida. On and on they go and I try to envision Melissa taking charge of this, of her and Mom and Dad fanning across town to talk to local businesses. It seems impossible that that woman is the same woman we moved next door to, but like I said, she's smarter than she thinks.

Kyle falls asleep listening to the kids tell him everything from how Micah at school can put a spaghetti noodle in his nose and pull it out of his mouth to why pink is no longer Emma's favorite color. The kids doze off soon afterward, and I watch them all, touching Kyle again to make sure he's really with us.

My insides are still shaking in the dark, and I don't know if it's from feeling grateful or overwhelmed. I know so many others have come home from a tour of duty and have not been offered a free car wash, let alone a word of appreciation. They come home and work themselves back into a community without much of a rustle one way or the other. It's what I expected, but sometimes the unexpected can really take a bite out of expectations. I reach across Ethan, who is breathing heavy in sleep, lay my hand on Kyle's chest, and close my eyes.

Seventeen

At the touch of love, everyone becomes a poet.
—PLATO

MELISSA

I've never done anything for anybody and that's the truth. I've lived inside myself, which is a pretty lonely and depressing place for thirty-nine years and I wanted out. I was scared to death when I walked into businesses in town and asked if they could do something to welcome Kyle home. Phillip and Miriam went with me on the first two visits, and then we branched out on our own. There was something mischievous, something that felt like electricity beneath my skin, in keeping this a secret from Gretchen and the kids. I went in earlier each morning to Wilson's, and Robert gave me three days off so I could "work the streets" as Gloria said.

I replay the image of Kyle walking through the civic center doors and watching Gretchen, unaware

Donna VanLiere

of his presence and helping someone buy a cake for the fund-raiser. Phillip was grinning and Miriam was crying. For the rest of my life I'll remember Gretchen's scream and her face. It was the best night of my life.

The roll of wrapping paper I bought two days ago is on the kitchen table and I open it. I haven't purchased a Christmas gift in years, so I never had a use for wrapping paper. Gloria helped me find a gift for Miriam: trouser socks. They sounded boring, but Gloria said nothing brings a smile to Miriam's face like a good pair of trouser socks, so I bought her three pairs. I'm giving Phillip cigars, Emma a game that the lady in the toy department at Wilson's said was popular, Ethan a football, and Kyle some gloves and a new winter hat to keep his head warm.

I pick up Gretchen's gift and stare at it; it's a frame that says "sisters" at the top with a photo of us together in front of her Christmas tree, and below it is the note she found in Ramona's apartment. I had it mounted and framed in town, and since I've picked it up, I can't stop looking at it. What if Kyle and Gretchen had decided to move closer to his parents rather than Miriam? What if Ramona's landlord had left the message about her death with someone else on the street or given up altogether? If one thing, however small, would have been different, I would have never known Gretchen as my sister and I doubt I ever would have known her as my neighbor. I would have just stayed behind my closed door and wished she and her children would do the same. If I strain, I swear I can hear that finger snap from heaven again.

Once I finish wrapping the presents I grab a cup of coffee and a piece of Mrs. Claus Coffee Cake I bought last night and head to work. Wilson's will be swamped today with last-minute shoppers.

My cell phone rings at one when I'm on break and I assume it's Gretchen because she wants me at her house after work for Christmas Eve dinner at six. I know she's calling to pester me again about how to make pistachio salad. It's pudding, marshmallows, pineapple, and Cool Whip! How hard can it be? I muster up a spring in my voice because she says I always sound grumpy when I answer the phone.

"Melissa, it's Robert." He's been out of the law office since Monday; his grandchildren are in town. My heart skips a beat, wondering if he has news. "It was a great night last night. You did tremendous work."

"Thanks, Robert," I say, putting a dollar bill inside the slot of the vending machine. "Gretchen and her kids were surprised."

"They were," he says. "And if you're ready, I have one for you." My heart starts that wild beating again as I bend down and pull out a bag of pretzels. "I received a call about your brother." I'm smiling and flop down on a chair in the break room. "Are you ready?"

"Yes."

"He took a bit longer to track down because the name his adoptive mother used on his adoption papers was her stepfather's name and not her birth name. That stepfather's name tracked to several men with the same name, and long story short, we finally tracked her back to her birth name and came up with a little boy born in 1976 to Ramona McCreary and adopted by Les and Susan Linton." My mind is racing as I try to write all this down on the back of a magazine lying on the table. "I have Bruce's information if you want it." I scribble everything down on the magazine and take a breath before I thank Robert and hang up the phone.

I dial Gretchen's cell but it goes to voice mail. I don't leave a message because I want to tell her in person. I feel as nervous this time around as I did when Robert told me he'd discovered my sister. The names Les and Susan Linton bounce off my brain as I eat the pretzels, and I keep staring at their names written on the back of the magazine. I try calling Gretchen's home and cell numbers again before I go back to work, but both phones go to voice mail. I put the magazine in my locker and try to keep my mind busy for the remainder of the afternoon, but it's like putting a piece of candy in front of a kid and telling him not to touch it for four more hours.

The afternoon is busy and goes fast, and the names Les and Susan Linton continue to roll through my mind. At four thirty, I'm organizing the mail room when a face pops into my mind and my pulse surges. I run upstairs to the break room and roll through the combination on the lock and yank open my locker, snatching the magazine off the top shelf. I read the names again, feeling my heart in my throat.

I run out the door and ask every employee in sight if they've seen my supervisor, Pat. "He was in the office," the lady in jewelry, whose name I never can remember, says.

I take the stairs by two and fling open the office door. He's standing at the copy machine. "Pat!" He turns and sees me standing with the door open. "Something huge has come up. I'm off in thirty. Can I go now?"

"How huge is it?" he asks, smiling.

"I'm going to be a sister!"

He looks confused but waves his hand in the air. "Go! Have a great Christmas." I'm yelling the same thing to him as I bolt down the stairs and grab my coat and backpack from my locker and clock out.

I can feel my heart beating high in my chest as I ring the doorbell. Karla opens the door and smiles. "Merry Christmas!" I say. "I hope I'm not bothering you on Christmas Eve."

She steps aside. "Get in here! Mom and I were having some coffee and some of the cake I bought last night. Want some?"

"Which one did you buy?" I ask, following her to the kitchen.

"Frosting the Snowman."

I laugh at another one of Gloria's names. "What kind is that?"

"White," she says, which makes me laugh harder.

Mrs. Schweiger is at the kitchen table with her box of photos sitting on top of it, so I know she's already been busy today. The kitchen smells yummy and I wonder why they're having cake so close to dinnertime. "Cake before dinner?" I say.

"Mom has to have something on her stomach for her medicine," Karla says. "I said, 'how about some cheese and crackers' and she said, 'how about some cake?' You see who won."

I hug Mrs. Schweiger, and she cuts a slice of cake for me while Karla sets a cup of coffee in front of me. "I don't need any cake," I say.

"It's Christmas. You do out-of-ordinary things at Christmas and wear big pants."

That makes me laugh and I take a bite. "Mrs. Schweiger," I say, getting right to it. "Do the names Les and Susan Linton sound familiar?"

Her eyes are big and she smiles. "From the apartments. Of course. They were wonderful people. Very kind."

"Did you know much about them?" She opens her mouth to answer, but I rephrase what I said. "Did you ever suspect or imagine anything about them?"

She leans forward, looking at me and I see something in her eyes. She points her finger at me, grinning. "What are you up to, Melissy?"

I smile. "I think you know." Karla looks from me to her mother and waits.

"It would have only been a thought," says Mrs. Schweiger.

"And what was that thought?"

"I knew how their family was brought together. They were always very open about adopting all their children."

"What else?" I ask, taking another bite of Frosting the Snowman cake.

"You and your mother had already lived at the apartments nearly three years when I saw Ramona watching the little Linton boy play one day in the parking lot. You remember how the children would play tag in that big, circular end of the lot. Your mother *never* stopped to watch the children, but that day she did, and as she looked at him, I looked at her and then back at him, trying to see what she was looking at. Something jiggled somewhere in my brain, and I didn't know what to think by what I was seeing but noticed that your mother was upset." She pats my hand. "In the couple of weeks following, all I could do was try to steal a glance of Ramona from time to time and look at that little boy and wonder, but I never knew anything for sure." She pulls out the stack of photos from her box and flips through them.

I lean back in my chair. "That's why Ramona moved out of there so fast, isn't it? She knew that the Linton boy was the little boy she'd given up for adoption."

Mrs. Schweiger's mouth puckers and she cocks her head. "I think she suspected. And long after you left, I always wondered."

"And the Lintons?"

"They never knew Ramona. Never even saw her, as far as I know."

I hand her the magazine. "My boss just located my brother. His name is Bruce Linton."

Karla says, "Are you kidding?" and tears fill Mrs. Schweiger's eyes.

"His parents are Les and Susan Linton."

Mrs. Schweiger lets out a whoop and plops Bruce's picture down in front of me.

"And he's a fire chief in California!"

There's no time to make pistachio salad, but I hope everyone will forgive me, considering I've been a bit busy tracking down my brother! I forget to knock and walk into Kyle and Gretchen's, holding up the magazine. "We have a baby brother!" I shout, hoping too late that no one is napping. The house is full, with Kyle's parents and Phillip and Miriam. Gretchen steps out of the kitchen and she hurries to me, taking the magazine. She reads over the information and looks at me. "I played with him for three years. He and his family lived above us in the same apartments where the Schweigers lived. When Ramona figured out who he was, we moved away."

"What are you going to do?" Gretchen asks.

"You mean what are *we* going to do," I say. I pull out my cell phone, and her eyes are big, watching me. For the rest of my life I'll wonder how all of this happened. I'll go through the what-if's countless times and settle on the same conclusion: I am seen. I dial the phone and put it on speaker so everyone can hear. Gretchen and I take our places in the wings, waiting. When a man's voice answers, Gretchen grabs my arm and we both smile.

The next act is about to begin.

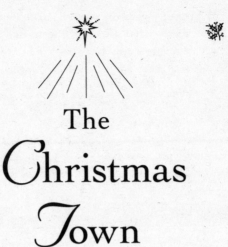

The Christmas Town

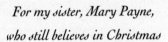

For my sister, Mary Payne,

who still believes in Christmas

Acknowledgments

Many thanks and much love to . . .

Troy, Gracie, Kate, David, Lucy, CoCo, Katrina, and Cindy for being the sweetest part of my life.

Jen Enderlin and the St. Martin's Press crew for continued belief and encouragement.

Ursula Houghton and Barb Cramer, who would make any town kinder and more neighborly.

Hope Chiasson and JoEllen Thatcher for your heart.

And thanks to our nephew, Desmond VanLiere, for inspiring Cassondra's story line. A faulty heart wasn't going to keep him down for long!

I don't know who my grandfather was; I am much more concerned to know what his grandson will be.

—ABRAHAM LINCOLN

One

November 2010

Lauren Gabriel slides her card into the time clock and punches out of work at 6:02. It would have been six o'clock exactly if her last customer hadn't taken a minute to dig through her purse for seventeen cents in change and then another minute to tell Lauren how annoying it is to find those last few pennies at the bottom of her purse. She grabs her bag from her locker before pushing open the double doors to walk back through the grocery store.

"See you tomorrow, Lauren," Jay says, bagging groceries for a mom with two young children.

She smiles and waves as she walks through the front door to the parking lot, wishing she did not have to come here tomorrow. She had wished a few weeks ago when Gordon's Grocery was transformed from Halloween to Thanksgiving and then to Christmas in a matter of days that she could work someplace else. Someplace where what to cook for the holidays wasn't first on everyone's mind. Lauren hadn't celebrated Thanksgiving or Christmas in two years, since leaving her last foster home. She had been with Jim and Lori, her final foster family, for three years and although they were good people, after ten years of being in the system, she had had enough of foster homes. She started working at the grocery store during her junior year in high school and had been there for four years now. She'd do anything else but can't imagine what that would be.

The streets glow with Christmas lights and Lauren feels that hollowed-out place behind her ribs again. Images, snapshots really, of being with her mom on Christmas cross her mind from time to time but the recollections are so short (the man who was her father smoking on the couch, her mom petting the cat, sleet tapping the window) that she can't piece them together into any sort of memory. Her father, Victor, would come and go out of her life until she was four when he decided to go for good. Her mother lived trapped in some sort of romantic haze, thinking that she could attract a good man, but managed to hook up with a string of users and losers. She was sentenced to five years for selling drugs when Lauren was eight. She told Lauren that she would be out in no time and they would be together again. Lauren watches a mom and her young daughter walk down the street and feels that dull, painful jerk at her heart again. She thinks of her mom with equal parts love and hatred. Cassie tried to be a mom but wasn't cut out for it. When she got out of jail when Lauren was thirteen, Cassie told her that she was going to find a job and an apartment and be back for her. That was seven years ago.

Lauren's life has been so much like a short, unful-filling magic show, full of failed tricks and disappoint-ing illusions. She looks in the rearview mirror and catches a glimpse of herself. She has dark, quiet eyes, not like her mother's, olive skin, and wavy, dark brown hair. She pulls up that snapshot of her father smoking and knows she looks more like him than Cassie.

In their cluttered apartment where smoke hung like thin veils, she used to reach under the bed that her parents shared and pull out a dark wooden box her aunt had given her, with words carved into the top, and dash into her closet, closing the door. Sitting against the wall she would run her tiny fingers over the grooves of the words and imagine them as magi-cal. Lifting the lid she pretended it was filled with precious gems and dazzling jewels, a portal of sorts that led to a charmed kingdom. She even attempted to carve her name on the underside of the lid with a pair of scissors but it proved too difficult and she didn't get further than the letter *L*.

When her aunt had given it to Lauren, she had read the words to her, but Lauren had forgotten what they said. One day she ran with the box to her mom. "What does this say again?" she asked, barely able to contain her excitement. Cassie kept her eyes on the TV. "Mommy, what do these words say?" Cassie was not paying attention. Lauren tapped her on the leg. "Mommy! What does this say?"

Cassie snapped her head around to look at her. "It doesn't say anything! I'm trying to hear this!"

Lauren stepped away and hurried back inside her closet, where she once more ran her fingers over the words.

The Lord says, "I will guide you along the best path-
way for your life.
    I will advise you and watch over you."
                                    —PSALM 32:8

Each time she played, she would dream and imagine what those words said until the day she reached
for the box and it wasn't there. Her father had taken
it when he left.

She can go home now, to a small, cramped apartment she shares with a girl she barely knows, catch
a movie she's not interested in seeing, hook up with
friends, or just keep driving past this infinity of
buildings and restaurants, sidewalks and people, to
someplace new. She passes Walmart and Lowe's, the
housing development that is being built on the edge of
the city, the park where all the Little League games
are played, and the city limits sign.

An hour into the drive the sky is still hung with
grays and deep purples, when she notices her gas
tank is almost empty. She pulls onto the main street
in Grandon and reads a banner hung over the road:
"Annual Christmas Parade December 18! Vote for the Grand
Marshal at Participating Retailers." The streetlights
are wrapped in garlands and topped with large, red
bows. Store windows are decorated with everything
from hanging stars and waving Santas to Nativity
scenes.

She spots a gas station in front of Clauson's, a supermarket, and realizes she hasn't eaten since lunch.
She hadn't intended to drive this far. Once the tank
is full Lauren walks into the grocery store for something to eat. At first glance it doesn't look too different from Gordon's Grocery except for an especially

long checkout line. Her manager at Gordon's would always call another cashier to the front if one line got too long. She makes her way to the deli and finds a premade ham and cheese sandwich and a small bag of chips hanging within arm's reach. The next cooler is filled with every soft drink, tea, lemonade, juice, and various flavored water available. Grocery stores make these grab-and-go sections as easy as possible.

At the checkout she sees that there are two cashiers working but one line is empty while the other has five people waiting. She assumes that the other cashier is either getting ready to leave or just coming onto her shift and isn't set up for customers yet. She takes her place in the long line and wonders if she has done the right thing. The other cashier looks ready.

"Register three is open," a black man with a round face, glasses, and graying temples says. His name badge reads LES, GENERAL MANAGER. HOW CAN I HELP YOU?

No one in the long line moves toward the open register and Lauren starts to step over there when the man in front of her says, "I'm staying right here, Les. I want my message from Ben."

The manager looks at the others in line and motions toward the second cashier. "We're fine waiting," a woman with a child in her grocery cart says. "We want our message, too."

Curious to know what they are talking about, Lauren decides to stay where she is to wait her turn. She watches as the second cashier rings out a customer while two more people join her in the long line. The manager looks on in dismay or awe; she can't determine what his face is saying.

When she gets close enough, Lauren cranes her

neck to see around the person in front of her and watches what looks like a typical transaction. However, when the customer gets to the exit doors, she stops and looks into her bags, pulling out a piece of paper. The next customer does the same thing. Lauren notices that as the man in front of her puts groceries onto the conveyer belt, the grocery bagger sifts through a pile of notes in his hand, before slipping one into a bag. As the man walks away he gives the bagger a high five and moves toward the exit. The cashier asks Lauren if she found everything she was looking for but Lauren doesn't answer. She is watching the bagger, a young man around eighteen or nineteen, as he looks at her and then shuffles through the notes, slipping one into a bag.

"Have a great day!" he says, handing the bag to her.

She takes the bag from him and looks behind her at the line that continues to form before heading to the parking lot. She stands just outside the doors and opens the bag, pulling out a small, simple piece of white paper.

> *It's a great day because you're in it!*
> *You are welcome here!*
> *Ben*

"What?" Lauren looks through the front window and watches as Ben shuffles through the notes and puts them into bags. She glances down at the note again and shakes her head. "That's freaky," she says, walking to her car.

She had intended to eat the sandwich while driving but sits in the parking lot. Her thoughts aren't consumed with the misery of her job or the drudgery of her life but rather with the note that is crumpled up on the seat next to her. She wants to turn the key and start the car and begin her drive home but can't. The sandwich either has no taste or she's unable to taste it because her thoughts aren't on eating.

When she finishes she wads the wrapper and the empty chip bag together, throwing them back into the grocery bag. She watches as people come and go from the store before opening her door. Ben is still bagging groceries as she approaches him. He's taller than her and skinny with a rebellious head of dark hair. "Excuse me."

Ben turns and smiles. "Hey!" He says it as if they haven't seen each other in a few days and he's happy to see her here. "Everything okay?"

"It's fine." She sounds annoyed and changes her tone. "You put a note in my bag."

He's busy bagging but seems thrilled to be talking with her. "It's a great day because you're in it! You are welcome here."

"You put that in all the bags, right?"

He shakes his head as he places bags into the empty grocery cart in front of him. "Nope. That was the only one."

Lauren doesn't understand. "That was the only note like that and you chose it for me? Why? You don't know me. How do you know it's a great day because I'm in it? Why would you say that I'm welcome here?"

Ben shrugs. "Because if you weren't in this day, then somebody would be sad. Your mom or dad or your grandma or people you go to school with or work with. The day wouldn't be the same." He looks at her and smiles again. This kid sure smiles a lot but it's not a smile that could be perceived as mocking. "And you *are* welcome here! You can come anytime. We have lots of different kinds of food and cleaning supplies and we even have an aisle full of toys and one with makeup for girls. I hope you come back."

At that moment the manager comes over and asks, "Did you find everything that you need?" and she feels stupid for coming back in.

Lauren takes a step toward the door. "Yes! Thank you." She looks at Ben but he is busy riffling through the notes in his hand. "Crazy," she mumbles, walking out the doors. "Gordon's would never allow baggers to do that."

She slips in behind the wheel of the car and pulls away from the store. No one has ever said it is a great day because she was part of it. No one ever made her believe that the world would be in need of something simply because she wasn't in it. How is it possible that some kid, a stranger in another town, made her feel that way? How did he, with one note, instill a spark of wild hope at a time of year that is notorious for dashing dreams and hopes?

She is driving behind a car through a green light when a pickup truck drives into the intersection, slamming into the side of the car in front of her. Lauren screams and slams on the brakes. She is jumping out of the car when she sees the pickup truck back up and pull away from the accident.

She grabs her cell phone and dials 911 while running to the car in front of her. "A truck just slammed into the car in front of me and then raced away," she says into the phone. She looks at the driver, a woman who looks to be in her forties, and yells through the closed window, "Are you okay?" The driver nods and rolls down her window. "The truck came right through the intersection and slammed right into her and then just raced away. I watched him," Lauren says to the 911 operator.

"A patrol unit is on the way. Is anyone injured?"

Lauren looks at the woman inside the car who looks shocked but unhurt. "Are you okay? Do you need an ambulance?"

"No. I'm not hurt. Just shaking."

"Did you happen to see the make or model of the truck or the license plate?" the operator asks Lauren.

"It was a smaller gray Nissan pickup. I didn't see the entire license plate but the first number was a three and it looked like the last letter was a *D*."

"Thank you. Please stay on the line until the officer arrives."

In a few minutes she sees the police lights just down the street and hangs up when the officer arrives. Lauren tells him what she had seen and a description of the driver, a man around thirty with shaggy light brown hair and wearing a dark T-shirt.

Lauren leaves as soon as she is able and the woman thanks her for remembering so much about the truck and driver. "You were at the right place at the right time. Without you the police wouldn't have much to go on."

"I hope they catch him," Lauren says.

It feels as if adrenaline is still rushing through her on the drive home, but when the images of the accident begin to subside a thought begins to bubble. What if she found a family for Christmas? What if she found people who would look at her and not think of her as a stranger or someone they kind of know from the grocery store, but people who would actually think of her as flesh and blood? A woman who would think of her as her daughter or a man with a receding hairline and a paunchy belly who would teach her how to change a tire or give her advice about boys? Surely there has to be some young kid out there who always wanted an older sister or someone who wanted a kid sister. Her brain buzzes with the thought: between social media and Craigslist, she will put out the word that she is looking for a family for Christmas.

Two

Nineteen-year-old Bennett Engler had handed his application to Les Gentry, Clauson's manager, over a year ago. "I'll be a real good worker. I promise," Ben had said.

Les had been the general manager for eight years at that time and was known for keeping his employees on task. If any of them were repeat offenders for failing to show up for work, he was quick to inform them that they were welcome to find another job. He had no doubt that Ben would be an outstanding employee. He had watched Ben and his family visit the store each week over the last several years and every time Ben would tell him that one day he was going to work for him. "Ben," Les had said, looking at Ben and Ben's mom, Stacy, "Jo will show you around the store for a few minutes."

"But I've been through the store at least a thousand times," Ben said.

Les laughed and opened the door to his office.

"But you've never seen our loading dock or any of the back rooms."

"Cool! Mom, can I have your phone to take pictures?"

Stacy handed the phone to him and said, "I'll be here waiting."

"Have a seat," Les said, closing the office door.

Although he was a senior when she was a freshman in high school, Stacy still remembers Les from the football team. At that time, everyone thought he would marry Ashley, a beautiful black cheerleader, but he went off to college and fell in love with Maura. He played football in college and all of Grandon assumed he was headed into professional football, but some things aren't meant to be. Once college was over he surprised everyone and moved back to Grandon with Maura. Their children were in college now: his daughter was a senior and their son a freshman. Stacy sat in a chair opposite his desk and smiled, feeling a rush of pride and nervousness for Ben.

Les sat in a seat next to her. "Can he handle this job, Stacy?"

She hadn't anticipated them but tears sprang to her eyes and her throat swelled. She nodded her head, smiling. "He can! He'll be great!" She wiped the tears away. "I don't know why I'm crying. He's so excited!"

Reaching for a box of tissues on his desk, Les handed it to her. "Maura will tear up when she does laundry because there's not as much to do anymore."

Stacy laughed and wiped her nose. "He will be one of the hardest workers that you have and I can assure you that he will always be happy to be here. He is the most grateful person I have ever known in my life."

She dabbed at tears in her eyes, looked down at the wadded tissue. "I always wish that I could be more like him."

"I've never asked but . . ." He wrung his hands in front of him. "What . . . ?"

"When he was born the doctor thought everything was normal. We thought everything was normal. But during the pregnancy fluid had built up in his brain. Nobody knew. Three months after we brought him home we could tell there was something wrong. He just wasn't like other babies that we had been around and he wasn't growing that much. He would never really look at us but kept his eyes downward. He wasn't active like other babies his age. His head was bigger than most. Tests revealed hydrocephalus and doctors put the first of many shunts in his brain to redirect the fluid."

Les looked to the door to make sure that Jo and Ben weren't coming back yet. "Does he still get them?"

There were no more tears as Stacy shook her head. "His last shunt revision was when he was thirteen. It doesn't mean he won't need another one someday. Because of the length of time before diagnosis and the severity of Ben's case, doctors had said he wouldn't be able to do this or he would only be able to do that, but at every milestone he has proven them wrong. He can't drive; his reflexes aren't quick enough. Controlling the steering wheel while putting pressure on the accelerator or brake requires great motor skills and he doesn't have them. He won't drive but so what? In June he graduated with his class. It took him longer. He was nineteen when he got his diploma but it didn't bother him. He worked hard and did it with an unbelievable attitude." She looked at Les. "He'll be just like that here."

Stacy was right. Ben loved his job and the people he worked with. However, on many days when she picked him up at the end of his shift, he seemed lost in thought. Six months into the job, he walked in the door one day and flopped down on the couch, which was out of character for Ben. Stacy set her purse on the kitchen counter and walked toward him. "What's the matter? Did something happen at work?" He shook his head. "Did an employee or a customer say something to you?"

She braced herself for his answer. Over the course of his nineteen years Stacy has had a harder time dealing with the comments and opinions of others than with Ben's own struggles. She cringes each time she remembers snapping at a child who would say something cruel to him. She assumed that the day would come when a fellow worker or customer would choose to use harsh or demeaning words toward him.

"Nobody said anything, Mom." He flung open his hands and rested his head against the back of the sofa. "It's just that I don't feel like I'm doing enough bagging groceries. Anybody can bag groceries."

Lucy had heard her mom come into the house and yelled to her from upstairs, asking for help with her homework. Stacy knew she didn't have much time and prayed that she could say the right thing to Ben. Through the years, she and her husband, Jacob, had felt overwhelmed by Ben's special needs at school and often walked into meetings with school staff with the simple prayer *Help me do the next right thing for Ben* on their lips. "Do you mean you want a different job at the store? You want more responsibility?"

He rolled his head from side to side on the back of the couch. "No! I love my job! It's just that people come into the store and sometimes they look so sad or angry or something and I wish that there was something I could do for them."

Stacy sat beside him and pulled his head toward her, kissing his forehead. "That's what's bothering you?"

"Yeah, Mom! What do you think would be bothering me?"

He gave her a look that said she really should know him by now, and she smiled, wrapping her arms around him and squeezing him. She and Jacob had said many times that the areas of Ben's brain that built up fluid during her pregnancy were given a double portion of mercy and love. Of course he would pick up on the weariness, sadness, disappointment, and loneliness of people throughout the day. Lucy called again from upstairs and Stacy patted Ben's leg. "I'm going to run upstairs and help Lucy for a few minutes. While I'm gone why don't you think of something that you could do at work that might be able to help brighten someone's day."

Stacy was still in Lucy's bedroom, helping with English, when they heard Ben bound up the stairs. "Mom! Lucy! I know what I can do!"

"Do about what?" Lucy asked. Lucy was fifteen at the time and although she was younger than Ben, she had always been fiercely protective of him.

"About customers who look sad or lonely or upset when they come into the store," Stacy said.

Ben grabbed Lucy's bumblebee Pillow Pet and paced the floor, squeezing it. "Put Buzzie down before you squeeze the stuffing out of him," Lucy said.

Ben threw the Pillow Pet back onto the bed and sat on the end of it. His whole body was trembling with excitement and Stacy hoped he had not come up with an over-the-top idea that could never happen. "Every day when I get home from work I will write notes that I can give to each customer."

Stacy and Lucy looked at each other then back at Ben. "You mean like you'll find quotes and stuff off the Internet?" Lucy asked.

He shook his head. "No, I'll come up with each thing that I want to say." His eyes were bright as he glanced from his mom to his sister, looking for support.

Stacy couldn't imagine him writing that many notes per night but there was no way she was going to discourage him. "It's awesome!" She hugged him and said, "I think it's an amazing idea!"

He wrote notes for three hours that first night. He started writing them as Stacy was making dinner, and before long the kitchen table was littered with different-colored pieces of paper. Although she tried to steal a glance occasionally, Ben wouldn't let Stacy or any of his family see the notes while he worked. He moved them aside during dinner but continued to write. When Jacob asked how his day was, Ben shook his head, never looking at his dad, and said, "Not right now, Dad. I have work to do."

Jacob was in the garage and Stacy was folding laundry in their bedroom when Ben finally called to them. In the kitchen he held the papers, a jumble of different colors and sizes, and handed several to each of them. Jacob and Stacy read aloud what was written on each paper.

*You are more awesome than you know! Have a
great day! Ben*

*Flowers, trees, and lakes are beautiful but not as
much as you! Ben*

*Our dog will give up chasing our cat and walk
away. Sometimes you just have to know when to walk
away. Have a great day! Ben*

*Whoever is happy will make others happy, too.
Anne Frank said that and I think she's right! Ben*

*A man who is honest and has great character can
change a town. I'm so glad you're changing this one!
Ben*

Stacy and Jacob flipped through each one and
looked up at Ben, slack-jawed. "You came up with all
of these?" Jacob asked.

Ben shrugged and nodded.

Stacy struggled for words. "You didn't look on the
Internet or in a book?"

"No. Why?"

"I . . . They're incredible! I thought they would all
say the same thing but they're different." She sifted
through the papers in her hands. "Every single one of
them is different."

Ben fell asleep that night realizing that his job
might be one of the most important in the entire store.

His first shift for slipping notes inside grocery bags
was on a Saturday. He ran the idea by Les (in hind-
sight, that was something Stacy realized they should
have done first) and Les said he would allow Ben to

try it. Ben watched as people stood in line and he selected just the right note for each one.

For the customer who wouldn't make eye contact with him or the cashier: *Maybe what's happening isn't really a problem but a gift! Have a great day! Ben*

For the single mom: *You aren't everything to your kids. You are just enough! Have a great day! Ben*

For the cranky man: *My grandma says that if we are not careful we can lose the song in our soul. I hope your soul keeps singing! Ben*

For the sad-looking teen: *Without sadness happiness wouldn't mean as much. Everything comes and goes. I hope you'll stay! Ben*

Customers came and went those first three days without much to say. Most assumed the notes were a one-time thing. At the end of the week, when customers were coming in again and receiving another note, they began to thank Ben for "making their day" or for "doing a great job." In fact, Les didn't think Ben would be able to keep up with the notes, but six months later he realized Ben would continue to do them as long as he worked at Clauson's. Les thought the notes were cute and some people found them inspirational, encouraging, and motivational, but he had no idea they could be life-changing. Sometimes that's just the way it is with things that seem too simple to matter.

Three

"Are you serious? You put a listing on Craigslist looking for a family at Christmas?" Lauren took two days to tell her roommate, Brooke, about the idea and wishes now she had kept it to herself. "Do you know how many crazy people you're going to hear from? What does the listing say?"

Lauren shrugs, slipping her bag over her shoulder. "Just that I'm looking for a family at Christmas."

Brooke opens the refrigerator and pulls out a carton of milk, putting it on the counter. "Some guy could say he'd be"—she uses her fingers as quotes in the air—"'happy to be your dad' and turn out to be a rapist!"

Lauren digs for her keys in her bag and heads toward the door before she's late for work. "I really don't think most people are like that."

Brooke shakes her head. "It doesn't take most people. All it takes is one lunatic."

"I know all about lunatics," Lauren says under her breath, closing the door.

She reasons that there are decent people—unlike her own parents—who would respond to a listing and want to be part of her family. Lauren discovered years ago that when a child is born it doesn't necessarily mean that a father and mother are also born. She imagined her father standing outside the glass window of the hospital as a nurse held up a pink bundle, roughly the size of a loaf of bread, and the look on his face. Was it at that moment he saw she had his eyes that he decided to take off? Was it when he heard her cry that he realized his own cries had never been answered? Could the nurse tell that he was planning his escape as she held up that six-pound newly born life for him to see? Lauren has stopped wondering if that image nags him because it has nagged her enough for both of them.

Seven years after her mom's release from jail she wonders if her mom ever hears her voice. Does she see Lauren in a young woman her age a thousand miles away or wherever she lives? Does she think about Lauren on her birthday or Christmas? Does she mark the days off as she marks the end of another day?

The thought of home is what Lauren always returns to in her mind. Every home is a little created world furnished with things and people. The furnishings in her home were all shabby and unreliable. She is often homesick for a home she never had.

She pulls into a parking space at Gordon's and reaches for her phone to read her Craigslist ad again: *I am a 20-year-old woman looking for a family this Christmas. I've been in many foster homes and some of them have been very good homes, but I've never felt as if I have a family to call my own. A family would be the best Christmas present because a family isn't there for just a day but for life.*

So far, she has received no e-mails or phone calls regarding her listing. She opens Facebook and thinks for a moment before posting, *I'm looking for a family at Christmas. Maybe one who has always wanted a daughter or maybe one who needs another daughter.* Lauren looks at the words and then deletes them. She then posts, *Anybody interested in starting a family at Christmas?* She realizes how that sounds and groans, erasing it. She tries again: *Anyone interested in an extra family member at Christmas?* She reads it again, clicks post, and tosses the phone into her bag.

Time moves way too slowly as she stands at her cash register. She wonders how people are responding to her ad on Craigslist and her post on Facebook. Since being on her own she has not had close friends. In truth, she has never had a close friend. While living with her mom, she was ashamed of her and never asked to have a friend over. When she entered the foster home system, she was too ashamed to let the kids at school know anything about her home life. She went from one foster home and school to another without ever attending a birthday party or a play date or after-school activity of any kind. The closest thing she has to friendship is with her roommate, who worked briefly at Gordon's, and the seventy-nine people on Facebook and fifty followers on Instagram who claim to be her friends.

On her break she races for her locker and reaches for the phone. Her heart sinks when she sees there are only four likes and three comments to her Facebook post.

Donna VanLiere

Sure! Lanny commented. *Come on down to Florida!*

Can you cook? You're free to use my kitchen! LOL! Bethany said.

Lori just put a smiley face as her comment.

"What sort of answer is that?" Lauren says, looking at the bright yellow face. "I have no idea what that means." She sighs and deletes the entire post, feeling stupid for putting it up in the first place.

She checks her e-mail and notices one from Craigslist. She opens it and reads, *How lame are you to put an ad like this on Craigslist?* Her heart pounds and tension stretches through her chest. She is working on opening her post so she can delete it when her phone buzzes. Someone just left a voice mail from a number she doesn't recognize. She puts the phone to her ear to listen.

"Miss Gabriel, my name is Darrell Jamison with the district attorney's office in Grandon. Could you return my call at your earliest convenience?"

Lauren can't imagine why he called as she presses the "call back" button on her phone. "I'm returning Darrell Jamison's call," she says. She gives her name and listens to instrumental music as she digs in her purse for change for snacks out of the vending machine.

"Darrell Jamison."

She slides seventy-five cents into the vending machine and pushes the button for peanut butter pretzels. "This is Lauren Gabriel returning your call."

"Miss Gabriel, we have a suspect in the hit-and-run accident that you witnessed two days ago and we would like you to come to Grandon in order to identify him."

Lauren rips open the bag and sits at one of the

tables in the break room. "What? Why? If you picked him up and he looks like the guy that I described, then obviously he's the guy! Why do I have to make a trip there to tell you what you already know?"

"We found the truck parked on a side street, and when an officer saw the suspect advancing toward the truck, he approached, but the suspect denied that the truck was his. He was brought in on suspicion and we're quite sure he is linked to several robberies in Grandon, but at this time we are unable to hold him on those possible charges. The only one that we could hold him on is the hit-and-run and that is with a positive identification. We really need your cooperation, Miss Gabriel. We would need you this afternoon or tomorrow morning at the latest at the police station."

Lauren can't believe what she's hearing. "Are you serious? I can't be there this afternoon. I'm at work!" She groans. "I shouldn't have even got involved!"

"I understand the inconvenience. Please understand that we firmly believe he is linked to several crimes but we are unable to hold him without an identification. Nine A.M. tomorrow would be great if you can make it."

She sighs, not believing her bad luck. "Fine. I don't have to work until late tomorrow afternoon so I'll be there."

On her way into Grandon, Lauren decides to stop once again at Clauson's. She has just enough time to grab something to drink before making her way to the police station. A Salvation Army bell ringer is outside the front doors and twinkly lights outline the store windows. On entering, she glances to the cash registers to see if the young man who had slipped the note inside her bag is working. He's not. She's looking over the refrigerated drink options when she hears, "Hi! Good to see you back!" Ben is carrying a box of instant rice. "We have a price check on register two," he says, rushing to the front.

She grabs an orange juice and follows behind him, standing in his line. She watches to see if he is still putting notes inside shoppers' bags. An older woman reaches for her bag from Ben and puts her hand on his face, patting it. The next man in line grabs his bag, oblivious to the fact that Ben studied him before picking out just the right note. When Lauren steps up to the register, Ben has a stack of notes close to his face, looking through them. "This is my new friend," he tells the cashier.

"You have so many friends, Ben," the cashier says, smiling at Lauren.

"She's new here," he says. "This is only her second time in the store. Well, really, it's her third time because she came back twice on the first day she was here."

Lauren hands money to the cashier and says, "Wow! You remember all of that?"

Ben slips a note on top of her sandwich, juice, and chips, and hands the bag to her. "I remember all of my customers. Even the little babies. "

The cashier looks at Lauren and nods. "It's true. He does. He puts the rest of us to shame, don't you, Ben?"

"Customers are the most important part of our business."

Lauren moves out of the way for the next customer and looks at Ben. "I think that's really cool."

"Thanks!" His mouth is open to ask her name when a little boy standing next in line with his father misses the conveyor belt and drops a jar of olives to the floor, breaking it. "It's okay," he says to the little boy. "I'll get a mop."

Lauren walks to her car and opens the door, getting inside. She reaches for the note in her bag. It's on a plain green piece of paper.

> *Sometimes family is disguised as the neighbor down the street, the waitress at Betty's Bakery, or the bag boy at Clauson's.*
> *Have a great day!*
> *Ben*

Her heart pounds in her ears as she stares at the note.

Four

The gazebo and three large pine trees in the Grandon town square are heavy with decorations and simply beautiful. Lauren imagines they must be stunning at night. The storefronts, restaurants, and offices on the square are fully dressed for Christmas as people come and go from Wilson's Department Store, Betty's Bakery, and Maggie's Flowers. The police station sits three blocks off the square and Lauren hopes this won't take long.

A male and female officer are working behind the counter as she approaches. "You're Lauren, right?" Lauren turns and sees a petite woman in her forties getting up from her seat in the waiting room.

"Yeah."

"I'm Stacy Engler. I was the one hit a couple of days ago."

Lauren nods. "Yeah, right. You're okay?"

"Yes, but I don't think I stopped shaking that night." Stacy notices there isn't much to read in Lauren's face: no hint of joy, not really a smirk of displeasure or sense of sadness. "Do you live around here? I've never seen you."

"Miss Gabriel?" A man in his fifties with short, cropped brown hair enters through a door and sticks out his hand, saying, "Darrell Jamison, DA's office. Thank you so much for coming." He pats Stacy on the shoulder. "Mrs. Engler, why don't you and Miss Gabriel step back here?" He ushers them through a door leading into the heart of the station. Opening another door he says, "This is Officer Lutrell." A uniformed police officer shakes their hands. "He was the arresting officer that brought the suspect in. The police department has put together a lineup and in a moment we'll bring them into that room right through there," he says, pointing to a window. "They are unable to see into this room. We need both of you ladies to look at the men and let us know if you see the man who struck Mrs. Engler's car on Baxter Street."

"Bring them in," Officer Luttrell says.

Seven men roughly the same age and stature enter the room next door and line up, facing the window. Lauren scans their faces and sees the man responsible for the hit-and-run. It looks like he has tried to comb back his untamed hair but the face is the same. "That's him," she says. "The third one from the left in the black T-shirt."

"You're sure?" the DA says. She nods. "Mrs. Engler?"

"I'm sorry. Like I said on the phone, I never got a look at his face."

He holds out his hand for a final shake and opens the door. "Thank you both for coming in. I'll be in touch."

Stacy and Lauren step into the hall and Officer Lutrell walks them toward the front of the station.

"That was fast," Stacy says. "You knew he was the guy?"

"Yep. He tried to do something with his hair but couldn't do anything to improve his face." The officer pushes open the door and both women walk past the clerks again and through the front door.

Stacy wants to get in her car but there is that unnamed sadness on Lauren's face again. "You didn't get to tell me where you live."

"In Whitall."

"Are you headed back right away? I'd love to buy you a coffee or late breakfast at Betty's. She makes amazing pastries."

Lauren jangles the keys in her hand. She doesn't want to sit around and talk to a woman she doesn't know, but there is something kind about Stacy and she is hungry. "Sure. I don't have to be at work until this afternoon."

"Great! Follow me. It's just up on the square."

The aroma of Betty's Bakery is unlike anything Lauren has ever smelled. The glass display cases in front of her are filled with muffins, pastries, cookies, pies, and cakes of all colors and sizes. "Wow! How do people work here without gaining weight?"

Stacy leads her to a table by the window. "Who says they don't gain weight? Betty herself has gained and lost so much weight over the years that she could star in her own reality show." She leans in to whisper, "You didn't hear that from me." She picks up a menu that is propped up on the table and hands it to Lauren, sitting down. "Everything is great here." Stacy snaps her menu closed and Lauren looks over the menu at her. "I always get the same thing: eggs Benedict."

"What's eggs Benedict?"

"It's a poached egg on an English muffin with hollandaise sauce over it." Lauren shrugs. "Hollandaise sauce is made out of egg yolks, butter, and lemon juice."

"No, thanks," Lauren says.

A waitress comes and asks if they'd like coffee. "It's the best if you're a coffee drinker," Stacy says. The waitress fills both cups and takes their orders: eggs Benedict for Stacy and pancakes with bacon for Lauren. "My kids would eat pancakes every day if I made them."

"I never eat them." Lauren feels awkward and reaches for her phone in her bag. "I've probably eaten them four or five times."

Stacy pours cream into her coffee and stirs it. "Four or five times this year or in your life?"

Lauren rips open three sugar packets. "My life. My mom never cooked. She never did much of anything, really." She sips the coffee and grips her phone with the other hand.

Stacy wonders if Lauren is hoping that her phone will ring or a text will come through. "Do you still live with your mom?" Lauren shakes her head. It's all she wants her to know, so Stacy changes the subject. "Are you a student?" Lauren looks at her phone and Stacy realizes this girl isn't much into conversation.

"I'm not really college material."

Stacy nods. "Not everybody is. There are blue-collar people and white-collar people and the world needs both. My father has worked as an upholsterer for forty-five years. He started in a little shop his senior year of high school and by the time he was twenty he was running his own business in his parents' garage. I remember watching him many years ago in his shop and he was covering a chair with this beautiful, silky-looking fabric and my dad has big, rough hands. That beautiful fabric didn't even look like it belonged in those hands, but I noticed the care he took when he touched it. I thought that in other hands the fabric would be destroyed but in my dad's hands he knew just how much pressure it could take and just what he needed to do to get it on that chair so the final product would be beautiful. And I started to cry watching him. It could have something to do with the fact that I was pregnant at the time," she says, laughing. "But more than that it was because my father was so good at what he did and he never went to college. He raised four kids reupholstering furniture all over this town. So all that to say that it's okay that not everybody is meant for college because somebody has to do the upholstery work and the maintenance work and the roadwork and the grocery store work."

Lauren's eyes widen. "I'm a cashier at Gordon's Grocery in Whitall."

"No kidding? My son works at a grocery store, too. He won't be going to college either but he'll be happy working with the public for the rest of his life."

Before Lauren can respond two older women step to their table and one of them wraps her arms around Stacy's neck. "How are you, sugar pop?" The woman looks at Lauren and smiles. "Hi, sweetie. I'm Gloria." Her accent is from the South and she has a warm, open face and short rings of salt-and-pepper hair.

"My apologies for a complete stranger calling you 'sweetie,'" the other woman says. She is in a long black coat, which looks striking against her blondish bobbed hair and is a complete contrast to the red Christmas sweater with candy canes, bells, and miniature wreaths that Gloria is wearing. "Unfortunately, 'sweetie' and 'sugar pop' and my personal favorite, 'honey babe', is what she calls most everyone except me. I'm Miriam."

Lauren smiles and looks at Stacy, wondering what to do with these two. "This is Lauren," Stacy says. "She saw that guy crash into me the other day. These are two of my friends, Gloria Wilson . . . most everybody calls her Miss Glory."

"Not me!" Miriam says.

"And this is Miriam Davies."

"Well, I'll make this quick because we don't want to stand around here and ruin your breakfast," Gloria says.

"Too late for that," Miriam says.

Gloria sighs and looks at Stacy. "The annual fundraiser for Glory's Place is fast approaching. It's only three weeks away and we normally have Glory's Place decorated by now and all the items in for the auction. I had hoped to come up with another idea to raise money but I've been down with the misery in my back—"

"She threw her back out," Miriam says.

Gloria turns to Miriam and scrunches up her face. "That's what I said."

"No one except for a handful of people in Georgia refers to throwing her back out as having 'the misery in my back.'"

"Well, nobody can ever figure out your British jargon. 'Bob's your uncle?' All of Grandon is still trying to figure that one out!" She rolls her eyes and turns back to Stacy. "Anyway, I'm way behind. I have people all across town helping us find auction items but I need help decorating Glory's Place."

"What's Glory's Place?" Lauren says between bites.

"It's a center that Miss Glory runs for single moms and families who are down on their luck. She has a food pantry there and does after-school tutoring for children," Stacy says.

"It's probably way too late to come up with another idea to raise money. 'A day late and a dollar short.' That's me! We're just always so busy throughout the year that I can never think of fund-raising until it's almost too late."

"How many kids come to Glory's Place?" Lauren asks.

Gloria and Miriam look at each other. "Heddy would know the exact number," Gloria says. "But I know that throughout the week we see at least fifty different kids."

"Why don't you do a sing-a-thon in the gazebo?" Lauren looks at their faces and wonders whether she has overstepped her bounds.

Gloria grabs Miriam's arm. "A sing-a-thon!" She begins to yank on Miriam's arm and Miriam tries to shake her off. "The kids could come in shifts throughout the day!" She tugs and shakes Miriam's arm again and says, "Can you see it, Miriam? Can you see a day where the kids are singing in that beautiful gazebo?"

Miriam pushes Gloria's hand away. "Yes, I can see it, Gloria, but I won't be able to work that day with only one good arm!"

Gloria folds her hands and puts them under her chin, smiling at Lauren. "Where have you been all these years? I have been hoping and praying for someone like you but have only been given Miriam."

"God gave you what you needed. It takes a person of strong constitution to work beside you," Miriam says, winking at Lauren.

Gloria sits down in the booth next to Lauren and pats her hand. "Could you lead the sing-a-thon for me?"

Stacy holds up her hand. "She doesn't live—"

Gloria doesn't let her finish. "The children would respond so well to someone your age. They would really look up to you. Every day they see me and Dalton and Heddy . . ."

"And me!" Miriam says, sighing, sitting next to Stacy.

"And we have wonderful volunteers to help but we don't have a lot of young people your age." Gloria is smiling and Lauren looks to Stacy for help. "Don't worry. Stacy could help." She reaches across the table and squeezes Stacy's hand. "Is that okay, babe? Would you be able to help Lauren with the sing-a-thon?"

Stacy laughs and waves her white napkin in the air. "I surrender. I may as well not put up a fight because in the end I know I'll be helping anyway."

"Annoying, isn't it?" Miriam says.

They look at Lauren and she feels something trembling beneath her skin. "I'll help." That rolled off her tongue quicker than she anticipated and she wonders if she can take it back.

"You are a doll!" Gloria says, squeezing Lauren to her. Nope. It's too late to take anything back now. "We are on our way to a fabulous Christmas!"

Lauren smiles, wondering if it's true. Hoping that it's true.

Five

Maria Delgado has worked for the chamber of commerce for five years but this is the first year she has been in charge of the annual Christmas parade. She wants everything from the floats to the food trucks to the games and booths to be exceptional. Normally, a man or woman is chosen by chamber members to sit atop the lead carriage in the processional and to host the day's festivities as the grand marshal, but it was her idea to have the residents of Grandon vote for the GM this year. As she gathers her purse and coat, Maria sticks her head into the office of Jessie Klein, the chamber president. "Just wanted to remind you that I'm taking Cassondra to the doctor."

Jessie looks up from her computer. "Is this just a follow-up or is there more going on that I don't know about?"

Maria smiles. "Just a follow-up. Dr. Andrews assured us that her heart is ticking right along like it's supposed to."

A year earlier, Maria and her husband, Craig, were at home with Cassondra and her older brother, Aidan, who were running and chasing each other in the back yard, when Cassondra collapsed, her body seizing. Aidan screamed for his parents, and as they ran across the deck and down the stairs they could see her crumpled in the grass. When Craig scooped her into his arms, her eyes fluttered open.

They raced her to the emergency room where a doctor assumed it was something neurological but could not say that with certainty, and issued a transfer to the nearby Children's Hospital. One test after another was performed with nothing definitive revealed. A seizure two weeks later led them to a neurologist named Dr. Leonard Craig. Antiseizure medication was prescribed and months went by without another episode, until six months ago when Cassondra seized again.

Dr. Craig recommended that Cassondra see Dr. Nathan Andrews, a pediatric cardiologist. "Sometimes," Dr. Craig said, "seizures aren't related to the brain after all but to the heart. I'd like to send you to Dr. Andrews for further tests."

Dr. Andrews looked to be in his thirties with short, sandy-brown hair and blue eyes when he entered the hospital room where Cassondra and Maria and Craig waited. They were anxious as he stuck out his hand. "I'm Dr. Andrews," he said, shaking each of their hands. When he got to Cassondra, he stood by the hospital bed and said, "Well! You are just the prettiest thing I've seen all day!" She grinned and folded her hands in her lap. "Don't tell my wife I said that. She can be insanely jealous."

Maria and Craig never sensed that he was in a hurry to get to another patient. He had a file with him but it was closed. "Are you in school yet?" Cassondra nodded. "Let me guess. You are in seventh grade." She shook her head. "Twelfth grade!" She laughed and shook her head again. "Don't tell me you're already in college."

"Kindergarten!" she said, laughing.

"Kindergarten! You mean with ABCs and 1,2,3, and crisscross applesauce?" She nodded, smiling. "What is your favorite part about kindergarten?"

She thought, resting her chin on her index finger. "I like math tubs."

He crossed his arms, looking impressed. "Math tubs? Is that like a bathtub but instead of water it's filled with numbers?"

"They're filled with math games!"

He nodded. "And you get this love of math from which parent?"

"Neither," Maria said, smiling.

"They don't like math," Cassondra said.

"So you are going to have to be the one at the grocery store figuring out the best price for the macaroni and cheese when your mom buys it or at the dealership when your dad goes to buy a new car, right?" She nodded and Maria and Craig relaxed. Dr. Andrews was not in a hurry. He was going to take the time that he needed to get to know his newest patient. "From what I understand, you have a big brother. What's he like?"

"He's good," Cassondra said.

"He's good? When I was a kid I don't think I would've described my sister as being good." He leaned in, whispering to her. "Did he tell you to say that in front of your parents? Is he holding something over your head?"

She laughed, opening her hands on her lap. "No! I'm serious. He's good. He's okay. He can be mean sometimes but not all the time."

Dr. Andrews nodded. "Ah! That sounds more like it. I could be mean sometimes, too. What's your brother's name?"

"Aidan."

"You were playing with Aidan outside one day when you fell in the yard. Is that right?" She nodded. "What were you and Aidan doing?"

"We were playing *Star Wars* with our dog."

He looked captivated. "And who were you and Aidan?"

She shrugged. "He was a storm trooper and I was a Jedi."

"Just as I assumed! And who was the dog?" Maria and Craig smiled, listening to them.

"He didn't have a name. Just a bad guy with the dark force that I was fighting."

"So you were running around the yard, chasing each other?" She nodded. "And two weeks later when you had another seizure, what were you doing?"

Cassondra looked at her parents. "She was at a birthday party," Maria said.

"What was she doing at that time? Eating cake? Playing a game?"

"It was at a place where there are trampolines and big pits filled with foam balls. Things like that. She had just gotten off a trampoline with a friend."

Dr. Andrews was still not referring to the folder in his hand, but it was obvious he had already read through it. "And when she got off was that the moment she began to seize?" Maria nodded. "The next few months brought no other seizures but then what happened late yesterday?" He looked at Cassondra, wanting to hear it from her.

"I was swimming at our community pool and a bunch of us were playing mermaids and we were swimming to get away from the sea witch."

"And who was the sea witch? The dog again?"

"No! Dogs aren't allowed in the pool! Katrina was the sea witch because she can swim fast."

"So the faster Katrina swam the faster you swam?" She nodded.

It was here that Dr. Andrews finally opened the folder and looked at Maria and Craig. "Were you with her?"

"I was," Maria said. "Craig was at a job interview. His company downsized and he's been . . ." Dr. Andrews can see on their faces that the last few months have been stressful and nods for her to continue. "One of the kids saw her immediately and started screaming. I jumped in along with some other adults and the lifeguard and we got her out." Maria wiped her face and cleared her throat, reminding herself not to get too emotional in front of Cassondra. She didn't want her to be afraid.

"And there has been no major illness or heart surgery prior to this?" Maria and Craig both shook their heads. Dr. Andrews looked at Cassondra and asked, "How do you feel right now?"

"Good."

He smiled, placing his hand on her head. "Well, let's make sure that you stay feeling good, okay?" She nodded and he closed the file. "I'm going to take a listen to your heart, all right?" She leaned forward and he put his stethoscope first on her chest and then her back. "You know you have a heart that sits right about here," he said, touching her chest. "And it is an amazing organ! When it works right it's wonderful but when there's a glitch in it things aren't so wonderful and somebody might not feel so good." He crossed his arms and looked directly into Cassondra's eyes. "Now, I want to try to explain this to you in a way that you can understand. So if you don't understand I want you to tell me, okay?" She nodded. He pulled a cartoon picture of a heart out of the folder, pointing to it as he spoke. "Everybody is born with their own natural pacemaker inside their heart. The upper chamber sends out a signal and that moves to the lower chamber and the ventricles squeeze and blood gets pumped all through your body. All the way down to your toes and back. Isn't that awesome?"

She nodded and he continued. "The cells inside your heart are called pacemakers because if you're exercising they need to work faster, and if you're sitting around and watching TV with your dog, then they work slower. Those cells send out little electrical pulses and regulate the pace of your heart. Make sense?"

She shrugged. "Sometimes, babies are born with a glitch somewhere in that system. A glitch means that there is some sort of little issue that might be causing a roadblock, which means that the little electrical impulse isn't working right and blood can't get all the way to your toes after all and that's called an arrhythmia, a doctor's word for a heartbeat that's too fast or too slow or irregular. So!" He patted her on the leg. "When I listened to your heart with this," he said, indicating his stethoscope, "I didn't hear anything unusual, but your history clearly tells me that we need to test your heart so we can get to the bottom of all this seizure stuff. Does that sound all right?"

"Do the tests hurt?"

He opened his arms wide. "Do I look like the kind of guy who would put my patients through tests that hurt? I'll tell you who that hurts . . . It hurts me that you would even think that!"

"So they don't hurt?"

Dr. Andrews laughed. "No, they don't, but you can pretend that they do so that the nurses feel sorry for you and give you a handful of candy. How does that sound?"

It sounded just fine to Cassondra, and after she'd had the tests she was happy to relay back to him that they indeed did not hurt!

Two days later Dr. Andrews implanted a pacemaker inside Cassondra's chest. If the length of time stretched too long between heartbeats, the pacemaker would send out an electrical impulse to make her heart contract and beat. "When can it come out?" Cassondra asked prior to the surgery.

"More than likely it will be there for the rest of your life," Dr. Andrews said. "The battery can last for years and you'll just get that changed out when needed, and as you grow and get bigger we'll need to change out the wires to longer ones."

"Can I still play *Star Wars* and mermaid?"

"Absolutely! But I would advise against boxing or football."

When Cassondra and Maria followed up with Dr. Andrews two weeks later it was inside his medical office. A nurse led them to the office and they looked at pictures on his wall and his desk of his wife and two children as they waited. Cassondra noticed a wooden box on the bookshelves behind Dr. Andrew's desk and walked to it, opening the lid, noticing an *L* scratched into the underside. "Cassondra," Maria said. "Don't touch his things. Come back on this side of the desk."

"It's so beautiful," Cassondra said. "I could pretend it held dreams and when I opened it I could be right in the middle of them!" She traced her fingers over words engraved on the top. "What does this say?"

"It says," Dr. Andrews said, entering the room, walking behind the desk and reading the words, "'The Lord says, "I will guide you along the best pathway for your life. I will advise you and watch over you." Psalm 32:8.'"

"We're so sorry, Dr. Andrews," Maria said. "Cassondra, come over here please."

"Don't be," Dr. Andrews said. "She wasn't hurting anything. I think it's beautiful, too." He picked up the box and held it in front of him. "My wife found this at a garage sale a year or so ago and thought it'd look good sitting in my office. She loved what it said because it's kind of like both of our lives: how I became a doctor and how she survived a heart defect of her own and a liver transplant when she was a young woman." Cassondra's eyes widened as she listened. "But you know what? I never knew what to put inside of it. That's why it's still empty. You, however, saw it and immediately knew that it could hold dreams, so why don't you have it?" He held it out and Maria leaned forward in her chair.

"Oh, no, Dr. Andrews! She couldn't take that."

"Why not? I completely missed its purpose and Cassondra took one look at it and knew what it was for. I'd like her to have it. Would you like it?" Cassondra smiled and he put the box in her hands. "There you go, pretty lady! I hope all your dreams come true!"

Six

Gloria sits at her kitchen table with Miriam and Dalton and Heddy Gregory, longtime friends who have helped her with Glory's Place. Dalton was the first black school superintendent for Grandon. He taught in the classroom for many years before working on the school board and then as superintendent. In their retirement, he and Heddy have been the hands and feet of Glory's Place.

"New this week . . . JoAnn and Marty have donated one week's use of their condo in Florida to the auction," Heddy says. "And Gerri at Spark's Travel has donated a four-day cruise to the Caribbean."

Gloria slaps the table. "Amazing!"

Dalton shuffles papers around in front of him and moves his reading glasses farther down on his nose. "Sarah's Glassworks has donated a two-day glassworks class and a handblown vase. The value of the vase alone is a hundred and fifty dollars but we all know what Sarah's work looks like and it is worth far more than that."

"Monet wishes that he could've created art like Sarah's," Gloria says.

"Monet wasn't a glassblower," Miriam says.

"I know that, Miriam. I'm merely suggesting that Sarah is an incredible artist." She looks at Dalton and Heddy and rolls her eyes.

"And I'm merely suggesting that you not compare her to Monet in front of her. He was not a famous glassblower." Miriam looks at Dalton and Heddy and rolls her eyes.

"Who is a famous glassblower? Can you name one?" Gloria snaps.

"Girls! Girls!" Dalton says. "You're both pretty. Calm down and carry on." Heddy puts her hand on her forehead, laughing. "Serendipity Cakes has donated a special-occasion cake."

"Does that include a wedding cake?" Gloria asks. Dalton looks at her over his glasses and smiles. She pumps her fist into the air. "Yes!" She uses the napkin in front of her to fan herself. "Combined with the auction items we already have we must be nearly double the items we had last year, right?"

Heddy smiles. "It's looking good. With the sing-a-thon maybe we'll raise more money than ever before. Someone does need to call the parks department to make sure the gazebo is free on that day and to allow us to set up tables for the auction items and chairs for anyone who wants to listen to the kids."

"Who do we even need to talk to at the parks department?" Miriam says.

Dalton picks up his coffee cup and talks over it. "Travis Mabrey."

"Ugh!" Miriam says. "Is he still there? Forget it! He won't be any help at all! We may as well come up with another idea."

"Would you get over it!" Gloria says. Dalton and Heddy look confused. "Madame Grumpy Puss here parked in a spot one day marked for parks and rec vehicles only and got a ticket. She appealed her case first to the officer who issued the ticket and then made a call to parks and rec, asking them for help. Travis had the unfortunate task of speaking with Miriam that day." Miriam crosses her arms in silence. "Note to committee," Gloria says, writing something on the legal pad in front of her. "Do not have Miriam contact parks and rec!"

Dalton laughs and stands to leave and Heddy drinks the last of her hot tea before taking her cup and Dalton's to the dishwasher. "We have several stores to visit this morning so we will keep you posted," she says. She grabs her coat from the back of her chair and looks at Gloria and Miriam. "So Stacy and her friend are running with the sing-a-thon?"

"On board as of yesterday and Lauren will be working with the kids starting today! Stacy did ask if we could help find some risers for the gazebo but they'll do everything else."

"Just call one of the schools," Miriam says.

"They're all too big for the space in the gazebo," Dalton says. "We just need a riser with two levels and it can't be too long."

Gloria raises her finger in the air. "Don't worry! We're on it!"

Miriam looks at her. "What do you mean 'we're on it'? Why is Madame Grumpy Puss on it with you?"

Dalton and Heddy head for the door as Dalton

says, "Remember, girls, keep calm and carry on!" Heddy waves and they close the door behind them.

Gloria pulls her laptop across the table in front of her. "I bet I can find risers in no time." She looks at Miriam. "Where should I look?"

Miriam stands up for more coffee, hissing at Gloria. "Why do you even own a computer? No one knows less about a computer than you do!" Gloria types something and makes a thinking sound in her throat. "What are you typing over there?" Miriam grabs another pumpkin muffin from the tray and takes a bite.

"I'm typing 'garage sales' for Grandon!" Gloria says, as if that is the most obvious thing she'd be typing.

"In December?" Miriam says, setting her coffee and muffin down with a thud. "You think you're going to find a riser . . . at a garage sale . . . in December . . . in Grandon?" She sighs, reaching for the computer. "Give me that before you accidentally land on porn." She types something and makes a couple of clicks with the mouse before sliding the computer back in front of Gloria. "There. Craigslist. That's one huge garage sale online. You can type in risers and see what comes up."

Gloria does and frowns. "It says there are zero matches."

Miriam bites into the muffin and shrugs. "Huge surprise! Shocking!" Gloria types in something else and makes a few more clicks with the mouse. "You're typing and clicking again and that makes me very nervous."

Gloria scowls at her and says, "I typed in 'Christmas.' You know, thinking I could find some extra Christmas decorations for Glory's Place and this popped up: *I am a 20-year-old woman looking for a fam-*

ily this Christmas. I've been in many foster homes and some of them have been very good homes, but I've never felt as if I have a family to call my own. A family would be the best Christmas present because a family isn't there for just a day but for life." She looks at Miriam. "What do you make of that?"

Miriam crosses her arms on the table, leaning on them. "I think the better question is, what do *you* make of that?"

Gloria reads the listing again. "I think I'm going to contact her."

Miriam closes the computer. "I knew it! This is why you are not allowed on the computer!"

"Why can't I respond to her?"

Miriam grabs her head. "Who puts an ad like that on Craigslist? Only a murderer!"

Gloria gets up for more coffee. "You watch way too many of those crime-scene TV shows."

Miriam turns to look over her shoulder. "All right, let's say she's not a murderer, but you give her the address of your home and she comes in here and robs you blind. Of course you'll be able to simply explain it to Marshall by saying, 'At least she wasn't a murderer!'"

The pumpkin muffins are too hard to resist and Gloria picks one up, bites into it and then sets it back down onto the pan. "Look at this," Gloria says, lifting the computer lid. "She's lived in several foster homes and is looking for a family this Christmas."

Miriam shakes her head. "She's looking for a family to strip bare! Not everyone is honest and good, Gloria."

"Not everyone is rotten either, Miriam." She picks up her coffee cup and looks into it, whispering, "Just you."

Miriam stands, pulling her coat from the back of her chair, and walks to the front door. "I heard that, Gloria! And one day when you're not murdered or robbed you'll thank me."

Gloria watches as Miriam walks across the yard to her home next door. She glances at the computer screen again and reads the words. She clicks reply to send an e-mail and types. *I saw your ad and must ask the obvious question . . . Are you a murderer?* She wonders if there's anything else she must ask at this point and decides there isn't, but wonders if she should sign her real name just in case the girl really is a murderer. She thinks for a moment and types "Lana Turner." She looks down at her sweatshirt with Snoopy wearing a Santa hat and says, "No, I'm definitely not a 'Lana.'" She types "Ethel Mertz" and stares at the name. "That makes me sound old and frumpy." She deletes the name and stares at the screen. "How in the world do criminals come up with so many aliases?" A grin spreads across her face and she types "Mary Richards." A twenty-year-old would not know who Mary Richards was. She looks at the name and nods, content with herself and clicks send. This would be her secret.

Three years earlier, Gloria's prayers after seven long Christmases had been answered. Her son Zach had returned home. He had run away at seventeen, and day after day she wondered where he was, if he was alive and if anyone was being kind to him at Christmas. Did he even remember what Christmas had been like in their home or even believe in the power and hope of Christmas anymore? She lost Zach to the streets, and then lost her husband after a short illness and felt her own faith in Christmas slipping away. She couldn't imagine a twenty-year-old facing that same loss of Christmas. She started Glory's Place because there were people right there in Grandon who didn't have socks or the money to pay the electric bill or a bed to sleep on or shampoo to wash their hair. Through the years, Glory's Place morphed into a center for single moms and families who needed extra help, because she knew that Christmas wasn't for the people who had their lives in order. Christmas wasn't for the ones who had no need for anything. It was for the ones who are messy and hopeless and feeling alone. It was for the ones who keep making the same mistake over and over and for the ones whose relationships are wrecked before they've even begun. Christmas was for all of the Zachs out on the street and for the twenty-year-old young woman looking for a family on Craigslist.

She would wait to hear from this young woman and figure out what to do next. One thing was certain . . . since she and Marshall had space at their kitchen table she wasn't about to deny that spot to someone who was desperate for a family at Christmas.

Seven

Lauren's phone alarm wakes her and she reaches for it, turning it off. She sits up in bed and opens her e-mail. Her heart quickens when she sees two from Craigslist. She reads the first and laughs, replying, *I am wondering the same thing about you, Mary Richards! No, I'm not a murderer. Just looking for someone to be my family. My dad left when I was a kid and my mom has been in and out of my life, but mostly out. Christmas is supposed to be about love and miracles and I guess that's what I'm looking for.* She thinks for a moment and types, *Don't worry if being part of a stranger's family isn't for you. I hope you have a great Christmas.* She wonders if she should sign her real name but types "Kelly" before clicking send.

The other e-mail reads, *Losers show up everywhere. Even on Craigslist. Get a life!* She considers deleting the ad again but Mary Richards has given her enough hope to keep it on Craigslist at least for a few more days.

She has arranged to switch her schedule from the afternoon to the morning shift for two days in a row, clocking out at three o'clock and running to her car. In some unexplained way she is looking forward to working with the kids in Grandon. Stacy said that most parents pick their kids up between five and seventy-thirty at Glory's Place so if they got an hour's worth of work with the kids between four and five that would be a good start.

On the drive there she goes over Christmas carols and songs in her head and feels something like a jolt of electricity pulsing inside of her. For the first time in her life she feels as if she's part of something and hopes she doesn't blow it. Lauren approaches Clauson's and decides to stop for no other reason than to stand in Ben's line and read the message he has for her today. Stevie Wonder's "What Christmas Means to Me" is playing throughout the store and the baggers are all wearing Santa hats, Ben included. She stands just inside the door and watches as customers take their place in his line.

"Line two is open," the manager says. Lauren smiles. No one is moving. "Ben! Why don't you come over here and bag for Mattie on line two?"

"No way, Les!" a woman holding a five-pound bag of flour says. "I've waited in line this long and I intend to get my message!"

"I can give you a message if that's all you need," the manager says.

"We don't want to hear your message," an elderly woman says, winking at Ben.

Lauren takes her place at the end of the line and watches as people interact with Ben. So many of them seem like part of his family. She imagines that some of them were there on the day he was born. Others came alongside and helped when doctors gave his parents a diagnosis that probably took their breath away. While some here resemble a grumpy uncle or distant aunt, others most likely have been there for every birthday, Thanksgiving feast, school program, scraped knee, broken heart, or belly laugh. Some may have picked up the phone in the middle of the night or showed up at the door holding a casserole. They have become his family, and Lauren realizes that after four years of standing behind a cash register, she still doesn't know any of her customers' names.

She grabs a pack of gum and slides it in front of the cashier.

"You're back!" Ben says. She watches as he sorts through the notes in front of him. He nods his head and slips the note inside a grocery bag, along with the gum. "You've been here a lot lately!" The cashier is already ringing out the next customer as Lauren grabs her gum.

There isn't enough time and too many groceries to bag for Ben to ask her name. "Have a great day!"

"You, too!" she says, walking away and pulling the note out to read it.

Christmas means we get to unwrap something new.
I hope it's everything you wanted.
Merry Christmas,
Ben

Lauren folds the note and puts it inside the pocket of her jeans and drives to Glory's Place, a simple building one mile from the town square. Pulling into the parking lot she reads the sign:

Donna VanLiere

GLORY'S PLACE
A Place of Help and Hope

An older black woman with a kind face and broad
smile greets her behind a desk. "You must be Lauren,
right?" She stands up and steps to her. "I recognize
you from your paperwork. Thanks for getting all of
that to me ahead of time so we could run the background check. I'm Heddy!" She hugs Lauren and
the sweet, soft scent of flowers remains on her coat.
"Stacy said you were coming and we're all very excited about the sing-a-thon!" She is leading Lauren
beyond the desk into a large open room with a basket-
ball hoop on one side, two Ping-Pong tables on the
other, and areas that are set up with different games
like corn hole, four-square, and jump rope. Tables are
set up near shelves full of board games, books, and
puzzles. There are at least twenty children who are
either shooting hoops, playing Ping-Pong, jumping
rope, or spread across the tables playing games. There
are three adults playing with the children and Heddy
points, while leading Lauren. "This is my husband,
Dalton." His smile is as broad as Heddy's and Lauren
notices the way a small girl, no older than five or six
with huge brown eyes and long black hair, holds on
to his leg. "This is Lauren. The young woman Gloria
and Stacy told us about."

Dalton bends to pick up the little girl. "Boy, are
we ever glad to see you! What an idea you've come
up with!"

"I hope it works," Lauren says.

"If we could get Cassondra out there singing, then it
is sure to work!" Dalton says, looking at the little girl.
"Will you sing in the gazebo to help Glory's Place?"

She lays her head on Dalton's shoulder and shakes it. "Well, if you don't sing, then we won't be able to raise any money! We were counting on you to be one of our loudest singers." He pokes a finger into her ribs and she squirms, grinning. "You won't help us sing?" She shakes her head again and buries it in Dalton's neck. He pats her back and Lauren notices the care he takes with her. He looks at Lauren. "Well, it's up to you to unlock Cassondra's beautiful voice!"

The task feels overwhelming now but Lauren musters a smile. She steps over so she can see the little girl's face and says, "My name's Lauren. I love your shirt. I'm a big Pooh Bear fan, too, but I could never rock that shirt the way you do." Cassondra smiles and Heddy directs Lauren to a door that says SHH, GENIUSES AT WORK above it.

Lauren stops at the door and looks at all of the children playing. "Do any of them come from abusive homes?"

"More than we probably know about." Heddy shakes her head. "Some kids don't exhibit the typical signs because they're really good at hiding their feelings." Lauren feels something catch in her throat as she watches the children and she turns away so Heddy can't see her face. "Gloria is through here. This is where the children do their homework after school and where the tutoring takes place."

Children are seated at every other chair at three long tables, where they are working independently. Small cubicles are set up throughout the rest of the room for one-on-one tutoring. Gloria peeks her head around one of the cubicle walls when she hears the door close. "Lauren! You made it!" She jumps up and hugs Lauren to her. Several children look up from their work. "This is Lauren! The young woman I told you about who is going to be teaching you some songs for the sing-a-thon!"

"I still don't know what a sing-a-thon is," a young boy around twelve says.

Gloria turns and smiles at Lauren. "I've already explained it and apparently I have done a poor job so the floor is yours."

There have never been so many eyes on Lauren at one time and her back gets hot. She takes off her coat and holds it, feeling awkward in the silence.

"So what is it?" the boy says again.

"Well, Stacy and I will be teaching you some songs and you'll sing them in the gazebo."

The boy slaps his pencil to the table and looks exasperated. "We know what singing means. What does 'a-thon' mean?"

Lauren thinks for a moment and Gloria laughs. "The 'a-thon' part is like a marathon," Lauren says. "You know, where people run for a long distance. We thought that you could sing all day in the gazebo to help raise money for Glory's Place."

The young boy shakes his head as if something is rattling about in there. "All day? What if I have to pee?"

"I *know* I'll need to pee!" a little boy around eight says.

"Do we just pee right there while we're singing?" a little girl about six or seven says.

Lauren glances at Gloria and Gloria opens her arms, laughing. "Welcome to Glory's Place!"

"We'll rotate singers in and out all day, and if you need to pee then you'll just leave your spot and go to the bathroom."

This sounds reasonable to the young boy and he nods. "How old are you?"

"Twenty."

"I like your hair," a little girl with fair skin and red hair says.

"Thanks," Lauren says.

A boy with brown skin, huge brown eyes, and black hair that looks like it was buzzed impatiently, says, "Are you going to help us every day? We don't sing around here so this could be pretty awful."

Gloria steps forward. "You will all do great! It is impossible for children to make a Christmas carol sound awful."

A little girl chewing on her pencil raises her hand. "Did you grow up here?"

Gloria waves an arm in the air. "Everybody finish your homework in the next few minutes, then you'll work with Lauren and Stacy and you can ask all the questions you want." She leads Lauren back into the main room, chuckling. "I may have just set you up for some of the craziest questions you have ever heard!" They walk across the room and Gloria spreads her arms. "This space is nice and open and a good area to work with some of the kids on the songs." She crosses her arms, looking at her. "Stacy will be here any minute. So while we wait . . . tell me about yourself."

From anybody else that may have sounded trite but Lauren can tell by the look on Gloria's face that she can't wait to know about her and her palms feel slippery. "There's really not that much to me."

"'There is more in you than you know.' That's from *The Hobbit*. Not me. I mean, I believe it and think it's true. I just didn't come up with that on my own. At least I think that's how it goes. So . . ." She sits on a plastic chair and gestures for Lauren to sit on the other one. "How long have you lived here?"

"I don't live here. I live in Whitall." She sits and holds her coat and bag on her lap.

Gloria's eyes are huge and she grabs her head. "What? I thought you . . . That's an hour from here. Why didn't you tell me when I asked for your help?"

"Stacy tried to tell you but—"

Gloria leaps to her feet. "I have done it again! Miriam says I am like a bull in a china shop. Oh, I hate it when she's right! She will never let me live this down. And if I even tell her about the woman on the computer!" Lauren watches her and doesn't know if she should laugh or be afraid. Gloria sits again. "I never should have assumed that you live here. I am so sorry, babe. You don't have to feel obligated in any way."

She doesn't know Gloria's last name but it doesn't matter. At this moment she would do anything for her. "I could have said no. I want to do this. It feels like some of these kids are probably me." She feels tears in her eyes and hopes that Gloria doesn't notice.

Gloria reaches for her hand and squeezes it. "You are making this one of the most memorable Christmases for these kids and for me. I hope you know that's true."

If tears came easily to Lauren she would cry now, but years of sucking it up and stuffing it down have made her a pro at this face she wears. But Gloria's face, like Ben's face and Stacy's face, are so unlike hers. For some reason, their faces, their voices, have the power to make her want to believe.

Eight

Stacy arrived prepped with the lyrics to "Jingle Bells," "Silent Night," "Away in a Manger," "Rudolph the Red-Nosed Reindeer," "Have Yourself a Merry Little Christmas," "O Holy Night," and "Santa Claus Is Coming to Town," but they've been unable to get through all of the songs with the children. Most of the time has been taken up with questions, giggling, and an unannounced contest of who could sing the loudest. Trevor won, hands down. True to her word, Cassondra will not sing. She sits on a chair where her legs dangle just above the floor and watches Lauren and Stacy with keen interest.

Lauren bends down in front of her, pointing to her ear. "I can't hear you." She uses her palm to smack her ear. "There must be something wrong with my ears. Can you see anything in there?" Cassondra grins and shakes her head. "Oh, I see! You're not singing!" She taps her on top of the head. "Would you sing for a dollar?" The little girl shakes her head.

"Would you sing for a candy bar?" Cassondra grins but shakes her head. She whispers something and Lauren strains to hear. "What?"

"Gummy bears."

Lauren laughs and finds herself pulling the bird-like tiny shoulders into her. "I'll see what I can do."

Numbers dwindle as parents arrive to pick up their children. Lauren watches as each one leaves and notices that some run to a mom or dad while others hang their head and slump toward the door, heading for home.

"That went better than I expected," Stacy says, as the last two children bolt for their things.

They pick up the song lyric sheets and stack the chairs as Lauren watches the children file out and into cars waiting for them. She notices one boy who isn't wearing a coat but shrugs it off, assuming he forgot it at home.

Miriam waves at her from the front door and Lauren pauses, unsure if she's waving at her. "Lauren! Please hurry!" Lauren glances at Stacy and hands her the song lyrics. "Run! Please!" Miriam says, waving her arms. Lauren runs to her and Miriam grabs her arm. "Do you see that man getting out of that truck? That's Travis Mabrey from parks and rec. Gloria called yesterday about the use of the gazebo on the eighteenth. As you can see, Gloria and Dalton and Heddy are all busy loading the children into cars and I'm unable to speak with him."

"Are you helping get the kids into cars?"

Miriam sighs. "No. Unfortunately, Mr. Mabrey and I have an ugly past together." Lauren looks at the young man walking across the parking lot heading toward Miriam. "Not in an unseemly way!" Travis opens the door and Miriam steps behind Lauren. "He and I should not face one another. Would you please take care of his questions?"

Lauren looks to see if Stacy is near but she has slipped into another room and Miriam disappears into the office. "I'm looking for Gloria," Travis says, approaching her. He looks twenty-something with sandy blond hair and a stocky build.

"She's out with the kids right now getting them in cars."

"I'm with the parks department. She called me yesterday but I haven't had a chance to get back with her. I was driving by and thought I'd stop in."

"Yeah. She wanted to see if the gazebo could be used on the eighteenth for the fund-raiser."

"In the gazebo?"

She nods. "We're doing a sing-a-thon. They're going to do the auction items like usual and would need to put out tables for those."

"Around the gazebo?"

She doesn't feel as if she's answering well and talks faster. "Yeah. Auction items would go on top of the tables and people will bid on them. And she needs chairs placed around the gazebo in order for people to listen to the children singing." He crosses his arms, thinking. "We hope to have the children singing throughout the day and raising money that way. So . . . is it available?"

He looks down at his phone and taps the screen. "Actually, no. That's the day of the Christmas parade. The chamber blocked that day off for the gazebo months ago."

"That means the sing-a-thon won't work. And it was my idea! Miss Glory will be so disappointed."

"Why don't you talk with Maria or Jessie at the chamber. They might not need the gazebo for the parade and I bet they'd love to see kids filling it up." She smiles and he extends his hand. "I'm Travis Mabrey, by the way."

"Lauren Gabriel."

He slips his phone into his pocket. "Related to Victor Gabriel?"

Lauren stops breathing and hopes there is color in her face. "Um, yeah. I mean, I've met him but I don't know him."

"Distant family?"

She nods. "Yeah. Just part of the family tree somewhere." She concentrates on keeping her feet from moving. "How do you know him?"

"He worked in the department for a couple of years."

"He's not there anymore?"

He shakes his head. "Left two and a half to three years ago, after he got the divorce. We were happy to see him go."

A wave of sadness sweeps over Lauren. For a moment she found herself hoping that her father was a man who carried his lunch to work and made jokes with his coworkers before jumping in his truck and doing his job of mowing, raking, weeding, or repairing playground equipment at parks around the city. For a moment she believed that he took his paycheck home and provided for a family that she didn't know about and used that money for his son's Little League jersey or his daughter's tennis racket. For a moment she saw him holding hands with his wife or carrying his child atop his shoulders.

"If you don't really know him, then you've probably never seen that side of Victor."

He's looking at her but her throat feels full of cotton. Her breath is catching and she turns to look behind her. "I'm sorry. I have to help clean up."

He watches as she dashes across the floor, grabs her bag, and disappears through a door.

"So do you need any help tonight organizing for the sale?" Jessie asks Maria as she gathers her things at the end of the day.

Maria laughs. "We have been moving things into the garage for the last week. I don't have that much to sell. Hopefully between tonight and Saturday it will all be gone. Who knew a move across town could be so time-consuming?"

On her way home from work Maria drops by Wilson's Department Store, Betty's Bakery, and City Auto Service to pick up the votes for grand marshal. The final stop is Clauson's. She walks to the customer service counter and reaches inside the box she placed there a week earlier and pulls out a small handful of papers. She grabs a take-home pizza for a quick dinner tonight and decides that since Ben's line is short that she will stand in it. "You're coming to the Christmas parade, right, Ben?" she asks, opening her wallet.

"If I have the day off I will! Christmas is our busiest time of year!"

She watches as he puts the pizza into a bag and sifts through the notes in his hand. "I wish you could move to the other side of town so that I can keep getting these notes at Bixby's Food and Pharmacy! You know that's going to be so much closer to me."

Ben grins, looking sheepish. "I can mail you some."

The cashier and Maria laugh. "It just wouldn't be the same without you putting it inside a grocery bag!" She reaches for the bag and says, "Because of you, Ben, I will never look at a grocery bag the same way again." She pats his shoulder then digs for her car keys as she walks into the parking lot. After opening the car door, she places the bag on the passenger seat. She pulls out the note and then starts the car, letting the heater warm up as she reads Ben's words.

Christmas isn't a parade or concert but a piece of home you keep in your heart wherever you go.
Merry Christmas! Ben

Maria smiles as she puts the car in reverse. "I'll just have to make the drive across town for these."

The offices of the Grandon Chamber of Commerce are just three blocks from Glory's Place. Lauren wants to talk with Jessie or Maria before saying anything to Miss Glory about the gazebo mix-up.

"Is Jessie or Maria available?" she asks a woman around fifty sitting behind a desk in the main office.

"Maria left early today and Jessie is in a meeting. Can I help you with something?"

"I'm helping out with the Glory's Place fund-raiser and we wanted to do a sing-a-thon with the kids in the gazebo on the eighteenth, but parks and rec said you have the gazebo reserved that day." Lauren watches the woman's face for understanding but she isn't revealing much. "I was just seeing if there's any way that maybe Glory's Place could use the gazebo . . . for at least part of the day."

The woman nods and reaches for a notepad. "Give me your name and number and I'll have one of them call you back."

Lauren had wanted to have this taken care of before she saw Gloria again, but she gives the information to the woman, hoping that one of the ladies will call her back soon.

Before heading for home she orders a sandwich, chips, and a glass of water at Betty's and watches as snow falls outside. She feels stupid for running away from Travis and guilty for suggesting the sing-a-thon. What if it can't happen inside the gazebo? Snowflakes leave frosty patterns on the window and she watches as one lands on the glass and then slides to the ledge, piling up with the others. Her head throbs with the thought, *Why did I run away?* She didn't even come face to face with her dad, just his shadow as it passed through this town. Who runs from a shadow? Stacy must wonder what happened to her. She considers calling her but doesn't want to explain herself. She doesn't want tears in her eyes when the waitress arrives with her food but there they are anyway. The waitress sets her sandwich and chips in front of her as a tear makes its way down her cheek.

"Are you okay?" the waitress asks. She's in her mid-twenties with shoulder-length blond hair that she has pulled back into a ponytail.

"Yeah, thanks." Lauren swipes away the tear and reaches for the sandwich.

"Can I bring you anything else?" Lauren shakes her head and the waitress walks away. She is used to this . . . being alone. In a house full of foster children she could always find a corner or a front porch step where she wouldn't have much fuss from anyone. It was there, observing the cracks between the wall and baseboard or the patch of dry grass at the edge of the sidewalk, that she became aware of a loneliness that no person would ever fill. It was something she could not name or put her finger on.

"You're lonely for home," her last foster mom, Lori, had said.

"Which home?" Lauren had asked.

"The one you *wanted* to grow up in." Lori was kind. Lauren had known a few kind foster mothers and fathers. Others seemed to be working in the system for the wrong reasons, but Lori did it because she cared about kids. There are moments when Lauren wishes she had not left Lori and Jim's home so abruptly.

"Hey, I don't mean to be nosy but . . ." Lauren looks up at the waitress. "Are you okay?"

"Yeah." Lauren puts a chip in her mouth and looks out the window, hoping the waitress will go away.

The waitress sits across from her at the table and Lauren turns to look at her. "You're my last table. I never do anything like this but I hate to watch you cry alone. I'm Holly, by the way."

Lauren avoids eye contact while pushing the sandwich into her mouth. "Lauren."

"Is there anything that I can help you with? Like is your car broken down or something?"

Lauren stares at what's left of her sandwich and shakes her head. "No. Just old stuff." Holly is quiet, not wanting to pry. "I just found out that my dad used to live here in Grandon."

Holly leans her arms onto the table. "And you didn't know that because . . ."

A couple leaving at the next table attracts Lauren's attention and she watches as they put on their coats and grab their packages before leaving. "Because he left when I was little. I live in Whitall. I never knew where he was. I just assumed that he was hundreds of miles away. I had no idea he was only an hour away with a brand-new wife. Maybe some kids. I don't know. But, true to form, he packed up and left them, too."

Holly sighs, watching the customers around them. "He's an idiot." Lauren looks at her and Holly shrugs. "He is. You might want to believe that life would've been better with him in it, but it sounds like it would have been worse. He couldn't stay then. He can't stay now. He couldn't be a dad then. He can't be a dad now. And now there might be other kids like you who are going to be wishing that he'd stuck around, but he's incapable of sticking around because he's an idiot!" Lauren finds herself grinning and Holly jumps on the opening. "Deep down you know it's true even though deep down you also want him to be different—but that's never going to happen. There is no going back and changing anything, especially him! He's the one who missed out and not just on watching you grow up. He's missed everything in life."

"Did he miss out on eating this turkey and bacon club sandwich?"

"I bet he did!" Holly says. "He's strictly a fast food guy because he doesn't know anything about what good food is!" She points her finger at Lauren. "And he never once looked out this window to see that gazebo all lit up at Christmastime!"

Lauren tries to hide her smile and takes a final bite. "So he missed sitting here at this booth and getting yelled at?"

Holly laughs. "Yes, he did! Nobody takes the time

to yell at customers at Taco Bell. Only at Betty's Bakery." She leans forward, resting her chin on her hand. "I'm really sorry that he was your dad."

"I am, too."

"If it helps, you can share my dad. He's a horrible dresser and, no matter what he tells you, he is awful at impressions, but other than that he's a good dad."

"Thanks."

"Why are you in Grandon, anyway?"

Lauren pushes her plate away and pulls her water glass in front of her. "At first I was brought here to identify a guy in a lineup, but now I'm helping with a Christmas fund-raiser for Glory's Place."

"That's kind of wild. How'd you go from a lineup to a fund-raiser?"

Lauren shakes her head. "I'm still not sure." She opens her purse and pulls out her wallet.

"It's okay," Holly says. "I'll get this one today." She taps the table. "And that's another thing your dad has missed out on!"

As Lauren slips her wallet back into her bag she realizes that Holly doesn't mean that her dad missed out on free food, rather the generosity of others who help people feel less alone.

Nine

Gloria stares at the computer screen on her kitchen table and reads. *Dear Mary, I am not a murderer. I've never even had a parking ticket. I would never hurt you or anyone. I have never had a normal Christmas and I would like one very much. I have never had a normal family and I would like one very much. You don't have to lecture me on how no family is normal because I know that. I have been in lots of foster homes so I know what homes and families are like. But what you may see as frustrations—dirty dishes, laundry, trips to the grocery store, cooking dinner, unloading the dishwasher, cleaning house, going to baseball games and soccer matches, walking the dog, cleaning out the car, and sweeping the garage—all sound pretty good and normal to me. If you want to meet somewhere that's great, but don't worry if this whole thing sounds weird to you. I've never done anything like this before and it sounds pretty weird to me right now, too. Kelly*

Gloria's heart beats inside her ears. She wonders if she should tell Marshall about this and knows beyond certainty that she cannot tell Miriam. She wonders if Kelly feels as frightened and unsure as she does. She thinks for a moment before replying. *Dear Kelly, I would love to meet you! I cannot imagine life without my family or life without Christmas with my family. No one should be alone at Christmas because Christmas is for the lonely. I would love to meet you, and after that, if you think that you would like to join my husband and me and our families for Christmas (we are a big, blended bunch with a nosy neighbor thrown in as well), then I would be honored to set a plate for you at our table. We live in Grandon. Just set the date and time and I can meet you at Betty's Bakery.*

Gloria looks at the e-mail and contemplates signing her real name this time but decides against it. *I look forward to hearing from you. Your friend, Mary Richards*

She clicks send as Miriam walks through her front door. "Any word on the risers yet?"

"It wouldn't kill you to say good morning, you know!" Gloria says, closing the computer. "Have you had your coffee yet?"

"No, I haven't," Miriam says, pulling out a chair at the table.

"That might explain the rudeness this morning. Now we just need an explanation for all the other hours of the day." Gloria pours Miriam a cup of coffee and sets it in front of her. "As a matter of fact, I have found some risers that will work. The church has a small riser that will work just great." She sits down and folds her arms, looking satisfied.

"No need to look smug, Gloria. There is still so much work to be done." Miriam scowls, pushing a crumb off the red place mat in front of her. "What is this that you and Marshall ate for breakfast?"

"It was a spinach and cheese quiche. Would you like some?"

"It would help the coffee go down."

Gloria sighs, standing back up. "Why don't you just say you've got a gnawing in your stomach and need something to eat?"

"Because no one would say that, Gloria!"

Gloria cuts a piece of quiche and warms it for a few seconds in the microwave before setting it in front of Miriam. They make small talk about the weather and sales at Wilson's before Gloria says, "I'm headed out in a few minutes to find more items that we can auction off."

"Where are you going? The travel agency? Restaurants? Jewelry stores?"

Gloria pours herself another cup of coffee. "To the church rummage sale."

Miriam stares at her. "To the rummage sale?"

"Yes! All the money goes to that orphanage in Haiti."

"Gloria! We need high-ticket items for the auction, not dog bowls and knickknacks."

Gloria waves the words away. "I found a whole set of relief glass there last year. Remember? That alone sold for two hundred dollars. Don't pooh-pooh my rummage sales."

"I'm not pooh-poohing anything. I'm not entirely sure what that even means. I'm just saying—"

Gloria won't let her finish. "I promise to wow and astonish you when I get done shopping there. I will find the most valuable gift of all." She raises her finger in the air and Miriam leaves it at that.

"What did you do about that Craigslist woman you mentioned?" Miriam asks.

Gloria is surprised and hopes Miriam doesn't catch her eyes bugging out. "You told me not to do anything!"

Miriam finishes the quiche and picks up her coffee. "I know what I told you but what I tell you to do rarely coincides with what you actually do."

Grabbing her napkin, Gloria twists it around one finger and then does it again. "You are absolutely right. That woman could have been a murderer." She stands and picks up her coffee cup, taking it to the dishwasher. "I want to be first in line at the rummage sale so I better go."

Miriam walks to the dishwasher and places her dishes inside. "Sometimes you surprise me, Gloria! I'm sorry I doubted you."

"Apology accepted." She walks Miriam to the door and can feel the wintery air as she opens it. "I'm off to buy something truly great now!" Miriam opens her mouth to say something else but Gloria closes the door, breathing a sigh of relief.

Gloria cringes as she walks by a table in the Grandon Community Church lobby with not one but three ceramic dog bowls on it. She finds it so annoying when Miriam is right. The bric-a-brac is mostly broken and there's not a sign of relief glass anywhere. A painting of a barn by Grandon's former mayor holds promise for the silent auction but it's not in a frame. Buying a frame for it would cost more than the painting is worth. In the end, she walks away from the rummage sale with a stack of classic literature books dating as early as 1923. She looks at her purchases as she loads them into her car and realizes there is nothing that will "wow and astonish" anyone. Why did she have to use such highfalutin words with Miriam?

On her way home she notices a MOVING SALE sign at the corner of Jefferson Street. She turns onto the street and drives to the end to a modest ranch house where the contents of the home spill out onto the driveway. She recognizes the homeowner and waves. "Maria! Are you moving soon?"

Maria is handing change to a couple who is hauling away a twin bed headboard, frame, and mattress. "In January. I have to get through the Christmas parade first!"

Gloria walks over to her, wrapping her arms around her. "Any job for Craig yet?"

"Nothing beyond his part-time work at Wilson's. But at least we won't have a mortgage on our backs. We can get by in a two-bedroom apartment until something full-time comes along for him."

Cassondra peeks through the window of the garage door and opens it, yelling, "Miss Glory! I have something for you!"

"I know! A piece of my heart, right?"

Cassondra smiles and slams the door, running through the house. Maria shrugs. "I have no idea what she has for you. I'm almost nervous to see what it could be."

The garage door opens and Cassondra is clutching a wooden box to her chest. "I thought you could sell this at the auction for Glory's Place." She hands the box, made of dark mahogany wood, to Gloria, and Maria steps close.

Gloria takes the box and reads the engraving on top. *The Lord says, 'I will guide you along the best pathway for your life. I will advise you and watch over you.' Psalm 32:8.*

"This is absolutely beautiful!"

"I thought you loved that box, Cassondra," Maria says. "You pretend that it holds dreams."

The little girl swings her arms and rocks back and forth on her heels. "I think there are a lot of people that Miss Glory knows who need dreams."

Gloria kneels down and smiles at Cassondra. "Are you sure about this?"

Cassondra nods. "My doctor gave it to me and now it's time for somebody else to use it."

"But what about all of your dreams?" Gloria asks.

Cassondra leans in to whisper. "Dreams don't really go in a box, Miss Glory. I thought you knew that."

Gloria laughs and hugs Cassondra, kissing her on the forehead. "You know what? Miriam said that I wouldn't be able to find anything at sales like this and I believe that you have just given me something that is absolutely priceless."

Miriam closes the door to the office and sits down at the computer at Glory's Place. With a few clicks she has logged on to Craigslist and has found the listing for the young girl looking for a family at Christmas. Miriam clicks to send her an e-mail and types.

Needing more information. My greatest concern is that this is a fraudulent listing and that you are a morally corrupt soul trying to take advantage of people's good intentions. If you are indeed looking for someone to spend Christmas with then I think that you would find me and the town in which I live to be

*most friendly. However, before we get down to sharing
ham and scalloped potatoes I must know some things
about you:*

   Are you a criminal?
   Are you currently incarcerated?
   *Have you ever pulled a gun on someone or caused
anyone bodily harm?*

   *These questions may seem a bit odd but surely
you understand my need to take precautions.*
   Thank you for taking time to answer them.

She pauses, thinking it best not to use her real
name. She mentally lists some of her favorite TV
characters and types in a name.

Laura Petrie

She realizes the last name isn't necessary and deletes it, ending the e-mail simply with "Laura."

A knock on the door startles Miriam and she
clicks send before closing out of Craigslist.

"Excuse me. Miriam?" Lauren is peeking around
the door and Miriam rises.

"I'm all done. Did you need the computer?"

"I just wanted to let you know that I spoke with
Travis from parks and rec about the use of the gazebo
but I still don't have an answer."

Miriam claps her hands together. "Thank you so
much for talking with him."

Lauren steps into the hallway with Miriam and
watches as children enter through the main doors.

"I actually thought he was a really nice guy. I can't imagine what he could have done that would have made you not want to talk to him."

Miriam holds up her hand. "He knows. Trust me. He knows."

Miriam takes her place behind the desk and helps sign the children in for the afternoon. Lauren spots Cassondra coming through the doors. The little girl catches her eye and Lauren waves. Her mother signs her in and then kisses the top of her head as she leaves.

Lauren walks to her and kneels down beside her, pulling something from her bag. "Gummy bears," she says. Cassondra reaches for them and Lauren pulls the bag away from her grasp. "Uh, uh, uh. Remember our deal? I would bring you gummy bears and you would sing?" Cassondra's eyes are big and brown and Lauren doesn't know if she'll have the strength to keep the candy away from her. "Will you sing today?" Cassondra looks up at the ceiling and shrugs. She sticks out her hand and Cassondra holds on to it. "Was that your mom?" Cassondra nods. "Was she headed to work?"

"Yep!"

"Where does she work?"

"At the chamber of congress."

Lauren stops at the game tables and looks at her. "The chamber of commerce? What's your mom's name?"

"Maria."

Lauren sighs as she watches Maria pull out of the parking lot.

Cassondra pulls Guess Who from the shelves. She opens the box and pushes a yellow tray filled with row after row of illustrated faces in front of Lauren. "Am I playing this with you?" Cassondra smiles and Lauren can't resist. "I don't think I've played this game before so you go first and you can teach me."

Cassondra hands her a card but doesn't look at it. She takes one for herself and places it on the tray in front of her. "Does your person have yellow hair?"

Lauren looks at the card in front of her. "My person does not have yellow hair." She watches as Cassondra flips down tiles on her tray. "Okay. Does your person have dark hair like us?"

Cassondra shakes her head as Lauren flips down all the tiles with people with dark hair. "You remind me of my mommy."

"That's funny because I thought you reminded me of myself when I was your age. Except I was never as pretty as you."

Cassondra can't hide her smile. "Is your person a woman?"

"She *is* a woman!" Tiles are flipped down with great flourish and Cassondra beams. "Somehow I think I'm about to get beat! Okay, does your person wear glasses?" Cassondra shakes her head and Lauren flips down three tiles. She looks at her tray, which is mostly filled with upraised tiles and then to Cassondra's, where four tiles remain up.

"Does your woman's name start with *M*?"

"If you mean Megan, then yes!" The little girl crosses her arms and smiles. "I hope you're as good at singing as you are at this game!" Cassondra laughs and Lauren finds herself joining her.

"I called and left a message." Lauren looks over her shoulder to see Travis, holding some papers. "I brought paperwork for use of the gazebo. I didn't hear back from you so I thought I'd swing the paper-work by just in case you decided to move ahead."

Lauren stands, feeling awkward and sorry for running away yesterday. "Yes! I mean, no, I haven't heard back yet."

They each stand in the clumsy silence before Travis hands the papers to her. "Well, here they are just in case you get the answer to go ahead."

"I didn't mean to run away yesterday," she says, taking the papers.

"No! No problem! You aren't the first girl who's run away from me." She laughs out loud and thinks that despite what Miriam thinks of him, Travis is a good guy. "I hope I didn't say anything wrong. That's why I came today, because I wanted to apologize." He slips his hands into his coat pockets and shifts from one foot to the other.

She can feel Cassondra's eyes on them and turns to her, squinching up her face to make Cassondra smile. "You don't need to apologize. I was a jerk. I can't believe I did that."

"No. I've run from lots of things. Just last week a raccoon chased me and Barry through one of the parks." She laughs out loud again and knows that all is forgiven.

"Thanks for stopping by. You don't have to make another special trip. You can call and talk with me or Miriam."

"Who?"

"Miriam Davies. You know, you've talked to her before."

He looks down at the floor, trying to picture Miriam's face. "I don't remember her. Maybe I made her run away, too." Lauren smiles and he shifts his weight once more, clearing his throat. "Do you work here every day?"

Lauren tucks some hair behind an ear. "I don't work here at all. I'm just helping with the fund-raiser at the gazebo."

"Then I guess I'll see you around since the gazebo is kind of my thing."

Lauren wonders if that is something like his version of wanting to get to know her better and isn't sure how to respond. "Okay. And I promise not to run away again." She wishes she hadn't said that but he laughs, smiling. He waves and she watches as he walks through the front doors and back to his truck.

"Is he your boyfriend?" Cassondra's hands are over her mouth as if she is about to pop.

Lauren grabs her bag from the table. "No, he's not my boyfriend!"

"He should be."

Lauren looks shocked. "So this is why I came to Grandon? To take advice from a five-year-old?" She shakes her head, laughing, and reaches for her phone while she walks to the lockers. She checks her e-mails and notices a new one from Craigslist. She reads through the list of questions from a woman named Laura and sighs.

"Everything okay?" Stacy asks, putting her purse into a locker.

Lauren slips her phone into her back pocket and closes the locker. "It's great. Just weird people on the Internet."

"Is everyone fighting with each other on Facebook?" Stacy closes a locker and reaches for the door.

"No."

Stacy hands her the sheets with the lyrics and

begins to set the chairs in a circle. "I didn't see you leave yesterday."

Lauren is quiet, placing the lyrics on each chair. "I didn't mean to run off."

"I didn't know you ran off. I just didn't see you leave." She looks at her. "Did you run off because of something I did?"

"No!" Lauren stops what she's doing. "I'm just stupid sometimes."

Stacy reaches for the music stand and pulls it up, into position. "I'm stupid, too, sometimes."

Several children take their places, and Lauren feels Cassondra holding on to her leg. Lauren has never believed much in the miracles or magic of Christmas, but when these voices rise and fall to "O Holy Night" she finds herself believing. Maybe the home that she keeps looking back on is really in the manger from so long ago. Maybe her loneliness is swept away into those starry skies in which the angels appeared. Maybe the greatest gifts have never been received because she hasn't opened her hands. Maybe the greatest miracles of Christmas are here in this room or just around the corner. She realizes that a small voice, as clear and sharp as a bell, is rising above the others and she leans down to hear. Cassondra looks like a baby bird opening and closing her mouth and Lauren pulls her to her. She never realized that one of the miracles of Christmas was wrapped in the voice of a child.

Ten

Miriam sits at the computer in the spare bedroom of her home and checks her e-mail. The room is as tidy and organized as Miriam and in the same shades of gray and black with just a pop of red, like Miriam loves to wear. She sees the reply from Craigslist and opens it.

Dear Laura,
I am not a criminal and I'm not a prisoner. I never have been.
I've never pulled a gun on someone or caused anybody bodily harm. I know this whole thing sounds crazy but all I'm wanting is someone who would accept me into their family and make me a part of it. I'm not looking for money or even Christmas presents. I'm just looking for a family that I can sit around a table with and eat Christmas dinner. I can't cook but I could bring something! If you would like to meet before Christmas so you can be sure I'm not on

*the FBI's Most Wanted list I understand. It would be
nice to meet you, too.*
Thank you,
Kelly

Miriam reaches for her phone, thinking that she
would call Gloria to tell her about this but decides
against it. Gloria would never let her hear the end
of doing something that Miriam had advised her
against. Miriam still is not convinced that the woman
is not a grifter of some kind but feels the very least
she can do is meet her. She puts her fingers on the
keyboard and types.

*How lovely to hear from you and to learn that you
are not being tracked by the FBI. A meeting sounds
like a good idea. I also have been alone for several
years but am blessed with wonderful friends that I
call family and I have grown children and young
grandchildren who still make Christmas a magical
time for me. I will be spending Christmas with my
dearest friends and I'm sure they would be pleased
to have you as well. As audacious as her personal
tastes are, my friend is one of the kindest and most
generous people you will ever meet. Thankfully, she's
also a wonderful cook (not my strong suit). I am
willing and able to meet you at your convenience.*
Most sincerely,
Laura

Lauren sits at a table in the break room at Gordon's
Grocery and slides money into the vending machine
while looking up the number for the chamber of com-

merce in Grandon. She opens the bag of chips as the phone rings. "Is Maria available?"

"Who's calling?"

"This is Lauren. I work with her kids at Glory's Place." She is put on hold and hopes to come up with the right things to say.

"This is Maria."

Lauren sets the chip bag on the table and takes a breath. "Hi! My name is Lauren and I'm working with your kids and the others at Glory's Place for the sing-a-thon on the eighteenth."

"Cassondra mentioned that. Is everything okay? Did the kids get into trouble?"

"No!" Lauren stands up from the table and walks around the break room. "Miss Glory's fund-raiser is on the eighteenth, the same day as the Christmas parade. We had hoped to use the gazebo for the sing-a-thon but the parks department has said that the chamber is using it that day."

"Oh! I see. Yes, local vendors were going to set up in the gazebo and town square."

Lauren is nervous. Who is she to suggest anything regarding Grandon? "This is different for Glory's Place. Normally, Miss Glory does a fund-raiser with silent auction items and desserts at Glory's Place. It was my idea to use the kids in a sing-a-thon because Glory's Place is all about kids. I haven't even mentioned this scheduling problem to Miss Glory yet because she has her heart set on it. So do all the kids!"

"There must be another date that's available for the gazebo. I can even check with the parks department."

"All of the invitations have already gone out. I may

have single-handedly ruined this fund-raiser for Glory's Place, and those kids are so sweet. Your kids are awesome! I love Cassondra!"

Maria laughs on the other end. "This isn't a hard sell for me. Don't forget that I have a vested interest in Glory's Place. It was full but Gloria knew that my husband and I could not afford child care at this time and she made room for Cassondra and Aidan. I know that there are more people just like us out there who need this place. Cassondra loves it so much that she gave Gloria a special wooden box for the auction." Lauren can hear her shuffling things. "Let me talk with the chamber president and I'll get back with you."

Lauren sighs as she hangs up, looking at her phone. There are four Craigslist e-mails and she clicks on the first. She smiles when she reads that Mary lives in Grandon. She quickly clicks reply and uses her thumbs to type.

> *Hi, Mary! Awesome that you live in Grandon!*
> *I could meet you at Betty's Bakery on Thursday.*
> *I have the day off but I'm busy from 3:30–5:00 but*
> *could do anything before or after. Just let me know a*
> *time that works. I'm excited but a little bit nervous to*
> *meet you. Hope that makes sense.*
> *Kelly*

Lauren feels like a fraud using her middle name but she doesn't want kids she knew in high school or anyone she works with to see the posting and make fun of her or question her motives. When she meets Mary she will tell her the truth. She clicks on the next e-mail and smiles again before responding.

Hi, Laura! I forgot to ask where you live but if you are close to Grandon I could meet you at Betty's Bakery on Thursday. I'm busy from 3:30–5:00 and I know I will have one more meeting that day but I don't know the time yet. If you don't live close to Grandon then we could meet somewhere else. I'm excited AND nervous.
Kelly

The other two e-mails are from people who are calling her even more creative names for loser and telling her how lame she is. When she posted the listing, Lauren had no idea what to expect. There are those who think she's an idiot, but now there are also two women out there, one of them actually in Grandon, who have agreed to meet her. She slides the phone back into her bag and puts it inside her locker. She is either crazy for doing this or about to open a Christmas gift she's always wanted.

As Christmas draws closer, Clauson's gets busier every day. Ben's note writing has more than doubled each evening. Stacy and Jacob and even Lucy help him decorate each note with a Christmas star after his name. Les has compared sales from this year to last year and at each staff meeting he explains that sales are up, along with customer satisfaction. As he observes people standing in Ben's line each day, he wonders if those small notes of Christmas cheer are making the difference. Les has tacked these and other messages from Ben on the bulletin board in his office.

The Spirit of Christmas lives inside you and that is a great gift to me.

Merry Christmas! Ben

*Maybe Christmas, the Grinch thought, doesn't
come from a store.
Dr. Seuss said that and he's right!
Merry Christmas! Ben*

*Christmas is the celebration of Christ's birth but
we can have Christmas every day when we keep him in
our hearts!*

Merry Christmas! Ben

On Thursday, when Lauren drives into Grandon,
she makes her usual stop at Clauson's for a note from
Ben. "White Christmas" is playing throughout the
store as she opens a cooler near the cash registers
and pulls out a bottled water. This time, Ben's line
is so long that the end of it reaches into the baking
aisle. Again, Les encourages customers to step into
another line but his attempt is halfhearted; he doesn't
want them to move any more than they do. "Little
Drummer Boy" begins to play and then "Have Yourself a Merry Little Christmas." Lauren knows that if
customers stood in line this long at Gordon's, another
line would be opened. She smiles, looking at the other
two short lines and feels as if she's in on some sort of
secret, just as she felt all those years ago when she'd
sneak off to her closet and open the wooden box from
beneath her parents' bed. There is something magical
here that people don't want to miss.

"Hi!" Ben says, when he sees her back in the line.
"We're so busy because people are getting ready for
Christmas!"

"I think you're so busy because you're a rock star!" she says, making the others in line around her smile.

When she is able to put her water on the conveyor belt, Ben says, "Thanks for waiting in my line."

She hands money to the cashier and watches as Ben puts the note inside her grocery bag, handing it to her. Lauren steps toward him, taking the bag. "Ben, I'm so glad I discovered your line!"

"I'm glad you discovered Grandon!" he says, bagging the next customer's groceries.

Lauren reaches inside the bag and pulls out the note as she walks to the exit.

> *Everything is more beautiful at Christmas. I hope you see the beauty around you.*
> *Merry Christmas! Ben*

Lauren holds the note and puts it inside her back pocket. Perhaps it is Ben's reminder or just the fact that the town square is covered in fresh snow, but Lauren does notice how beautiful the white is as it clings to branches and sits atop the gazebo. Even the clouds are puffed up white and full as she drives beneath them toward Glory's Place. She was surprised to hear back from Laura and learn that she also lives in Grandon. What are the odds of *that* happening? She will help Dalton and Heddy and Stacy organize the items for the silent auction and begin assembling gift baskets before meeting Mary Richards first and then Laura at Betty's Bakery for coffee. She shouldn't be nervous but her palms are sweating. Who knew that meeting potential family members could be so nerve-racking!

Eleven

She finds Dalton, Heddy, and Stacy hauling boxes
to cafeteria tables where they unload them. There
are candles and candlesticks, gourmet foods, boxed
handmade candies, picture frames and glassware,
an apron and cookware, various books, small clocks,
vases, figurines, and more. Lauren is overwhelmed
looking at it all, but Heddy has a plan and is already
organizing the items in front of baskets. Dalton pulls
out a cardboard box from under the table and begins
to pull out the wooden keepsake box that Cassondra
gave Gloria. "Don't put that out," Heddy says.

Dalton looks inside the box. "Why not? I thought
Gloria wanted us to fill it with stationery and other
stuff."

"Heddy thinks it needs to be sanded and stained,"
Gloria says, behind them.

"It's beautiful!" Heddy says. "It just needs a little
TLC to bring out the full beauty!"

Gloria looks at Lauren and her eyes brighten.

"After we're through here, babe, would you mind dropping this off at Larry Maccabee's house?" She reaches for the cardboard box from Dalton and places two small, wooden bowls inside on top of the wooden box before handing it to Lauren. "He said that he would get these things looking brand-new again."

Lauren takes the cardboard box from her and sets it beneath the table. "Sure. Just let me know where he lives."

"He's not too far from here. I would drop it off myself but I have a meeting right after this and he said he would like them today." She looks over the tables, piled high with the generosity of the people of Grandon, and claps her hands together. "Just awesome! Weave your magic, Heddy!"

"I will if you'd get out of the way," Heddy says, raising her eyebrows at Gloria.

"I've always known when I'm not needed, so I'll leave you to it and make some calls to see how the baking is going for the fund-raiser."

Lauren, Dalton, and Stacy begin work on the basket that Heddy puts in front of each of them. "I've never put a basket together like this in my life," Lauren says. "What if it's ugly?"

Stacy picks up the decorative paper, ribbons, bows, and colored cellophane. "All of this makes the ugly beautiful."

Lauren's cell phone rings and she pulls it out of her pocket, looking at the number. She doesn't recognize it but answers anyway. "Hello."

"Lauren? It's Maria with the chamber of commerce." Lauren feels that pit in her stomach again and steps away from the table. "I spoke with the president and she is not crazy about the idea of giving up the gazebo on the day of the parade. I had thought vendors would be there, but actually Santa is supposed to set up inside." Lauren is disappointed and feels her palms sweating again. "But we both feel that the children singing in the gazebo can only add to the enjoyment of the parade." Lauren feels hopeful and finds herself holding her breath. "And I did pull, 'But what about the kids? They have their hearts set on this!' out of my hat."

"And it worked?"

"It worked. Have you mentioned this to Miss Glory since we spoke?"

Lauren looks at the others, who are busy putting together the baskets. "No."

"Then it will be our secret!"

"But what about Santa?"

"He's going to set up residence at the North Pole, which is on the ground floor of Wilson's."

Lauren smiles. "You have been so great! Thank you so much!"

"A friend of Cassondra's is a friend of mine, and since we're all part of the Glory's Place family then we need to stick together!"

Lauren hangs up, feeling relief and excitement, and joins Dalton and Stacy to assemble baskets, trying her best to make rectangle and square picture frames fit alongside a vase, figurines, a pewter clock, and boxed chocolates inside a round basket. As she works she says, "Do any of you know Mary Richards?"

Stacy looks up at her, thinking. "No, I don't believe I do."

"Sounds familiar," Dalton says.

"She works at WJM," Heddy says, sorting through the mass of gift cards in her hands.

"WJM?" Stacy says. "Where's that?"

"Minneapolis." She smiles, looking up over her reading glasses. "Mary Richards was the associate producer for the six o'clock news."

"Mary Tyler Moore!" Dalton says. "I knew that name rang a bell."

"Have you been watching *The Mary Tyler Moore Show*?" Stacy asks.

Lauren shakes her head. "No, I've never heard of it."

"Never heard of *The Mary Tyler Moore Show*?" Dalton asks. "I'm feeling like a dinosaur again."

"A woman named Mary Richards said she lives here in Grandon."

"Maybe she does," Stacy says. "Gloria might know her. Why?"

Reaching for some gold tissue paper Lauren feels embarrassed that she brought it up. She's not sure how Stacy, Dalton, and Heddy would react to her listing for a family on Craigslist. "I saw that she lived in Grandon and . . . was selling . . . her car," she says.

"Are you looking for a car?" Stacy asks.

"No. My roommate." She sprinkles some gold and silver stars over the items in her basket, and before anyone can ask more questions says, "How does this look?"

"Perfect!" Heddy says. "Now we'll wrap cellophane around it and tie it up with a huge bow and call it the Classic Home basket."

Lauren cuts some gold-tinted cellophane and works at wrapping it around the basket, creating a nice, long neck. Stacy moves beside her to tie it shut.

"By the way, the guy who hit me has officially been charged with hit-and-run, possession of drugs, and breaking and entering. They thought he was the guy who broke into the jewelry store and it turns out that he probably was."

"He sure stays busy," Dalton says.

"He'd still be busy if Lauren hadn't ID'd him as the guy who hit me."

"And you were just driving through that day, right?" he asks.

"Yeah. Bad day at work and I ended up driving away the demons, I guess."

Heddy puts a gift card among the goods for Lauren's next basket. "How long have you lived in Whitall?"

"I was born there," Lauren says, sorting through some of the ornate premade bows.

"That's so strange," Stacy says.

"What's strange?"

Stacy organizes the items in her basket and shrugs. "I don't know. It just feels like you've always lived here." She smiles at Lauren. "You know, 'I ran into Lauren today at Wilson's. She was looking at the dresses.'"

"She was *not* looking at dresses," Lauren says, laughing. "Trust me!"

Dalton wads up some tissue paper and stuffs it in the bottom of his basket, playing along. "Lauren was on the all-star team. Did you see her make that basket at the buzzer?"

"Lauren finally got her braces off but I thought she was beautiful when her teeth were crooked!" Heddy says, grinning.

"Lauren never had braces," Lauren says, feeling self-conscious at all the attention.

Donna VanLiere

"I wish there was a way we could keep you in Grandon," Stacy says. "But your family and friends in Whitall probably wouldn't like that."

Lauren's smile is sheepish as she finishes her basket. This building, this work, the kids who will run through here in the next few hours, these people . . . all of this, *this* is the beauty of Christmas that Ben hoped she would see.

Twelve

Dalton, Stacy, and Heddy are finishing the baskets when Lauren picks up the cardboard box from beneath the table. She needs to drop these things off for Gloria before her meeting with Mary Richards, her meeting with Laura, and then rehearsal with the kids. "Don't let Larry talk your ear off," Gloria says, after giving Lauren his address. "If you don't have one foot in the car, he can take you all the way back to 1953 and you'll be stuck there for an hour listening to stories about the first black walnut tree he cut down or the first canoe he made. He's very interesting, especially if you're not in a hurry!"

Lauren gets behind the wheel of her car and types the address into her map app: 115 High Smith Street. The location is found and it looks like it's five miles from Glory's Place. She'll have just enough time to get there and back to Betty's Bakery for coffee. She follows the directions down one street and up another and becomes puzzled when she finds herself in somewhat of an industrial area. Assuming that Larry's workshop is among these buildings she continues to drive. When she runs out of directions she cranes her neck to see the street signs: Poplar and Lafayette Street.

She stops her car and zooms in on High Smith Street. Smith Road appears to be one mile from here and she puts the car in drive again and heads in that direction. Smith Road turns to the right and she follows it. This is a country road with lots of bends and turns and she drives for several minutes before seeing the first house number: 705. She looks at the clock in her car dash and realizes it might take a while before she reaches number 115.

House number 521 has a long driveway and Lauren turns into it, studying the map again. She has to be at Betty's Bakery in ten minutes and calls the restaurant. "Is Holly there?" she asks, remembering her waitress. She's grateful when Holly picks up the phone. "Hi, Holly! This is Lauren Gabriel. You sat down and talked with me about a week and a half ago. I was sitting—"

"I totally remember you," Holly says. "How are you? What's up?"

"I'm supposed to be there in ten minutes to meet Mary Richards but I'm way out on some country road and will be late. Do you know her?" Lauren strains to hear over the noise of the restaurant.

"Hmm. Mary Richards? No. But hold on." Lauren hears her cover the mouthpiece of the phone as she shouts, "Hey, Betty! Do you know Mary Richards?" The faint sound of someone answering in the distance is heard. Holly uncovers the mouthpiece and says, "We don't know her. When are you supposed to meet her?"

"In about ten minutes."

"Okay. I'll keep my eyes open for a woman sitting alone who I don't know. When I see her I'll tell her that you're running late. How's that?"

"Perfect! Thanks so much, Holly! I'll get there as fast as I can." She pulls back onto the road in hopes she will arrive at Larry's house soon, but the homes are getting even farther apart now. After ten more minutes of driving she groans when she discovers that the numbers are now only in the four hundreds. She calls the restaurant again and asks for Holly. "Is she there yet?" she asks when Holly picks up.

"Nope. Just the regular crew. Same people who've been coming in for years."

Lauren sighs. "That's great! I'm still out on this never-ending road."

"What are you doing?"

"Delivering stuff to Larry Maccabee. Do you know where he lives?"

"The wood guy?"

Lauren slows down to see the worn-out numbers on a mailbox. "Yeah."

"I thought he lived somewhere closer to town but I'm not sure. His workshop may be out in the country."

The number on the box has a 7 in it so Lauren knows this isn't the house. "Thanks. If you see Mary, please tell her I'm coming. I really am!" She begins driving again but after another ten minutes she pulls into the end of a driveway and calls Miss Glory's cell phone.

"Hello!"

Lauren is so glad she answered. "Miss Glory, it's Lauren. I can't find Larry's house."

"You can't miss it, babe. It's got a great big wood carving of a bear in the front yard. I should've told you that."

Lauren backs onto the road and heads the way she was going, looking. "Do you know what color his house is?"

"Blue."

"Well, do you know how many miles he lives out on this road?" She groans before Gloria can answer.

"What's wrong, lamb?"

Lauren stops, putting her head on the steering wheel. "This road just ended! There wasn't a number 115 anywhere on this road."

Gloria puts her hand over her other ear so she can hear. "Which road are you on?"

"Well, High Smith showed up on the map but when I got to where it took me there wasn't a High Smith, so I looked on the map again and a mile away there was a Smith so I took that road."

"Are you on Smith Road? A country road?"

"Yes!"

"I am so sorry, babe! Larry only lives about a mile from Glory's Place. High Smith Street is right in town."

Lauren looks in her rearview mirror to make sure no one is behind her. There isn't. Of course there isn't because no one has been on this road in miles! "Okay. I'll turn around and head back toward town. What road does High Smith run off? I'll look that one up since High Smith doesn't show up on my map."

"He lives two houses down from the corner of High Smith and Bagley."

There is so much noise in the background that Lauren struggles to hear. "Bagley. Got it. Thanks, Miss Glory."

"I'm so sorry for your trouble. I should have asked Larry to pick up the box. He could have easily walked to Glory's Place. He could use the exercise."

Lauren turns the car around to head back toward town. "No big deal. Thanks, Miss Glory!" She taps the phone number for Betty's Bakery and this time Holly answers. "Holly! It's Lauren again."

"Mary Richards is a no-show," she says.

Lauren is relieved yet a bit hurt. "Okay. Maybe something came up. We were only going to meet for thirty minutes so I assume she's not coming. I'm also supposed to meet a woman named Laura. She should be there by now." There is a pause and Lauren pictures Holly looking across the restaurant at faces.

"Would she have anyone with her?"

"I don't think so."

"There's only one woman that I don't know and she's wearing a business suit but she's with a man and another woman. Could that be her?"

Lauren glances at the cardboard box on the seat next to her and feels doubt, frustration, and anger bubble up in her mind. "It doesn't sound like her."

"Hold on. I'll ask her." The line goes silent but before Holly can return Lauren already knows the answer. "She says her name is Audrey." Lauren feels her heart jerk a bit and lets up on the gas pedal. There is no point in hurrying any longer. "I'll keep a lookout for someone I don't know."

"Thanks, Holly." She hangs up and feels like a fool.

Miriam enters Betty's Bakery and spots Gloria sitting alone. "What are you doing here?" she says, taking a red cashmere scarf from around her neck.

"People commonly come here to eat, Miriam!"

"Especially you!" she says, sitting at the table. "What's strange is that you don't have any food in front of you. Nor do you have anything to drink. It appears as if you are waiting for someone. Are you meeting Marshall?"

Gloria is annoyed and crosses her arms. "No, I am not meeting Marshall. I came here for lunch."

Miriam turns to look behind her. "So your food is coming? What did you order?"

"What's with all the questions, Nancy Drew?"

Miriam leans onto the table, looking at her. "What are you doing here, Gloria Wilson? Who are you meeting?"

Gloria opens her mouth to answer but looks more like a carp gulping for air. "I think I can ask you that same question. What are you doing here? You told me you had a meeting. I don't see you meeting with anyone unless your meeting was supposed to be with me." She picks up her phone. "Let me check my calendar. No. It doesn't show that I have a meeting with you at this time so who are *you* meeting here, Miriam?"

Miriam runs her tongue under her upper lip, squinting at Gloria. "I already had my meeting. If you must know I got my brows waxed. I have come in here for a bite to eat." She glances toward the door and down at her watch.

"Are *you* expecting someone?"

"I'm not expecting anyone, big mouth! How about you? I saw you look at the door."

"I looked at the door because you looked at the door. I'm not expecting anyone. I just came here to eat like every other hungry person in here."

"Then you may as well eat with me," Miriam says, leaning back in the chair.

"Fine!" Gloria says, also leaning back in her chair. "*You* may as well eat with me."

And with that both women bury themselves in the menu.

Thirteen

The bells on the door ring as Lauren enters and Holly smiles from across the restaurant, waving. She shrugs and shakes her head, mouthing "She's not here" before refilling an iced tea for a customer. She is busy so Lauren looks for an empty table. She notices someone waving and smiles when she sees Gloria and Miriam. They wave her to their table and she takes off her coat, walking toward them. "Did you find Larry?" Gloria asks, moving her purse so Lauren can sit.

"Finally! I left him my cell number so he can call me when everything is done and I'll pick them up. I thought he was really nice."

"Did he tell you the story of making the mayor's desk?" Miriam says. "Or traveling ten hours one way for a load of curly maple?"

"No. He told me about making a kitchen table for his daughter's wedding gift. It started off as cherry but somehow the curly maple was speaking to him so the legs are curly maple."

Gloria and Miriam laugh and Gloria rests her hand on Lauren's. "Lunch is on me today."

"But you're both done eating," Lauren says, looking at their empty plates.

"There's always room for pastry," Gloria says.

"That's actually her motto," Miriam says. "She even had Larry engrave it on a piece of curly maple and has it hanging in her kitchen."

Gloria shakes her head and raises her hand, motioning for the waitress. It's not Holly but an older woman named Loni. "I'll take some coffee and a raspberry cream cheese pastry to share with Miriam. What would you like, babe?"

"A turkey club sandwich with chips," Lauren says.

"And a bowl of the chicken tortilla soup," Gloria says. Lauren opens her mouth and Gloria puts her hand in the air. "Trust me. You have to try Betty's chicken tortilla soup."

"What would you like to drink?" Loni asks.

"Just water," Lauren says.

"Peach tea," Miriam says. Lauren looks at her but Miriam isn't finished. "Do you just have peach today or do you have the raspberry-peach?"

"Raspberry peach," Loni says.

Miriam points at her. "That's the one! Just a little sugar, Loni. This isn't the South where they drink their tea so sweet it puts your teeth on edge." She looks at Lauren. "Trust me. It's much better than water."

Gloria and Miriam both look at Lauren and she smiles, feeling uncomfortable. "So what do you do when you're not being fabulous by helping nonprofits with their fund-raisers?" Gloria says.

"I just work at a grocery store in Whitall. I'm a cashier."

Gloria smacks the table. "I was a cashier once."

"That was when stores just kept their cash in a cigar box beneath the front counter," Miriam says.

Gloria glares at her. "It was at Sharp's Drugstore back home."

"Back when pharmaceuticals consisted of cat's claw and leeches."

Lauren laughs as Gloria's pastry is set before her and Loni sets down the raspberry peach iced tea. "Just for that I'm not sharing my pastry with you."

"I didn't want it anyway," Miriam says.

Picking up a knife, Gloria cuts it in half and slides one portion onto a plate and drops it in front of Miriam. "No you don't! You would love for me to eat this whole thing and gain weight just so you can shake your bony finger at me and tell me that you told me so. Well, no way, sister."

"Have you always fought like this?" Lauren says, sipping the tea.

"No," Miriam says. "The arguments began only after we met."

Loni brings the soup and Lauren's eyes bulge. "I'll never be able to finish this and a sandwich."

"Take it home!" Gloria says. "Marshall and I get lots of second meals from leftovers from Betty's."

"I wish they had a place like this in Whitall."

Miriam bites into the pastry and follows it with a sip of coffee. "So . . . what are your Christmas plans?"

Lauren eats the soup, thinking before she shrugs. "I don't really have a lot of plans."

"Are you eating Christmas dinner with your parents?" Gloria asks, glancing at Miriam.

"No."

"Do they live near you?" Miriam asks.

"Well, I didn't know it but my dad actually lived here at one time." Although she's looking into her soup she can feel Gloria and Miriam exchanging glances. "He's not here anymore."

"What's his name?" Gloria asks.

"Vic Gabriel. Travis told me he worked for the parks department before getting fired." She looks at them. "Did you know him?" They both shake their heads and she takes another spoonful of soup.

"When was the last time you saw him?" Gloria asks.

"Sixteen years ago." Loni sets the sandwich on the table and Lauren thanks her.

"Well, some people are not fit to be parents," Miriam says. Gloria looks at her but Miriam continues. "I think he's a coward and a fool for leaving you."

"Remind me not to have you counsel any of the children at Glory's Place," Gloria says.

"I wouldn't say that to a small child, Gloria, but Lauren needs to know that it wasn't her fault." Miriam looks at Lauren, raising her finger in the air. "It wasn't. His leaving was not your fault. He left because he is a little, little man without an ounce of courage or backbone or decency. Real men don't leave their children."

Gloria is using both of her hands, patting the air in front of her. "Would you calm down? Everyone is looking."

"My deepest apologies, Lauren. Forgive me for speaking the truth."

Lauren's throat tightens as she looks at Miriam. "It's okay. I've gotten angry lots of times."

"There are many things that Miriam and I do not agree on, and fortunately, this is not one of them," Gloria says. "Fathers protect and defend and provide for their children, and without a father's love and guidance a child will feel lost. I've seen it time and again. I've seen the struggle that single moms have, and it got to the point where I couldn't sit by and just keep watching it. I knew that I had to help bear some of their burdens. I knew that I had to pray for them and cry with them. I knew there were times that I had to get involved in their lives and other times that I just had to leave them alone."

"And that's huge for Gloria, by the way," Miriam says. "It's a struggle for her to leave people alone."

Lauren laughs but feels a tear making its way from her eye. She grabs her napkin and swipes it across her cheek.

"Basically, we just love on those kids and their moms or their dads or their grandparents or whoever brings them to Glory's Place," Gloria says. "We love on them the best we know how because we know that deep down there's something missing inside so many of their hearts. It could be because their dad walked away like yours or because their mom isn't there. Whatever it is we just love them and help them in whatever feeble way we can."

"I wish Glory's Place had been in Whitall." Her voice is so low that Gloria and Miriam strain to hear over the noise of the restaurant.

Gloria pats her hand. "Well, you just keep coming

any time you want and we'll love on you the best we can."

"And we'll always have pastries," Miriam says.

Lauren bursts out laughing and presses the napkin to her eyes. Gloria and Miriam smile sad, knowing smiles at each other, having had similar conversations before. If Christmas is a time for peace on earth then why do they encounter so many without it? If Christmas is filled with memories of warm smells, blazing fires, trees with twinkly lights and presents, and laughter so joyful that it reaches the tip of your toes, then why are so many memories as stark and bare as the winter trees? If Christmas is hope and joy and faith unending, then why are so many hopeless, joyless, and without faith?

Gloria squeezes Lauren's hand. "We know that we are not your family but we are both very grateful for your friendship this Christmas." Lauren tries to smile and catches more tears with her napkin. Even Miriam, who can always manage to pull her face into a stoic pose, turns away to keep her face together.

If this isn't a family, then Lauren doesn't know what one is.

Fourteen

The next morning before Lauren is awake, her phone rings. She wants to ignore it and go back to sleep but decides it could be someone from Glory's Place needing her. "Hello," she says, trying to make her voice sound awake.

"Is this Lauren?"

It's a man's voice but Lauren doesn't recognize it. "Yeah."

"This is Larry. From yesterday. You dropped off the stuff for Miss Glory."

She throws an arm over her forehead, wondering what he wants so early in the morning. "Right."

"Well, I wanted to let you know that I set the box down by the door. Now what I did not know was that my wife had other boxes and bags sitting there at the door that she was taking to the dump." Lauren sits up on the mattress, anticipating what he is going to say. "I didn't know about it until this morning when I went to look for the box that you dropped off."

"So all that stuff is gone?"

"I'm afraid so. But I'm happy to make a box for the fund-raiser. It won't take much time and since I'm the one who's in charge of this mess-up, then I'm the one who needs to make it right."

Lauren swings her legs to the floor, careful not to bang them against the metal frame. She feels like such a vagabond sleeping this way but at least it's an upgrade from her usual mattress on the floor. "Thanks, Larry! I'll call Miss Glory and let her know."

"You tell her I've got some real nice curly maple here that can make a beautiful box. I could even make it out of curly maple and do an inlay of cherry or black walnut. Or I could just make the whole box out of black walnut or mahogany or something. You just run it by her and give her my deepest apologies. But like I said, I will make it right!"

Hanging up, Lauren looks at the time on her phone: seven o'clock. Miss Glory would definitely be up by now. As she dials she realizes that Heddy said the box she gave Larry needed a lot of work. Obviously, the one he would make would be new and beautiful and worth more. "Miss Glory! Are you awake? It's Lauren."

"Marshall and I are sitting here having breakfast. Is everything okay?"

"I think so. I just wanted to tell you that Larry called me and said that the box of stuff that I dropped off with him was accidentally taken to the dump." She can hear Gloria gasp on the other end.

"Oh! This is awful!"

"No! Larry said he would make you a brand-new box, more beautiful than the last one. He said he would make it out of any kind of wood that you wanted."

"She'll be so devastated."

Lauren leans on to her knees, looking at her toes. "Who will be devastated, Miss Glory?"

"Cassondra! She gave me that box for the fundraiser. She said it held dreams. I can't tell her it's been thrown away."

Lauren gets up and paces in her bedroom, thinking. "Can't Larry make a similar box without her knowing?"

Gloria sighs on the other end. "I'm afraid not. She is way too sharp for that! Plus, the box had a verse written on the top of it and of course I can't remember what it was!"

"I'm sorry, Miss Glory."

"Don't be! It's not your fault. Well, I'll just have to put on my big-girl pants and tell Cassondra what happened. In the meantime, if you can call Larry back and ask him to make a box that would be great. I would still like to fill it with beautiful stationery and pens and offer that in the auction."

Hanging up, Lauren walks into her bathroom and turns on the water. "She loves that box," she says, realizing she's praying. "Would you show us where it is?" The moment the words slip past her lips she knows how absurd they are and splashes water over her face. Sometimes things are lost forever and that's just the way it is.

Before leaving for work Lauren checks e-mail and sees a few new ones from Craigslist. There are two of the obligatory hate-filled ones, calling her a moron and idiot and she quickly trashes those. The others are from Mary Richards and Laura. She reads the one from Mary first.

Hi, Kelly! Well, I am assuming that I blew it again. I must have gotten our date and time wrong for getting together at Betty's Bakery. I am so sorry that I missed you and I do hope that you did not wait too long for me on the day that you were there. On the upside, I ended up having a lovely lunch. I hope that you did, too. Could we try this again? Hoping that I have not scared you off. Mary Richards

Lauren feels a wave of relief to know that Mary did not blow her off. She opens the e-mail from Laura and discovers that she, too, had waited at Betty's.

Dear Kelly, apparently I got the time mixed up for our meeting. I would like to say that this is the first time that something like this has happened, but alas, it has happened before. Perhaps I input the wrong time in my phone. I send you my deepest apologies. Do you think there is another time that would work for us to get together? Things are ramping up here with work and all things Christmas and I imagine that your schedule is getting quite busy as well. Please let me know if there is another opportunity to meet. Yours, Laura

Lauren looks back at the calendar on her phone and wonders if she is the one who input the wrong date or time. She sits on the edge of her mattress studying the calendar. She will be back in Grandon in two days, on Monday. *Dear Mary,* she types. *Thanks for letting me know! I thought that maybe you had second thoughts. Maybe I'm the one who got the date wrong. I did have a great lunch that day. What does Monday look like for you? I'm free after six. Working before that. We could try Betty's again. Kelly*

She sends a duplicate letter to Laura and hopes for the best.

Maria Delgado finishes her grocery shopping before collecting the votes for grand marshal of the Christmas parade from the box on Clauson's customer service counter. She smiles as she pulls each one from the box, reading them. Whether she is collecting them from Clauson's, Wilson's, Betty's Bakery, Patterson's, City Auto Service, or other businesses throughout town, the overwhelming majority of votes have been cast for the one particular citizen that the residents of Grandon wish to see riding high on the horse-drawn coach that day. She puts the votes inside a Ziploc bag and then inside her purse before looking for an open cashier. One of the lines stretches longer than the others that are open and she notices Ben hard at work. Even though the line will take longer than the others, she'll wait. How could she neglect having a message from Ben this close to Christmas? The man in front of her notices that another cashier is open and moves to that line. "You don't know what you're missing," Maria says, under her breath.

"Hi, Ben," she says, pushing her grocery cart closer when she's next in line. "Have you found out if you can come to the Christmas parade?"

"We don't have the schedule yet," Ben says, careful to put the boxes of cereal in one bag and cans of soup in another.

"Les!" Maria says, noticing the manager walking toward customer service. "I've spoken with Ben and

Donna VanLiere

Alice at customer service and Jim in meats and none of them know if they can go to the Christmas parade yet."

Les walks toward them, smiling. "What do you suggest? That I let everyone off to go to the Christmas parade?"

"Of course not!" Maria says. "But since the entire town will be at the parade I think it's safe to say that the store could operate with just a couple of people here."

"Well, I'd keep my best employees here but you're saying you want Ben to go to the parade."

Ben hurries to bag the last of Maria's groceries before picking out a message for her. "I'll stay here if you want me to."

Les winks at Maria. "That'd be great, Ben. I know the store would be safe in your hands, but maybe Maria's right. Maybe you should go to the parade that day and I bag the groceries."

"Are you sure, Mr. Gentry? I can come in after the parade."

Les walks toward his office, talking over his shoulder. "I might just take you up on that. I'll schedule you off that day right now before I forget, and hopefully, this means that Maria will get off my back."

Ben loads Maria's groceries into her cart and says, "I don't think he meant that you're really on his back."

Maria laughs. "He might have meant that! I've been needling him pretty hard about letting you off work that day so you can see the parade."

He hands her the last bag before turning his attention to the next load of groceries. Outside Maria places the bags in her car trunk and pulls out her note. It's written on a small red piece of paper with a star at the end of Ben's name.

* 284 *

Christmas is a great time for celebrating, so dance today! You know you want to inside!
Merry Christmas! Ben

"I just love that kid," Maria says, closing the trunk.

Fifteen

On Thursday, Lauren is early getting into Grandon and decides to make a stop at Betty's Bakery for a quick cup of coffee before heading to Glory's Place. The smells of homemade bread and soup and fresh-brewed coffee welcome her as she opens the door. "My section's over there," Holly says, pointing.

"I'm only getting coffee," Lauren says. "I don't want to take up a whole table."

"It doesn't matter." Holly delivers two meals to a man and woman in front of her as Lauren picks the table closest to the back.

Holly places a cup on the table and fills it with coffee. "I'm sorry I never saw the women you were supposed to meet the other day."

Lauren reaches for the creamer on the table. "I heard from both of them. We got the date and time all mixed up. We're going to try again later today."

Holly turns to look over her shoulder, checking on

her tables. "Do you want to go see a movie tonight? Do you have time?"

"Uh, sure! I'm in no hurry to get back to Whitall."

"I get off at seven-thirty."

"That's perfect. I'm supposed to meet Mary here at six-thirty and then Laura at seven-fifteen.

Holly takes a step back, to check on her customers. "Why are you meeting them again?"

Lauren hesitates, wondering if she should tell her about the Craigslist ad but then says, "They're supposed to help me with some family stuff."

Although it doesn't make any sense to her, Holly says okay and returns to work as Lauren rips open a sugar packet and pours it into her coffee.

"Is it okay if I join you for a second?"

She is surprised to look up and see Travis Mabrey from the parks department, but finds herself pleased that he's here. He has a face that often looks as if it's about to open a present and she likes that. There's something sincere about him. "Sure."

He pulls out the chair opposite her and sits, holding a to-go coffee cup. "Everything pulling together for the fund-raiser?"

She shrugs. "It's pulling together but little things keep going wrong."

He nods. "Like the use of the gazebo."

"And a box that was supposed to be auctioned off ended up going to the dump." She looks at him over the coffee cup. "Any chance of actually finding that at the dump?"

He laughs, shaking his head. "No."

"I didn't think so but it was worth a shot." He can tell by the way she scrunches the napkin beneath her hand and squirms in her seat that she feels clumsy talking to him and he finds her self-consciousness attractive. She crumples the napkin in her lap and clears her throat, looking into the cup. "When I ran away . . . you know . . . the other day . . ."

"Right! I'm still in counseling."

Lauren laughs out loud and relaxes her hand, giving the napkin a break. She looks at him and notices that if he didn't shave for a couple of days, he'd have a full beard and imagines what he'd look like. "Victor Gabriel is my dad. He left when I was four and I had no idea he lived here."

"So it really wasn't because of me that you ran away?"

She laughs again and he smiles. "I had no idea that I would react like that." She's quiet, drinking from the cup. "I think that deep down I hoped that one day he would show up again, but knowing that he has left again proves that he is probably not the showing-up kind of guy." She glances at him. "Did you know his wife? Did they have children?"

Travis straightens in the chair, folding his arms on the table. "I met his wife a couple of times. She seemed nice but I don't really know her. As far as I know they didn't have children together but she had a couple of children from another marriage." She nods, listening. "I don't know where he went when he left here but I could ask around and maybe find something out."

"No, thanks." The answer came from a place of strength and it surprises Lauren. "He's a stranger. If I'm going to meet a stranger I think I'd want to meet his ex-wife. I think we would have a whole lot more in common than I would with him." She taps the sugar packets on the table. "Where did he live?"

"I can drive you by there if you want. His ex-wife still lives there."

Although she can't explain it Lauren wants to see that house more than anything she's wanted in a long time.

The cab of Travis's truck is neat with the exception of two empty coffee cups in the cup holders and a stack of papers on the dash. He throws the empty cups in a nearby garbage can before placing the cup he has been holding in one of the empty holders. "You're sure you have time for this?" she asks.

He pulls out of the parking space, looking over at her. "I'm sure. My workday is done. All I had on my schedule for tonight was coffee at Betty's and then a drive over to a former coworker's house."

"How long have you been with the parks department?"

"Seven years. Right out of high school."

"You grew up here?"

He makes a turn onto Poplar Avenue, nodding. "I did."

She watches the passing scenery: snow wrapped around tree trunks and homes and covering the streets and lawns like a fluffy white carpet, one-foot deep. "You never wanted to leave?"

"Absolutely! When I was in high school I couldn't wait to leave. I was going to work for a year and then either go to college or find another place to live."

"And?"

He turns onto Belden Road and grins. "I got an associate's degree in arboriculture and stayed right here. I like working with trees and grass and ball fields. And I like this town. As far as places to live go—I think it has everything I need." He slows down and parks the truck in front of a modest, two-story gray home set close to the road. Yew shrubs line the front of the house and three grown trees fill the front yard. "This is it." Lauren stares at the house and he wonders what she's looking at or, rather, what she's looking for.

The gutters are in need of repair and paint hangs loose from the window trim. Hope left the house years ago, making it look defeated and small. Lauren sits in the silence, looking at it. This house, she thinks, is just like her: waiting for attention from someone who is long gone. The voices of her mother and father in their bedroom in the apartment had the popping, murmuring sound of something frying or hissing. She wonders if this home has heard any soft sounds and if this is the place her father came to after he left her and why it wasn't good enough, either. He doesn't live anywhere, she thinks. He just exists. Just like her. Some people settle and live and grow while others wander, never really living, just existing here in this space for a while before moving along. The realization chokes her and the sound of the heat blowing inside the cab seems deafening. She realizes Travis has been waiting in the quiet. She looks at him and smiles. "I'm sorry. This is weird."

"No. Don't be. Are you ready?"

She nods and keeps her eyes on the road ahead as he pulls away.

He parks in front of Betty's and she lifts her bag onto her lap before opening the door. "Thanks so much."

He watches as she steps out onto the sidewalk. "I hope it helped in some way."

She looks over the hood of his truck and then back at him. "It did. I can't explain it but it did."

His hands are clasped on top of the steering wheel. "Great. Maybe next time I can actually drive you someplace fun. I mean, if there is a next time, and I hope . . . I mean . . . well, glad it helped."

She smiles. He flounders as much as she does. "Thanks again." She closes the door and watches as he pulls away, fully believing that she'll notice every black truck just like his from now on.

Sixteen

Several children take their seats at Glory's Place for rehearsal and Lauren turns to look for Cassondra and her brother, Aidan. Cassondra is talking with Miriam, her hands fluttering in the air like butterflies. Lauren smiles watching her and crosses the room to hear what she is saying. "When I saw Miss Glory I got the idea that she should have the box for the auction!" Lauren groans, listening. "I hope it sells for hundreds of dollars!"

"I could think of a few people who would love to pay hundreds of dollars for your box," Miriam says.

Lauren opens her eyes wide and looks at Miriam, shaking her head, trying to send a signal to her.

Cassondra reaches both arms high into the air. "Maybe even a thousand dollars!"

"That's right," Miriam says, fist-bumping Cassondra. "Let's shoot for the stars!"

Stacy claps her hands to get the attention of the children and the final stragglers run and make their way to the chairs. "There is no box," Lauren says, whispering to Miriam.

Miriam lifts an eyebrow. "Yes. The box that Cassondra gave Gloria and you took to Larry."

"And the one that Larry's wife accidentally took to the dump."

Miriam grabs her head. "You must be joking!" Lauren shakes her head. "And I just told that sweet child that that box might bring in a thousand dollars!"

"We haven't had a chance to tell her about it. I'll tell her today. Larry is making another box for the auction."

"And it will no doubt be a better quality box but it sure won't have the heart."

Stacy begins leading the children through "The First Noel" and Lauren walks behind the children to listen. Casey, a little boy around ten, fidgets in his seat and Lauren leans down to him, asking, "Do you need to go to the bathroom?" He nods and she taps him on the shoulder, releasing him to run for the restrooms. Six-year-old Livvy's mouth forms a perfect *O* as she sings and Lauren smiles at how serious she is each time they practice. Jackson and Antoine need to be separated again and Lauren points to an empty chair for Jackson. He scowls at her and slumps toward the chair. Violet struggles to read the lyrics and Lauren kneels next to her, pointing at each word and helping her read them.

In just a short time Lauren has discovered the personality of each of these children and she marvels at how much she loves being around them. David's infectious laugh makes her laugh every time. Nobody gives a bigger hug than Isaiah. Callie looks at everything as if the glass is half empty while Lillian is grateful for the rain or snow and never minds losing a game. Kate is always in the middle of acting out a story from her imagination as Jarod acts out imaginary football plays. Each day Gracie is busy keeping the younger children in line and Marcus finds somebody new each day to tease. The names and ages of each of the rest of the children are as much a part of Lauren's life now as eating and breathing.

Collin raises his hand and Stacy pauses before moving on to the next song. "Yes, Collin?"

"Yeah. What do we wear to this thing? Do we dress like elves or something?"

Stacy laughs. "No. You don't have to dress like an elf. Since it will be cold, you will all be wearing coats and you can just wear what you want."

Grayson raises his hand and Stacy smiles at him. "Can we just wear a sweatshirt or something?"

There's something in his voice that makes Lauren wonder why he asked that question. As the children are picked up Lauren watches as Grayson leaves. He doesn't retrieve a coat or jacket from his hook as the others do and Lauren steps in next to Heddy. "Does Grayson have a coat? This is the second time I've seen him leave without one."

Heddy watches as Grayson makes his way out the door and to his mother's car. "He might have left it hanging up."

"It's not there," Lauren says, stopping Heddy from running to the line of hooks.

"He must have forgotten it today. Each child who didn't have a coat received one at the beginning of November. We start our coat drive in October each year."

Lauren helps other children into their coats and makes a mental note to watch for Grayson tomorrow as her phone buzzes inside her jeans pocket. Someone has sent a text, but they will just have to wait until all the children have been loaded into cars. She is helping Stacy stack the chairs when she remembers the text and pulls the phone out of her pocket. Looking at her phone she gasps.

"Are you okay?" Stacy asks.

Lauren is staring at the phone. "My mom just contacted me." She hands the phone to Stacy.

I'm coming through Whitall tonight. I'd love to have dinner with you. Can you make it? Stacy reads. She looks at Lauren. "How long did you say it's been since you've seen her?"

"Seven years."

She hands the phone back to Lauren. "Do you want to see her?"

Lauren feels sick to her stomach. "I don't know anymore." She sits on a chair and looks up at Stacy. "What should I do?"

Stacy sits next to her and shakes her head. "I don't know what you should do. If it was me I would want to see her. I would want to know if there's any chance that this could open the door for a relationship."

Lauren leans onto her knees and puts her face in her hands. "Are you okay, babe?" She raises her head to see Gloria wearing a green sweatshirt covered with gingerbread boys and girls.

"My mom's driving through Whitall and wants to meet me for dinner." She says it almost as a question and not a statement.

Gloria sits on the other side of her and pats her leg. "Hard things. I know."

"Just when things are going smoother in my life she has to show up." She leans back in her chair and looks up at the ceiling. "She always knew how to ruin things. Of course she did it close to Christmas so she could ruin it."

Gloria and Stacy exchange looks. "It is close to Christmas and she is family," Gloria says. "She may not be ruining anything."

"Right," Stacy says. "How do you know she's ruining your Christmas? This might be the first of many Christmases together."

Gloria pats her on the back and moves to Heddy who is calling her from across the room, while Stacy returns to stacking chairs. "I'm supposed to have a couple of meetings tonight," Lauren says.

"Meetings can be changed," Stacy says, stacking the lyric sheets into a neat pile. "Mothers only drive through town once in a blue moon."

"But this will be the second time these meetings have been changed."

Stacy smiles and slips on her coat. "Well! Third time will be a charm." She slips the lyric sheets into a manila folder and sighs. "I need to pick up my son from work. See you tomorrow?"

"I'll be here." She can hear Stacy's footsteps behind her as she looks at her phone, texting. *I can be back in Whitall by 6:30. Does that work?*

It only takes a moment for her mother to reply. *Yep! Where do u want 2 eat?*

Jake's BBQ is new and just off the highway. Sound good?

Her phone buzzes in her hand and she reads, *Sounds great! I'm sooooo excited 2 c u! I can't believe my baby girl is all grown-up.* It's followed by seven smiley faces.

Lauren grabs her coat and her bag and heads to the front doors. "Have you decided?" Gloria asks.

She nods, pulling her bag onto her shoulder. "I'm meeting her."

Gloria hugs her, squeezing the back of her neck. "I hope this dinner will bring you some peace of mind, babe."

Lauren takes a step toward the doors and then turns back to Gloria. "What if she hasn't changed?"

"What if she has?" Gloria waves, and Lauren pushes open the front doors, an icy blast hitting her in the face. What if her mother has changed? What if they can build a new life together? Lauren wonders if when she sees her mom the years of disappointment and anger and frustration will fade.

The hour back to Whitall goes quicker than she remembers and as she spots the flashing sign for Jake's BBQ in the distance she realizes she hasn't called Holly or e-mailed Laura or Mary Richards. Her heart races as she pulls into a parking spot and dials the number for Betty's Bakery. She's able to talk with Holly but makes the conversation quick, hurrying so she can find the e-mails for both Laura and Mary. She types, *Dear Mary, I'm so sorry but I can't come tonight. Something has come up that I didn't know about until today. Can we please reschedule?* She copies the e-mail before sending it to Mary and then pastes it into an e-mail for Laura and sends that one off, too.

Her heart is racing as she looks at herself in the rearview mirror and puts on lip gloss. She steps out into the wind and closes the car door. It's 6:25 and time to look for her mother.

Seventeen

Gloria spots an empty table at Betty's and waves at Holly. "Better make it decaf," she says, pushing the coffee cup toward the edge of the table. "Full lead would keep me up all night."

Holly fills the cup and checks the creamer pitcher to make sure it's full. "What are you doing in here this late? Is Marshall coming to meet you?"

Gloria stirs the cream into her coffee, shaking her head. "No. He's finishing up some things at the store. I'm meeting someone here."

Holly rests the coffeepot on her hip. "Do you want to wait to order?"

"I think I'll just stick with coffee." She pauses for a moment and leans over in her seat, looking at the bakery case. "You probably don't have any of those chocolate cream cheese pastries left at this hour, right?"

"I actually think we do. Would you like one?"

Gloria crosses her arms, shaking her head. "No.

I haven't had my supper." Holly steps away from the table when Gloria adds, "Warm it up just a bit before you bring it to me."

Jake's BBQ has filled up fast. Lauren checks the time on her phone: 6:30. She texts her mom, saying, *I'm in a booth against the back wall.*

As Lauren takes a sip of Coke her mom replies, *Be there in just a couple of minutes.*

Each time the front door opens Lauren turns to see who is walking into the lobby. Although it has been seven years she is convinced she would still recognize her mom. So far the people who've arrived are in pairs or groups, none are by themselves. To settle her nerves she reaches for her phone and checks e-mail, discovering that her e-mails to both Mary Richards and Laura have bounced back to her. She sends them again only to receive a bounce-back notification. She looks to the front door and wonders if she has enough time to call Holly at Betty's. She looks back on her phone log and redials the number, hoping that Holly will answer. "Betty's Bakery."

It's Holly's voice! "Holly! It's Lauren."

"Hey! Are you meeting your mom?"

Lauren keeps her eyes on the door. "She should be here any minute. I know you won't believe this, but I'm supposed to meet that same woman as before, Mary Richards, and a little later I'm meeting another woman named Laura there. I sent them e-mails but they keep bouncing back to me. If you see a woman waiting by herself, would you please tell Mary that I can't be there?"

"Sure. But I haven't seen anyone that I don't know yet."

"Maybe she's running as late as my mom. Thanks, Holly!"

At 6:50 Miriam walks into Betty's and heads for the bathroom to straighten her hair and freshen her lipstick. When Gloria spots her she lifts a menu in front of her face but it's too late. "Whatever are you doing here at this hour?" Miriam asks, removing her coat.

Gloria slaps the menu on the table. "Why is it that whenever you see me in Betty's you always have this accusatory tone in your voice?"

Miriam looks at her watch. "Because by this time of night you and Marshall have already eaten and you are about to put on that pair of ridiculous pajamas that you wear! You are never seen at Betty's at this hour eating a . . ." She taps the plate in front of Gloria. "What was that? A chocolate cream cheese pastry? At this hour? Have you eaten 'supper', as you call it?"

Gloria wipes her mouth and crumples the napkin, throwing it onto the empty plate. "Could I also say that *you* are never seen at Betty's at this hour! What exactly are *you* doing here?"

Miriam folds her coat over her arm. "Grabbing a coffee."

"At almost seven?" Gloria points her finger at her. "You're up to something, Miriam Davies!"

Miriam pulls out a chair and sits down. "I was just about to say the same thing to you, Gloria Wilson! I mean, I know you love pastries but to eat one before your precious supper?" She leans across the table, staring at Gloria. "What is up with you? What are you doing here?"

❋ ❋ ❋

Lauren checks the last text she received from her mom: *Be there in just a minute. Took the wrong exit.*

OK, Lauren had texted back. *It's the same exit for all the fast food chains and the city park.*

Turning around. Be there in five.

Five minutes turns into ten and Lauren tries calling. No answer. She texts: *Are you close?*

Very. Needed gas.

What a stupid time to get gas, Lauren thinks. She thinks of Holly and feels bad for taking up this waitress's table for so long without ordering. She asks for a barbecue sandwich and fries and a refill of Coke. She decides to text. *I just ordered. Do you want me to order something for you?*

No. Just about there.

"You seem disappointed to see me," Miriam says.

"I was just thinking the same thing about you!"

Miriam presses her elbow into the table and points at Gloria. "You are here to meet that young woman from the Internet!" Gloria's mouth opens wide as she gropes for words. "Aha! For once in your life you're speechless so I know I've caught you!"

Gloria narrows her eyes looking at her. "You're here to meet her too, Miriam! You have that little line of sweat on your upper lip that you always get when you're caught at something."

Miriam touches her lip, swiping away the moisture. "I told you not to meet her!"

"Since when do I take direction from you? And why are you allowed to meet her and not me?"

"Because I'm more street savvy than you!"

"Street savvy! You use words like 'collywobbles'

and 'bits and bobs'! Only someone at the intersection of Piccadilly Circus and Full of Hot Air Street would know what you're talking about!"

Miriam sighs. "Out of curiosity I checked out her ad on Craigslist and found myself taken by her story."

Gloria raises both her arms in the air. "It's a Christmas miracle! Miriam has a heart!"

Lauren pushes aside her empty plate at 7:40 and reads the last texts between her and her mom.

It's 7:15. Are you still getting gas?

Talking with the cashier. 2 mins.

7:20. Here yet?

Her mom never replied to the text and Lauren called again at 7:25. Her mom didn't answer and Lauren didn't leave a message.

"Would you like dessert?" Lauren looks up at the waitress and wishes for a moment that it was Holly.

"No. I'd just like to get out of here."

The waitress lays the bill on the table and says, "I can take it or you can pay at the front."

She leaves cash on the table and grabs her coat.

"I can't imagine what happened," Gloria says. "She seemed excited to meet."

"Maybe she looked through the window and saw you waiting in here and decided she didn't like the look of the merchandise," Miriam says.

"Or maybe she was running late and by the time she got here you were already sitting here and you looked too street savvy for her, scaring her off."

Miriam waves her hand in the air, dismissing Gloria. "So now what? Should we explain to her that we know one another and just meet her together?"

Gloria nods. "If she still wants to meet. I'm sure several people responded to her. She might have gotten the times mixed up and was meeting someone else tonight."

Miriam crosses her arms, looking at her. "So what did you cook for you and Marshall tonight?"

"Pot roast in the Crock-Pot."

"With the potatoes and carrots in there with it?"

Gloria puts her coat on and ties a red scarf around her neck. "For crying out loud, Miriam! Why don't you just say you'd like to come eat?"

"That would be rude, Gloria. But if you're asking I think I'm free."

Gloria reaches for her purse, shaking her head. "I really need to stop coming in here. Every time I come in to meet potential family members I keep running into you!"

They laugh that deep laugh that only friends can share, then leave together.

Eighteen

The workday is unending for Lauren. She stands be-hind the cash register and rings customers through without chitchat or any pleasantries. She is simply on autopilot and wishing for the day to be over. She is surrounded by coworkers: those she has known for the last four years and those who are new for the Christ-mas season. Many of the same customers make their way through her line and do their best to draw her into the world of the living, but she is unable to muster any interest or enthusiasm. Surrounded by people, she feels a loneliness she has never felt before. It is beyond loneliness; it is an emptiness that grows inside her chest. She slept little last night but kept replaying in her mind the time she spent waiting in the booth for her mother. She read the texts over and over hoping for a different outcome.

On her break she doesn't open her e-mail. She blew off Mary Richards and Laura and can't bear to read an e-mail from either one of them. She is supposed to be at Glory's Place after work today but decides not to go. She is tired of hoping and longing. She is tired of being disappointed and walking around always wanting a different outcome but getting more of the same. Glancing around the break room with its plain walls and metal chairs, she is convinced that this will be as good as it gets.

Gloria stands beside her grocery cart scanning the shelves of food in front of her.

"Can I help you find anything, ma'am?"

It's Maria Delgado and Gloria offers a quick hug. "Maria! How are you?"

"A little frazzled from pulling together both our move and the Christmas parade but it's all good."

Gloria sets Marshall's favorite natural peanut butter into the cart. "Can you give me a little hint as to who it might be, Maria?"

Maria looks shocked. "Miss Glory! You know I can't do that!"

"Is it okay if I voted at each location? If that's not okay then I won't admit that I did it."

Maria laughs. "I think you're well within the rules!" She hurries to the front of the store. "Sorry to run off. I'll be late for a meeting with Les!"

"I wanted to tell you something about Cassondra's box."

"Is there something wrong with it?"

Gloria sees she is in a hurry and shakes her head. "Go on. We can talk another time."

Maria waves and hurries to Les's office. Ben is talking with him and Maria smiles. "Hi, Ben! How's your day?"

"It's great, Mrs. Delgado."

She looks at Les and grins. "It *is* a great day, Ben! Thank you for reminding me of that!" She pauses, looking at him. "You are still coming to the Christmas parade, right?"

He is about to leave the office. "I have the day off. It's written on my calendar at home and the one here at the store."

She sets her purse down on the desk and folds her hands in front of her. "Ben, I came here to pick up the final votes for the grand marshal of the Christmas parade. Did you vote for anyone?"

He looks sheepish. "No, I didn't, Mrs. Delgado. I always wanted to but then I kept getting busy. I can vote now if you want."

Maria smiles. "Who would you vote for, Ben?"

"My dad or my mom."

"Not for me?" Les says, spreading his arms out.

"I can vote for you, too, if I'm allowed to put that many votes in."

Les and Maria laugh as she says, "That's okay, Ben. The voting period is over now and I get to let everyone know who is going to be the grand marshal."

"What does a grand marshal do, anyway?" Les asks.

She leans against the desk, folding her arms. "Well, the grand marshal sits in the carriage. You know, the tall red carriage that Mr. Lawson pulls with his horses?" Ben nods. "The grand marshal sits on top of that carriage and leads the parade, waving to everyone. He gets the parade started and sort of acts as the host of the parade."

Ben's mouth opens in surprise. "You mean he has to wave at everyone?"

"Yes."

"That's a lot of waving!"

"It is. But I know you'll be great at it, Ben." She and Les watch Ben and wait.

His face registers wonder and disbelief at the same time. "I would wave? Why would I . . ."

Maria steps forward to hug him. "The town voted for you, Ben. They want you to be the grand marshal of the Christmas parade."

He looks at Les and Les sticks out his hand for Ben to shake it. "The town got it right."

Ben grabs his head. "I need to tell my parents and Lucy!"

Les pushes the phone on his desk toward him. "Call them right now."

"Another thing," Maria says as Ben dials the number. "You get to have someone on the carriage with you. So you can think about which one of your family members or friends you'd like to sit next to you."

The very thought of choosing someone seems overwhelming right now and Ben shakes his head. "Mom!" he says into the phone. "Guess what just happened?"

When Ben hangs up the phone, Les waits for him to leave the office before picking up the phone and pushing a button. He winks at Maria and says, "Attention, all shoppers. It is my great honor to announce that our very own Ben Engler has been voted the grand marshal of the Christmas parade!" His enthusiasm is contagious as the employees and customers break out in cheers and applause.

Ben's smile feels like it's pulled up to his ears and if he could pop he would do it right here holding on to a bag of oranges.

"I voted for him," Gloria says, sneaking up next to Maria.

"You and most of the town," Maria says.

Grandon had written its own Christmas message and handed it to Ben.

Gloria waves off Les's offer to step into another line, looking exasperated with him. "Les! Don't you know me better than that by now?"

"It's just a suggestion for anyone who's in a hurry," Les says, straightening chip bags on an end cap.

"Congratulations, Ben!" she says, hugging him as he bags her groceries. "You will be the most handsome grand marshal the parade has ever had!"

"What about Mr. Wilson?"

Gloria laughs. "Oh yes, him too!"

She congratulates him again and pushes the cart to her car. Before closing the trunk she peeks inside each bag, looking for Ben's note. She pulls it out and closes the trunk, reading.

> *Everything happens for a reason. Christmas isn't an accident and neither is what is happening today.*
> *Merry Christmas! Ben*

She shakes her head and smiles, putting the note inside her coat pocket.

Cassondra raises her hand and Stacy looks at her. "What is it, Cassondra?"

"Where's Lauren?"

"I don't know. She might be running late today."

Cassondra looks over at the parking lot. "She's really late because we've been singing forever."

Stacy shuffles her papers, looking for the next song. "She might be stuck in traffic."

"For like six hours?" Aidan asks.

"We've only been singing for twenty minutes," she says. She doesn't tell them that she has already tried to call Lauren with no luck. Lauren was supposed to arrive at three o'clock today so they could meet at the gazebo along with Heddy and Dalton to figure out how the tables should be set up and where to put the risers. She tried calling at three-fifteen and then again at four-thirty.

At the end of practice Cassondra brings lyric sheets to Stacy and looks up at her. "Will Lauren be back tomorrow?"

"I'm sure she will. She might have gotten sick."

"I hope she doesn't get that stomach thing. Aidan had that and puked everywhere."

Stacy laughs, straightening the sheets Cassondra has given her. "I've heard it's pretty bad."

"Pretty gross," Cassondra says. "If she has that then we might never see her again."

Stacy assures her that they will see Lauren again, and as the children load into their cars for the afternoon she calls her number again.

Lauren ignores Jay as he waves good-bye to her at the end of her shift, just as she has ignored every phone call from Stacy today. Driving to her apartment she passes a church sign, which reads THE ANGEL TOLD THE SHEPHERDS NOT TO BE AFRAID. She stares at the sign as she passes. Was there really an angel? Did it really tell those shepherds not to be afraid? Did they realize they were part of an unfolding story? She tries to picture herself in that unfolding story but can only see herself in that booth at Jake's BBQ as the book slammed closed.

Nineteen

"Mrs. Delgado said that I get to have someone up on the carriage with me to wave during the parade," Ben says, cutting into a meatball.

Stacy sprinkles Parmesan cheese onto her spaghetti and Jacob spoons more sauce over his noodles. "That's awesome!" Stacy says. "You didn't tell me that part when you called."

Ben stops eating and puts his fork down. "When Mrs. Delgado told me about that, I knew who I wanted to ride with me right away, but I didn't want to hurt your feelings."

"It doesn't matter which one of us you want to take," Stacy says. "We're just crazy excited for you!"

Ben looks down at his food, tapping the fork on his plate. "Really, it's okay," Jacob says. "If you want to take your mom or Lucy that's great."

"Not me," Lucy says. "I don't want to do that!"

"It's actually not any of you," Ben says. His words come slowly, as if each one was handpicked.

Stacy and Jacob exchange glances. "A friend from school or work or church is great," Stacy says. "Who is it?"

"I don't know her name."

Lucy slams her fork onto her plate. "*Her* name? You like a girl? You have a girlfriend?"

"No, I don't have a girlfriend! She's not my girlfriend, Lucy!"

Stacy waves her hands in the air. "Okay, okay. It's all right. How do you know this girl, Ben?"

"She comes into the store."

"And you think she's hot!" Lucy says, shoving a huge bite of meatball into her mouth.

"No, I don't, Lucy!" Ben pushes his palm onto his head and leans on the table.

"Lucy, let him finish," Stacy says. "Go ahead, Ben."

Ben keeps his head down, not wanting to look at his sister. "She's new here and she always looks kind of sad. I thought maybe it would help her feel at home."

Stacy and Jacob look at one another again and smile. "But you don't know her name?" Jacob asks.

"There's never been time to really ask her. You know how busy the store is right now."

Stacy wipes her hands on a napkin and puts it back in her lap. "I think it's a great idea! The next time you see her you should ask her. Does she come in every day?"

He shakes his head. "I haven't seen her in a few days."

"The next time she's in you just slip away from bagging for a second and ask her," Jacob says. "But first . . . ask her what her name is!"

* * *

"Gloria, you cannot send her an e-mail," Miriam says.

Gloria rises to get more coffee. "Why not? Obviously we got the time wrong again. That's all."

Miriam closes her eyes and shakes her head. "Two times in a row? Gloria, can't you see it? We are just pawns in this girl's game. For all you know she was outside the windows taking pictures of us."

"Why in the world would she take pictures of us?"

"To prove to everyone that we're a couple of patsies."

Gloria screws up her face, pouring coffee into her cup. "How does a picture of us sitting at Betty's prove to everyone that we're a couple of patsies?"

Miriam waves her hand in the air as if erasing everything that Gloria has said. "You never understand anything!"

"No one in all of Grandon would understand what you're saying. We need to e-mail that young woman!"

Marshall enters the kitchen and raises his voice to get their attention. "Why are you arguing so early this morning?"

"Because she is batty and hardheaded," Miriam says.

Gloria gives Marshall an imploring look. "Does that even seem possible to you?"

"I'd like to stay married so I'll plead the fifth on that one." He slips his coat on and kisses Gloria's cheek. "I'm headed to the store." He looks at them. "Should I even ask what you're arguing about?" They open their mouths and he holds up his hand. "No, I shouldn't. But I know you'll both do the next right thing." Glancing at them again, he isn't so sure of that as he opens the garage door and heads to work.

"And the next right thing is to contact her," Gloria

says. "What if she's laid up in the hospital some-where?"

"What if she's been arrested?" Miriam says.

"Then the next right thing would still be to contact her!"

Miriam scowls, sighing, and reaches for Gloria's laptop on the table. "Let me contact her. I'm better with words than you are."

"You use words like 'scrummy' and 'kerfuffle'!"

"Exactly, Gloria. I am a woman of refinement," Miriam says, pulling up Craigslist on the computer.

Gloria looks over her shoulder. "Just keep your re-finement out of the e-mail."

Miriam looks at her. "Are we telling her that we know each other?"

Gloria shifts her eyes to the ceiling, thinking. "Yes. We need to let her know that we saw each other at Betty's, and after we got to talking we realized we were both there for the same meeting."

Miriam begins to type: *Unfortunately, it looks as if our time and place for meeting has been confused once again. We do hope that everything is tickety-boo for you—*

"Wait! Wait!" Gloria says. "'Tickety-boo'? Is that a cartoon character?"

Miriam turns her head slowly to stare at Gloria. "A cartoon character, Gloria? Are you mad?"

Gloria stands. "Am I mad? You just used the word 'tickety-boo' in an e-mail to a young girl who didn't grow up in England and who probably doesn't watch PBS."

Miriam begins typing again. *We hope that everything is going great for you.* She looks up at Gloria. "Happy?"

"Very," she says, sitting back down. "Keep going."

Gloria and I saw each other at Betty's and—

"Actually, she doesn't know me as Gloria."

"You didn't sign your name?"

Gloria hesitates. "I signed a name."

Miriam glares at her. "A name? What name?"

"Mary Richards."

"*The Mary Tyler Moore Show*?" Gloria nods. "Oh, that's rich, Gloria!" She deletes Gloria's name and continues. *Mary Richards and I saw each other at Betty's and because we have a close relationship—*

"That might be stretching it," Gloria says.

Miriam shoots her a glance and continues the e-mail.

we began to chat and discovered that we were both there to meet you. We are so sorry that it did not work out and hope nothing is wrong. Maybe you're getting ready for Christmas and no longer in need of a family. But if you are still looking for people to share your Christmas with, we would be happy to meet you.

She looks at Gloria. "I feel we need to make sure this is not some big game to this young woman."

Gloria purses her lips and narrows her eyes, looking at Miriam. "What do you mean?"

"We must question her sincerity." Gloria begins to answer but Miriam talks over her. "I know that it grates on you to think that anyone could have less than honorable motives, but this is not Mayberry, Gloria. It is the twenty-first century and we live in a very cynical world."

"Said the queen of cynicism," Gloria mumbles into her coffee cup.

Miriam crosses her arms and sits ramrod straight. "You call me cynical. I call me cautious. I call me wise. I call me—"

"Oh, for the love of Pete! Just write something!"

Placing her fingers on the keyboard Miriam types, talking aloud as she does. *"Please do not take offense at this but we must be assured of your sincerity. Are you looking for a family with an honest heart or is this a ploy or a ruse of some kind? We merely want to be assured that this is not a game on your part."*

Gloria rubs her temples as if plagued by an excruciating headache.

"What is wrong with you, Gloria?"

Gloria shakes her head. "I wouldn't blame her if she never wanted to meet us again."

"And this will inform us if we indeed want to try to meet her again." She types *Mary Richards and Laura* and positions the arrow over the send button.

"Wait! Who's Laura? Laura who?"

"Laura Petrie," Miriam says.

Gloria laughs. "Mary Tyler Moore's character from *The Dick Van Dyke Show*?" Miriam refuses to laugh. "Oh, we are quite the pair, aren't we?"

"Come on, Gloria! Should I press send?"

"Against my better judgment but yes."

Miriam clicks send and gets to her feet. "I need to run. I'm helping Dalton and Heddy pick up some final auction items."

Gloria groans. "That reminds me! I need to pick up the box that Frank was making for us."

Miriam reaches for her coat from the back of the chair. "Did you tell Cassondra about her box going to the dump?"

"No. But I will. I tried to tell Maria yesterday but she was about to tell Ben that he'd been voted grand marshal."

"Maybe Frank's box will bring in more money than Cassondra's," Miriam says, buttoning her coat.

Gloria puts the cups into the dishwasher and snaps it closed. "Maybe. But it was the spirit of the thing. She gave it with such a sincere heart and I thought for sure that box was meant for someone at the fundraiser."

"Maybe that box was meant for you alone." Miriam is pulling on her gloves, taking painstaking effort to make sure each finger is pushed as far as it can go.

"Why me?"

Miriam shrugs. "Who knows? Maybe Cassondra's giving of the box was to remind you to give like a child or have hope like a child."

Gloria walks her to the front door. "Listen to you being all deep!"

"You're not talking to a duffer, you know."

"I don't know what that means but I'm pretty sure I am."

Miriam bursts into laughter and opens the door.

Twenty

The air turned colder overnight and as Lauren drives to work that morning she finds herself thinking of Grayson, the little boy at Glory's Place who never wore a coat. "Not my problem," she says aloud. She decided last night that she would not go back to Glory's Place. She is embarrassed and disappointed and discouraged. She wanted so much to believe that there was a place for her somewhere, but the failed dinner with her mother has taken all hope from her. She is not up to facing Stacy, Miss Glory, Miriam, Holly, Travis, or even Ben at the grocery store. She isn't a part of their lives and can't pretend that she is.

When she arrives at work, the manager asks if she'd be interested in extra hours today and she says yes. Work just might keep her mind off her mother and the responsibilities that she's stepping away from in Grandon. She pictures Cassondra's mouth formed in that perfect *O* as she sings, but dismisses the thought. "Stacy doesn't need my help," she reasons.

On her break Lauren opens her e-mail and sees one from Craigslist. She is reluctant to read it but clicks it open anyway. As she reads the e-mail from Mary Richards and Laura she is confused to learn that they waited at Betty's for her to show up, even though Holly had told her that no one beyond the regular customers was there. She is interested to read that Mary and Laura know each other and doesn't blame them for questioning her motives. She doesn't respond but shuts her phone off, regretting having pulled strangers into the drama of her life.

Cassondra is sitting at her spot for rehearsal when Stacy arrives at Glory's Place. "She's not here yet," she says, watching Stacy take off her coat.

"Who's not here?"

"Lauren."

Stacy turns, looking around the room. Dalton, Heddy, Miriam, Gloria, and other volunteers are here but Lauren isn't among them. "I'm sure she'll be here and it is going to make her feel so good to know that you've missed her."

"She won't be here," Cassondra says, swinging her dangling legs.

"Why do you say that?" Stacy asks, placing sheets of lyrics on each chair.

"Something in my head told me last night that she left and she's not coming back."

Stacy stops what she's doing. "Of course she's coming back." She looks across the room toward the parking lot beyond the windows, watching for Lauren's car, and hopes she's right.

As Stacy leads the children through one song after another she gives Cassondra a wan smile. Lauren never returned any of her calls, but maybe she should have been more persistent about calling her. There has always been an unnamed sadness that surrounds her, and Stacy has wanted to be kind without being intrusive. Perhaps Lauren needs an intrusive friend. As the children sing she reaches for her phone inside her purse and quickly redials Lauren's number. It goes straight to voice mail. "Lauren, it's Stacy," she says, holding a hand over her exposed ear. "The kids are rehearsing and asking about you again. We're all hoping you're okay. Please call me back. Listen to them." She holds the phone out toward the children and records the chorus of "The First Noel" for her. "They're sounding great," she says. "Please call me."

As the final notes fade Grayson raises his hand. "Where's Lauren?"

Stacy shakes her head. "I don't know."

"Is she *ever* coming back?" Madison asks.

"Maybe she's a spy and got called out to a job," Isaiah says.

"She's not a spy," Landon says, pointing to his head. "She doesn't have a spy hat or the glasses or anything."

Stacy tries to regain control. "As soon as we contact her we'll ask if she's a spy, but for now let's keep singing so we can show her how good you've gotten!"

At the end of rehearsal Cassondra helps Stacy gather the lyric sheets. "So," Stacy says. "What's your head telling you now?"

"My mom was talking to my dad once and said that somebody they knew was like closed doors."

Stacy thinks for a second. "Did your mom say that someone was 'closed off'?"

Cassondra thinks, then shakes her head. "That

doesn't make sense. Closed doors makes sense because you can open and close a door. Lauren's got closed doors." She hands the papers to Stacy. "Can you get her to come back?"

She taps the papers on top of Cassondra's head. "I'm trying my best. I am determined to get to the bottom of this mystery!" She watches as Cassondra and Aidan and the other children gather their backpacks and coats to get ready for dismissal. Looking at her phone, she hopes a voice mail will be there from Lauren that she missed. There's no message and no text. *Open all the closed doors in Lauren's life, Lord, and bless all that you find inside!*

Stacy, Dalton, Heddy, Miriam, Gloria, and two of the volunteers are stacking chairs and spraying and cleaning tables when Travis Mabrey appears at the front door and waves to get someone's attention. "Your friend from the parks department is here, Miriam," Dalton says, trying to keep from smiling.

Miriam stiffens. "He is certainly no friend of mine. Gloria! Go see what he wants."

Gloria puts a fist on her hip. "And I thought that all of the children left for the day." Miriam shoos her with her hands and Gloria sighs, smiling at Travis. "Hi, Travis! I thought we sent the paperwork back for the gazebo. Didn't you get it?"

His eyes are scanning the room and Gloria looks behind her, wondering what he's looking for. "We did get it." There's an awkward pause and he sticks his hands in his coat pockets. "I was just wondering if Lauren has been able to practice at the gazebo and if it worked out okay." His eyes are still roaming the room and Gloria smiles.

"Stacy, could you come here for a minute?" Stacy

is putting on her coat as Gloria talks across the room to her. "Travis is wondering how the gazebo is working out for you and Lauren?"

"It'll be fine," Stacy says, a bit confused. "Lauren wasn't there but I took a look at it the other day and it'll be great."

Travis nods, glancing over her head. "Does Lauren need to see it?"

Stacy looks at Gloria, who's smiling like a Cheshire cat, and says, "Um. She should see it but she hasn't been here for two days."

He lifts the parks department cap off and scratches the side of his head. "Is she sick?"

"Nobody knows," Gloria says. "Stacy's called. I've called. She won't return any of our messages. I've even thought of calling Gordon's Grocery, where she works in Whitall, to see if she's there. We're very concerned about her."

Travis takes a step back toward the doors while pulling his keys out of his pocket. "Just let me know if I can help with anything!"

"Will do, Travis," Gloria says, waving as he leaves.

"He didn't seem to be too interested in what I thought about the gazebo," Stacy says, watching him get inside his truck. "That sure was helpful of you to let him know where Lauren works. You know, just in case he wants to call and talk about the gazebo." They look at each other and laugh. "What has happened to her, Gloria? Did something happen with her mom?"

Gloria shakes her head. "I wish I knew. I wish she'd open the door and let some of us in."

Cassondra's words echo in Stacy's mind and she prays for open doors again as she watches Travis pull away.

✳ ✳ ✳

Stacy walks inside Clauson's to let Ben know she's waiting in the parking lot. His line is long as shoppers wait for a message from him. She watches him chat with a customer as he bags the groceries and her heart swells. This isn't what she'd imagined for Ben when she was pregnant with him. She thought of sports and college and a good-paying job that would provide for his ever-increasing family. She and Jacob hadn't pictured long days at the end of a cashier's line and tossing canned tuna, grapes, and milk into plastic bags, yet through every doctor's appointment and stent adjustment for Ben, she has discovered that even broken dreams are a means of grace that she and her family may not have come to any other way. A year into this job and Ben is content and happy. She wishes again that she could be more like him: always hopeful, always observing, and always caring. He has taught her more about grace and hope than anyone, and her eyes glisten watching him. She waves when he notices her and he finishes bagging for the final customer in his line before clocking out and meeting her at the front of the store.

"How was your day, my love?" she asks.

"Good! We're getting busier." He zips his coat as he waves to the cashiers and the employees behind the customer service counter before exiting.

Stacy unlocks the car doors and as she gets in she says, "Did you see the friend you wanted to ride on top of the carriage with you?"

His face looks concerned. "No. I haven't seen her in a while."

"Well, some people only go to the grocery store once a week. Don't worry. She'll be back in."

Ben reaches for the seat belt and buckles himself in. "I hope so. She kind of seems sad to me."

Stacy looks at him. "I know a girl like that, too."

"What do you do for her?"

She smiles. "Probably not enough but I try to be kind and encourage her and I pray for her."

"That's what I do, Mom. I hope it works."

Twenty-one

Miriam opens the door to Thrifty Seconds, determined to find some last-minute discoveries for the silent auction. She makes her way through the aisle of home goods and picks up several pieces of artwork, glass vases, and dinnerware but nothing that is worth much. She moves into a section displaying furniture, but everything is worn out and tired. Hoping the book section will offer some hidden treasure, she takes several minutes to scan through the titles. Disappointed, she walks to an aisle that holds lamps and an array of knickknacks, then sighs when she sees the lack of prizes in this aisle as well. A pretty younger woman stands at the end of the aisle, and when she takes a step back, Miriam notices a wooden box and wonders if it could work as a replacement for Cassondra's. She walks closer to the box and reaches for it just as the other woman does.

"I'm so sorry," Miriam says. "Were you looking at that?"

The woman withdraws her hand and smiles. "Not really but sort of." She laughs at herself. "That didn't make any sense. This looks exactly like a box I gave my husband to take to his office. I got it for him because I thought it was one-of-a-kind, however, seeing this one makes me believe that it wasn't so unique after all."

"Did you want to get it? You were reaching for it first. I was just going to look at it because I was hoping it might replace a box that was inadvertently thrown away for a silent auction I'm helping with."

"No, no!" The woman picks up the box and lifts the lid. "I didn't know if I would buy it. I was just so curious when I saw it because it looks so much like the box I purchased a couple of years ago." She closes the lid and looks at the writing on the top. She shakes her head. "I remember it had this verse and everything." She hands the box to Miriam. "What is the silent auction for?"

Miriam holds the box and runs her fingers over the engraving on top. "Glory's Place. We hold a fundraiser each year but this year we're also having a sing-a-thon in the gazebo on the day of the parade. We'll have lots of silent auction items out there for sale. You should come."

"We make it to the parade every year. Our kids love it." She extends her hand to Miriam. "I'm Meghan Andrews."

"Miriam Davies. Lovely to meet you. Would you like to purchase the box?"

Meghan shakes her head. "No. You should buy it for the auction. As a matter of fact, could I purchase it for you? It'd be my donation to the auction."

"Of course! Yes! That's very kind of you." She walks with Meghan to the front of the store.

"Maybe I'll end up buying it on the day of the auction," Meghan says.

"That would be wonderful! We do hope to have it filled with lovely pieces of stationery and pens."

Meghan pays for the box and hands it over to Miriam. "I hope we get to see you that day and that it's your best fund-raiser ever!"

"Thank you, dear." She feels a tad awful that she has already forgotten the woman's name. "And thank you again for this lovely donation."

Lauren slides her card into the time clock and grabs her coat and bag from her locker. She has stopped checking her messages because she cannot bear to hear Stacy's and Miss Glory's voices asking her if everything is okay. She hasn't looked at e-mail, either. She smiles at Jay and one of the cashiers who catch her eye on her way out of the store, and is digging in her bag for her keys when the front doors slide open.

"Hi, Lauren."

She lets the keys fall back into her bag. "What are you doing here?"

"I was just driving through," Travis says. He looks at her and shuffles his feet. "Actually, that's not true. I drove here on purpose."

This is the first time she's seen him without his parks department clothing. He's wearing jeans and a flannel shirt and Carhartt coat. "Why?"

He sticks his bare hands into his pockets to keep warm. "Could we go somewhere else and talk?"

They are quiet inside the cab of his truck as Lauren directs him to a coffee shop just up the road. "Do they have real food in here?" Travis asks, turning into the parking lot. "I mean, besides crumpets and coffee, because I haven't eaten dinner and I'm . . ."

She laughs. "Yeah, they have sandwiches."

"That's awesome! I could eat a sandwich at every meal." He notices that she smiles and he feels more relaxed.

The coffee shop is filled with hipsters sporting beards, big glasses, knit caps, and flannel shirts, and Travis looks down at his own flannel shirt. "Do you think these guys will try to recruit me into their club?"

Lauren laughs, sitting down in a booth. "No. You have to have the beard and the right kind of boots. Your boots are clearly park department boots, not hipster boots."

He folds his hands in front of him on the table. "So how are you?"

She shrugs, looking away. "Fine. Busy with work."

He nods, taking a menu from the waiter. "A Coke is great," he says when asked what he'd like to drink.

"Same," Lauren says, avoiding Travis's eyes.

Travis keeps the menu closed and looks at her. "Nobody's been able to reach you, so everyone at Glory's Place is pretty worried."

"I've been so busy that I haven't been able to make it there."

"So busy that you can't even return phone calls?" The waiter returns and they place an order for a roast beef sandwich with Swiss cheese and a turkey club sandwich, each with a side of potato salad. "So what's up?" Not wanting to talk, she looks down at the table. "You seemed to really like helping at Glory's Place."

"I do like it," she says, glancing up at him.

"So why the big freeze?"

The Christmas Town

She feels her throat tightening and holds back tears. "I don't belong there."

He leans onto the table. "You don't belong at a place that helps children? I don't get what you're saying."

Tears are filling her eyes but she wills them back. "I thought things would be different if I helped but they're not. They're the same."

He's watching her, trying to meet her eyes but she keeps avoiding his. "I didn't think you knew anyone in Grandon. I thought helping at Glory's Place was new for you. How are things the same?"

His voice is low and kind, and despite Lauren's best efforts to keep them at bay, a tear sneaks down her cheek. "My mom is the same. I'm the same. My life is the same."

He wants to take hold of her face and force her to look at him, but instead he leans back, clasping his hands in his lap. "Of course you're the same. You're the person that everybody wants at Glory's Place."

She shakes her head. "I don't belong there."

"You keep saying that but I don't know what it means. Everyone there is wondering what happened to you. They told me they keep calling you. You were a huge help and now you're just gone. I know I'm a guy and I can be really stupid, but can you help a nonhipster doofus out?"

Lauren laughs and swipes the tear off her cheek. "You're not a doofus."

"I must be because I really don't get it."

She looks at him and smiles. "I wanted a family for Christmas. I've been in a lot of homes all my life, and even though a lot of them were great people, I never felt like a part of the family. When I was in Grandon

I began to feel like I was part of some kind of family. Then my mom contacted me and said she wanted to meet me for dinner a few days ago but she never showed up." The words are coming slower now and she shuts her eyes, holding them closed with her fingers, as tears squeeze out between the lids.

"I waited so long for her and she kept saying that she was coming and I believed her. I left the restaurant and realized that nothing has changed in my life. Everything is exactly the same." She uses a napkin to catch the tears and forces herself to look at Travis. His smile is soft as he leans forward onto the table.

"Your mom may be exactly the same but you're not. You're a rock star to those kids at Glory's Place. Miss Glory told me that they keep asking where you are and when you're coming back. It doesn't matter to them who your mom is or what she does or doesn't do. They love you. Miss Glory and Stacy love you."

"They don't know me."

He nods his head. "Oh, yes they do! They know that you show up. You care about kids who aren't even yours. You drive an hour one way just to help them. I don't know your mom but I doubt she is someone who would do that. And I worked with your dad and I know for a fact that he's not someone who would do that. You say that everything is the same, but actually, everything is different, mostly you."

She dabs her eyes with the napkin then looks at him. His voice and tone are sincere when he says, "You look like a raccoon," and she bursts into laughter. She uses the napkin to wipe underneath her eyes and looks at him again. He makes a face and quickly shakes his head. "You might actually be making it worse," he says, watching her rub away mascara and smear her eye shadow.

"Stop! I'm trying!" she says, laughing.

"First you ran away from me. Now I've made you cry. We're never going to get past the awkwardness to an actual first date."

She looks at him and her eyes are puffy and red and smeared with traces of black mascara. "You want to go on an actual first date?"

"Yes, if we could ever get past the running and the tears and the coffee shop filled with hipsters that make me feel awkward." She giggles as the waiter brings their food and sets it in front of them. "Well, would you actually go out on a date with me somewhere? Anywhere except this coffee shop?"

She laughs and nods, picking up her sandwich. "Yeah. I actually would."

"And would you pick up the phone and call Stacy or Miss Glory and let them know that you're alive and coming back to Grandon?"

She covers her mouth as she replies. "I'll tell them I'm alive."

"And that you're coming back to Grandon?"

She nods, chewing. "I was getting to that! And that I'm coming back to Grandon!"

Some things may never change but other things can be so completely different that they make the things that don't change bearable. Somehow, that's just enough to get her into tomorrow.

Twenty-two

Miriam walks into the office at Glory's Place and sets the box she purchased at Thrifty Seconds on the desk. She had wanted to show it to Gloria last night but she and Marshall were at an employee Christmas party for Wilson's Department Store. She is taking off her coat and hat when she hears a scream behind her, making her jump, clutching her chest. "What is wrong with you, Gloria? You should never walk up behind someone and scream!"

Gloria is holding the box and staring at Miriam. "Where did this come from?"

Miriam straightens her sweater and brushes off her slacks, still annoyed at Gloria. "I bought it yesterday, hoping it could be a replacement for the one that you lost." Gloria crosses to Miriam and grabs her face, kissing her on the forehead. "What is wrong with you, Gloria Wilson!"

"*This* is Cassondra's box. The one that was taken to the dump. Where did you find it?"

"I found it at Thrifty Seconds. Another woman was looking at it and it caught my attention. As a matter of fact, she bought it and donated it to the auction."

"You were in a thrift store?" Miriam nods her head in annoyance. "You always said that you felt like you were contracting hepatitis when you touched used merchandise."

Miriam ignores her and points to the box. "*This* is the exact box?"

Gloria lifts the lid and looks inside the box, smiling. "Yes! It had this *L* scratched into the wood and this same verse on top." She shakes her head in awe. "It wasn't taken to the dump. It was taken to the thrift store!" She looks at Miriam. "Miriam, I didn't think I would ever say this but you are an angel." Miriam rolls her eyes. "It's true! All this time I thought you were acerbic and pompous and really not much good for anything but I was wrong! You have single-handedly saved the auction for Cassondra. You are truly heaven-sent."

Miriam puts up her hand and walks to the door. "Charm does not suit you, Gloria! All you had to do was say 'thank you'."

Gloria sticks her head out the door and yells after her. "Thank you, Miriam! You're my hero!"

"That doesn't work for you, either!"

Gloria laughs and yells for Heddy, waving her into the office. "Look what Miriam found!"

Heddy's eyes are huge. "Where did she find it?"

"Okay, steady yourself . . . in a thrift store."

"Miriam was in a thrift store?"

"That's what I said! Yes, she was! This is the same woman who has never worn a used article of clothing on her body in her entire life or gone to a garage sale, but somehow she felt compelled to go to Thrifty Seconds!"

"It's a Christmas miracle," Heddy says.

They burst into laughter, and from outside the door they hear Miriam yell, "That's more like you, Gloria!"

They laugh harder as Gloria hands the box to Heddy. "Take this home and guard it with your life!"

Cassondra is the first to spot Lauren when she walks into Glory's Place and she runs to hug her. "Where have you been?"

"I got sidetracked," Lauren says, squeezing her.

"Are you on track again?"

"I hope so." Cassondra grabs her hand and leads her toward the rehearsal area.

"There you are!" Gloria says. "Is everything all right, babe?"

Lauren nods.

"She got sidetracked," Cassondra says.

"Well, that happens to me on a daily basis," Gloria says. She nods toward the rehearsal area. "The kids will be thrilled that you're back." She leans in, whispering. "You'll never believe it but Cassondra's box has been found!"

Lauren is amazed. "How," she mouths so Cassondra can't hear.

"A Christmas miracle," Gloria says, smiling.

Cassondra tugs on Lauren's hand, leading her toward several children, and they rush to her, giving her hugs. "I missed you guys," Lauren says. "How have rehearsals been?"

"We still stink," Caleb says.

Donna VanLiere

"I don't believe that's true," Lauren says. "Let me help Stacy get set up and then I can't wait to hear how far you've come!"

Stacy stops setting up the chairs to welcome Lauren. "I got your message," she says, hugging her. "We are so glad to have you back." She crosses her arms, looking at her. "Was it your mom?" Lauren nods. "It didn't go well?"

"She never showed up."

Stacy sighs. "I'm sorry. You could have called me."

Lauren knows that's true and wishes that she had. "It was just a bad night all the way around." She sits down and looks up at Stacy. "You're going to think I'm stupid but I put an ad on Craigslist asking for a family at Christmas." Stacy sits next to her. "Remember when I asked if you knew Mary Richards?" Stacy nods. "She responded to my ad and so did another lady named Laura. We tried to meet once before but it didn't work out because I was out trying to find Larry's house that day. So we set up a different time to meet and it was the night my mom wanted to get together for dinner. I tried sending them both an e-mail but it bounced back to me and when I called Holly at Betty's she said that they didn't show up."

Stacy is quiet as she processes it all. "You've been communicating with these two women?"

"Through e-mail."

"And they seem like honest, decent people?"

"I thought so but I'm not sure. They ask some really weird questions sometimes. They sound kind of crazy and unstable. I just can't figure out why neither one of them showed up."

"Have you heard anything from them?"

"They sent an e-mail. They wondered why I didn't

show up. I'm thinking they're just a couple of stupid kids who are playing games with me. I mean, if they were really going to meet me, then why didn't they show up? And what's with all the weird questions? They keep wondering if I'm a murderer!"

Stacy smiles. "Something does sound weird although it is possible they just got the time wrong."

"I don't think so. We made it clear when we'd be there. I just feel stupid because I believed that my mom would show up and I believed that those women would show up. I'm embarrassed I told you. I should keep that to myself."

"That's not embarrassing!" Stacy thinks for a moment and looks at Lauren. "If I had seen your ad I would have responded. My kids would love to have another sibling and Lucy always tells me I'm so bossy that I should have had ten kids!" Lauren laughs and Stacy pats her leg. "You are officially invited to our house for Christmas and I won't take no for an answer!"

"Thanks, Stacy."

Stacy hugs her and says, "Who knew a car accident could be such a great thing!" She looks at her. "Are you going to try to get together with the women again?"

Lauren shakes her head. "No. Now it's just weird."

At the end of rehearsal Lauren helps the children gather their things and put on their coats, making a special effort to help Grayson. "Where's your coat, Grayson?"

He shrugs, pulling the straps of his backpack over his shoulders. "At home, I guess."

She leans over onto her knees, looking him in the

eyes. "Heddy said coats were passed out in November. Where is yours?"

He looks sheepish and keeps his voice low. "Am I in trouble?"

"No! Not at all! It's just that it's been very cold and I never see you with a coat. You got one in November, right?" He shakes his head. "Why not?"

"I kept waiting to see if one had Spider-Man on it but none of them did. Then they were just all gone and I felt stupid and didn't tell anybody."

She puts her hand on his shoulder and squeezes it. "Grayson, Miss Glory would never want any of you to feel stupid. She would have had a coat in here the very next day if she had known."

He lifts his shoulders. "It's no big deal."

Lauren remembers being given coats or boots or gloves through local ministries and organizations when she was a kid and feeling awkward and ashamed. She looks up and smiles at Grayson. "It looks like your mom is here."

Several children hug her and wave good-bye and for a moment she can't remember sitting alone in a booth at Jake's BBQ and waiting for her mother. She just remembers the warmth of being loved here and the joy of tiny arms wrapped around her waist.

Twenty-three

"Well, how is she?" Gloria asks, stacking chairs on top of tables at the end of the day.

"I think she's okay," Stacy says. "Her mom didn't show up that night for dinner and that threw her into a tailspin."

"Poor lamb," Miriam says, wiping down the next table and spraying it with Lysol.

Stacy stacks chairs onto the table as Miriam moves to the next one. "On that same night she was supposed to meet two women for coffee at Betty's Bakery but they never showed up. That didn't help matters."

Gloria freezes and Miriam gasps. "What do you mean, 'she was supposed to meet two women'?" she asks.

Stacy moves to the next table and reaches to take the rag out of Miriam's hand. She bends over the table, scrubbing it. "Lauren put an ad on Craigslist looking for a family at Christmas." Miriam gasps again and her hand flies to her mouth. Stacy glances up at her. "I know. It's heartbreaking to think she was that lonely and desperate for a family. Makes me sad to think about it. She's so embarrassed and doesn't want anyone to know so please don't mention it." She picks up a chair to set it on top of the table. "But two women answered her ad. Somebody named Laura." Miriam makes a squeaking sound in the back of her throat like air being slowly released from a balloon. "And a woman named Mary Richards." Gloria hangs her head and shakes it. "They told Lauren they showed up but they never did."

Gloria hasn't moved from the spot she was frozen in moments earlier. "How does she know that?"

Stacy stacks the last chair on the table. "Holly told her." Gloria and Miriam stare at each other bug-eyed. "Lauren thinks it was some kids just playing a cruel joke on her."

"No!" Miriam shouts. "I'm sure it wasn't that!" Gloria pinches her arm and Miriam jerks it away.

"Who knows? It doesn't matter now. Lauren said they seemed kind of crazy and unstable. Kept asking if she was a murderer."

Gloria glares at Miriam. "I'm sure they're not unstable," she says.

"At least one of them isn't," Miriam says. Gloria pinches her again and Miriam pulls her arm away with a yelp.

Stacy puts the Lysol into the storage cabinet and closes it. "What do you mean?"

"We are—"

Gloria steps in front of Miriam, cutting her off. "Devastated for Lauren! I think we need to encourage her to set up another coffee with these ladies. Don't you think that would be a good idea, Miriam?"

Miriam looks ashen; her mouth is gaping open. "Oh, yes! I think that's a fabulous idea."

"She said she doesn't want to try to get together with them again," Stacy says.

"But it's Christmas!" Gloria says. "There could have been any number of reasons why they weren't there. Uh, plumbing issues or charity work or late-night choir practice."

"But they were there," Miriam says. Gloria turns to Miriam, screwing up her face. "In spirit! I just know they were there in spirit. I'm certain of it. I mean, I feel it very deeply that they were there in spirit and would want to meet with Lauren again. They would definitely want to be there in person." Gloria rolls her eyes and looks defeated.

Stacy crosses her arms, thinking. "You really think I should encourage her to try to get together with them again?"

Gloria raises her hand before Miriam can speak. "I do! I really do! She set out to find a family at Christmas and I truly believe that those two ladies are sincere. A bit daffy maybe—"

"Obnoxious," Miriam says.

"Overbearing and clueless," Gloria says, looking at her. "But sincere."

Stacy walks toward her locker, opening it. "You may be right. After all, they responded to her listing and have been e-mailing her. It seems like a really far-fetched thing to be a joke from young kids. Don't you think?"

"Absolutely! Definitely not a joke," Gloria says.

Stacy puts on her coat and zips it up. "I need to run and pick up Ben but I'll see you tomorrow!"

As she walks toward the door, Gloria yells after her, "Don't forget to talk to Lauren!"

"Let's make that meeting happen!" Miriam adds.

The door closes behind Stacy and Gloria turns to Miriam, throwing her arms in the air. "What is wrong with you?"

"I was very confused!" She rubs her arm. "And by the way, I am not a pincushion."

Gloria walks to her locker and begins to gather her things. "And I am not obnoxious!"

Miriam slips on her coat and pulls the collar up around her neck. "Why didn't we just tell Stacy the truth?"

"Because Lauren needs to know that someone saw her Craigslist ad and responded to it in all sincerity. You heard Stacy. Lauren is embarrassed and doesn't want anyone to know. If she knew that we knew all about this, then she would know that Stacy told us. If a meeting was set up she would think that we showed up out of pity just because Stacy told us."

Miriam pulls on her gloves. "So why can't Stacy know that we're Mary Richards and Laura?"

Gloria puts her hand on her hip, sighing. "Because when she tries to set up the next meeting it might come across as too forced. This way, she's a total innocent. I don't want Lauren to think that any of it was a setup."

"But it is a setup," Miriam says, slipping her purse strap over her shoulder.

Gloria pulls her hat on her head. "Of course. But nobody knows that except us. We simply must make her believe that we are her family!"

There have been no birthdays or holidays celebrated together, no track meets or soccer matches or dance recitals attended, but they are family. Lauren's happiness is fused with their happiness and her peace and joy are fused with theirs. Gloria and Miriam's joy cannot be complete until they share it with those who have no happiness or joy or peace. If they can't share their hope and love with someone at Christmas then why bother celebrating at all? To them it's what Christmas is all about and as simple as that.

Twenty-four

Gloria and Miriam sit at her kitchen table and stare at the computer screen. "Okay, now let's get this right," Gloria says. "How should we start it?"

Miriam nods, thinking. "Dear Kelly."

Gloria waits for more. "That's it? I could've come up with that."

Miriam pats the air in front of her. "Just hold on. I'm getting something good." Gloria keeps her fingers on the keyboard, waiting. Miriam nods. "We are not crazy people and would very much like to meet you."

Gloria shakes her head. "Just saying that we are not crazy people proves that we *are* crazy people!"

"Well, what is your idea?"

Gloria begins to type.

We are so sorry that we missed you again. Our hearts are in the right place and we truly would like to meet you. We can tell by your e-mails that you are a bright and sincere young woman.

"Oh, I like that," Miriam says. "That's good. Ask her if she can find it within herself to try one more time."

Gloria nods, typing again.

> *Christmas is our favorite time of year and we would be so honored if you would share it with us. We are not perfect people (as you are by now well aware), but we do have a lot of love to share, especially at Christmastime. Please forgive us for messing this up.*

"Technically, we didn't mess it up, Gloria."

"We need to eat some crow and fix this."

Miriam sighs. "I've never understood that expression. Sounds repulsive." She points to the screen. "Ask if she'd like to set the next date."

Gloria glances at her. "Good idea. We need to see if she really wants to meet. She shouldn't feel pressured to do it."

"But we do need Stacy to pressure her to set a date?"

"Absolutely."

Miriam shakes her head. "This is still very confusing to me."

"All of Grandon shakes its head at that revelation." Gloria finishes the e-mail.

> *Please let us know if and when and where you would like to meet again.*
> *Your friends (truly),*
> *Mary and Laura*

Miriam folds her hands on the table. "What if she doesn't reply?"

"She'll reply."

"But what if she doesn't?"

Gloria pushes send. "Why do you have to be negative? Let's just believe that she'll reply."

Miriam shrugs. "Okay. She'll reply."

Gloria closes the computer lid. "But what if she doesn't?"

Lauren watches as children arrive the next day at Glory's Place. When she sees Grayson and his mom walk into the building, she waits until he is all signed in and headed to his cubby. He stops when he notices a coat hanging on the hook inside. His face lights up when he picks it up. "Whoa!" Spider-Man's face is on the right shoulder and when Grayson turns the coat around, there is Spider-Man in midair shooting a web from his hand! "Awesome!" He looks up and notices Lauren smiling. "Did you see this?"

She nods. "I did. Try it on and see if it fits."

The sleeves are a little long but Grayson doesn't seem to notice. "Where did it come from?"

Lauren shrugs. "I told you that all you had to do was say something."

He runs to show some of the other boys as Gloria steps in next to Lauren. "That coat wasn't there when I got here a couple of hours ago." Lauren watches Grayson. "Now how do you figure that coat slipped into that cubby without my noticing?"

Lauren grins. "A Christmas miracle?"

Gloria throws her arms in the air. "Another one? What a red-letter Christmas this is turning out to be!"

With only two rehearsals left before the sing-a-thon the children's excitement ricochets off every wall inside Glory's Place. Dalton and Heddy have been

Donna VanLiere

busy the last two weeks finding red and green
scarves for all the children to wear on the day of the
parade. "Our treat," Heddy says, winking at Gloria.
Of course, all the children want to practice wearing the scarves during rehearsal and they shriek
and laugh, whipping the scarf ends at one another.
Lauren and Stacy try their best to maintain control,
leading their wiggling, giggling choir through each
Christmas song and carol as Gloria, Miriam, Dalton, and Heddy yell out "bravo, bravo" and "more,
more" at the end of each song. Cassondra's solo on
"Silent Night" brings tears to their eyes. They have
been graced (in Gloria's words because she doesn't
believe in luck) to work with these kids. They've seen
some families tear apart at the seams and others who
have mended themselves. They've watched as some
children have flourished while others have given up.
It hasn't been easy work, sometimes it hasn't been en-
joyable, but it has always come with its rewards: a
child who finally "gets" addition or division, one who
is put back into his home after a few months in foster
care, a single mom who lands a better job, a hug at
the end of the day from a child who'd had a melt-
down at the beginning, and a child's voice echoing
the sound of an angel as she sings.

Dalton and Heddy collect each scarf before the
children leave for home. "Don't worry," Dalton says,
smiling at their downcast faces. "We'll bring them
to the gazebo on Saturday and after the sing-a-thon
you can take them home." They hand each of the children a candy cane in place of the scarves and Lauren watches as Grayson carefully sticks his inside his
new coat's pocket and presses down to make sure the
Velcro sticks. He pulls the hood over his head and

pretends to release a web from his hand as he waits for his mom. When he sees her he runs as fast as he can and throws his arms around her. She marvels at his new coat and Lauren swears she can see his chest swelling inside it.

Gloria and Miriam work at wiping down the tables and chairs, Heddy straightens the front office area, and Stacy and Lauren begin to sweep as Dalton prepares the mop bucket. Lauren pulls her phone from her back pocket and Miriam grabs Gloria's arm. "She's looking at her phone!"

"Keep working," Gloria hisses, dipping her rag into the hot, sudsy water and wiping a chair.

They both bend low to the table, scrubbing the area in front of them over and over while keeping their eyes on Lauren. "She's moving," Miriam whispers, dunking her rag into the bucket of water on the table.

"I have eyes, Miriam! Move over, for crying out loud! We look suspicious!"

Miriam moves to the end of the table and watches as Lauren walks over to Stacy who's sweeping near the front door. Stacy holds on to the broom and leans over to look at Lauren's phone. Both of them look solemn, serious. "Are they reading an obituary?" Miriam asks.

"It doesn't look good," Gloria says, moving to a table closer to them. She cocks her head to make out what they're saying but Dalton's whistling is all that she can hear. Their faces are just too hard to read.

"They're laughing now," Miriam says between her teeth. "What does that mean? Do they think we really are nut jobs?"

Gloria glares at her. "You look like a puppet. Move

Donna VanLiere

your mouth before Dalton and Heddy think you're having a stroke!"

When Lauren moves away to finish her sweeping, Gloria and Miriam burst into activity. They keep their heads low as Stacy approaches. "Lauren has heard from the two women," she whispers. She continues to sweep as she notices Lauren looking over at them. Gloria and Miriam just catch each other's eye before stacking the chairs and assume that Lauren is answering their e-mail when they see her typing into her phone.

The door closes behind Dalton, Heddy, Lauren, and Stacy as they leave for the day, and Gloria locks it from the inside. She and Miriam scramble to the office where Gloria sits at the desk. "You have to pull up your personal e-mail, not Glory's Place's," Miriam says, twisting her hands in front of her.

Gloria begins typing on the keyboard. "I know that, Miriam!" They watch the screen load and Gloria clicks on an e-mail from Craigslist, reading aloud: *"Dear Mary and Laura, Thank you for contacting me. I really would like to meet you."*

"What a relief," Miriam says. "I was about to tell her the whole sordid story today."

Gloria continues, *"I will be in Grandon tomorrow and could meet you at noon at Betty's Bakery. Let me know if that works, Kelly."*

Gloria high-fives Miriam and then types *WE WILL BE THERE* in all caps.

Twenty-five

They watch for Lauren in Gloria's car across the street from Betty's. When her car pulls in front of the restaurant, Miriam reaches for her door handle. Gloria catches her arm. "Let her get inside and find a table."

"This wait is excruciating."

"I've had butterflies in my stomach all morning. This meeting has been running through my mind since yesterday. I put a piece of burned toast on Marshall's plate and called it breakfast. What would my mother think?"

Miriam looks at her watch. "It's 12:02!"

"Let's go!"

They lock arms and dart out to cross the road together, nearly getting themselves run over. A man honks and slams on his brakes as they laugh and hurry for the door. The restaurant is packed, the lunch crowd is in full swing, but they can see Lauren setting her things down at a corner table. They walk up behind her and Gloria puts her hand on her back. "Hi, Miss Glory!" Lauren says, hugging her.

"Hello, Kelly dear."

Lauren's smile fades and her eyes dart from Gloria to Miriam.

"We're so happy you replied to our e-mail," Miriam says.

"What?"

Gloria puts her hands on Lauren's shoulders, looking at her. "I'm Mary Richards and this is my friend Laura Petrie."

Tears spring to Lauren's eyes and she covers her mouth. "I don't . . ."

Gloria sits at the table and Miriam pulls a chair out for Lauren. "I saw your notice on Craigslist. I set out to answer you but someone thought I should be cautious."

"The news is filled with crazy people," Miriam says, slapping her hand on the table. "I thought I was responding to your ad in place of Gloria. I thought she had listened to me about not answering you but I should have known better. Since when has Gloria ever listened to me?"

Lauren places her fingers on each side of her head and shakes it. "You really are Mary Richards and Laura?"

Gloria nods. "Guilty as charged."

"When I was delivering the box to Frank that day, I kept calling here and asking Holly for Mary Richards . . ."

"She didn't see her," Gloria says. "She only saw the regular crowd, which includes us."

"And when I was supposed to meet my mom and Holly didn't see two women she didn't know . . ."

"Ta-da!" Miriam says.

"So you were here that night?" Gloria and Miriam nod. "Holly's never going to believe this."

"We were so glad that you decided to give us one more try," Gloria says. "But you didn't need to put an ad on Craigslist." Lauren looks confused. "You have a family right here in Grandon." She pats her hand. "You have me and Miriam and Dalton and Heddy and Holly and Stacy and that cute Travis Mabrey from the parks department." Lauren smiles and a tear sneaks its way down her cheek.

"We are imperfect people," Miriam says. She looks at Gloria. "Some are more imperfect than others, but we are closer to each other than we are to some of our own family. Dalton and Heddy are like siblings to me and Gloria is like a much older, dowdy aunt."

Gloria and Lauren laugh as Lauren wipes her eyes. "From the very first day I felt like you accepted me here."

"No," Gloria says. "You accepted us. Do you know how many people walk around with wounds and scars from their past and keep people at arm's length? Some people keep others at a distance their entire lives but you don't do that. God led you here to witness an accident and that led you to coffee with Stacy, which led you to helping with our fund-raiser and creating the sing-a-thon! None of that was us. That was you. Despite your past you've kept your heart open."

Lauren shakes her head.

"It's true," Miriam says. "It's much easier for people to shut down and close themselves off. Your Craigslist posting told us that this was a young woman who hadn't shut the world out yet. She was searching for what Christmas is all about."

"There were so many times that I felt so stupid for putting that ad on Craigslist."

Gloria hands Lauren a napkin. "Everybody wants to know why we're here, so we search for that answer. We want to know who we belong to so we search for those people and all the while God is whispering, 'Here I am.'"

"We search for something or somebody to believe in and for somebody to believe in us," Miriam adds. "It's what everybody wants."

"You searched for a family and we were all here right from the beginning," Gloria says. "Now all we have to do is get you to move here!"

Lauren laughs. "That won't be hard! I'm *so* ready to get out of Whitall."

Miriam thinks for a moment. "Who is Kelly, by the way?"

"My middle name. In case somebody I knew saw the posting on Craigslist."

She looks at both of them. "Who exactly are Mary Richards and Laura Petrie?"

"Oh, my!" Gloria says. "We have so many classic TV episodes to share with you."

"They're TV characters?"

Miriam nods. "From *The Mary Tyler Moore Show* and *The Dick Van Dyke Show*. Ironically, they're both played by the same woman and I'm not quite sure what that says about me and Gloria."

"It says that you think like me," Gloria says, winking at Lauren.

Miriam is horrified. Her back stiffens. "No. That's preposterous."

"It also says that I was right about answering the Craigslist ad from the beginning." Miriam's face is stony but her lip lifts into a curl. "Go ahead. Say I was right."

Miriam looks around the restaurant. "Who's ready for some nice tea and lunch? My treat!"

Gloria laughs out loud, looking at Lauren. "I'm afraid this is what you'll be dealing with in our family."

"It's okay. I'm kind of used to it already." Gloria and Miriam lift their heads to the ceiling and laugh out loud again. "I do wish I'd known you longer," Lauren says.

Gloria and Miriam put their hands on top of hers. "Families are built over time," Gloria says. "And you came along at just the right time."

The world is full of great sadness and loneliness, however here at this small Formica-topped table with its shiny metal napkin dispenser and sticky ketchup and mustard bottles, there is joy. Life can hurl a string of bad things our way and we can hurl a string of bad things at each other and ourselves, but home always calls to us. Tears of homecoming swim in their eyes as they laugh with the joy of being together. They are happy, in the sense of knowing that this happiness will be fleeting, as it always is, but that joy will live on long past this moment. The world can be cruel and offer good reason to give up hope but today proves that a corner spot at a coffee shop with unlikely family members can restore hope.

Twenty-six

Ben's line at work has gotten longer each day. Last night, he stayed up until eleven-thirty writing new messages.

My mom says the most beautiful mess she's ever seen is on the living room floor each Christmas! Enjoy the mess and Merry Christmas. Ben

Charles Dickens said to honor Christmas and keep it in your heart all year long. I think that's pretty good advice! Merry Christmas. Ben

For God so loved the world that He gave! Hoping you receive His gift at Christmas! Merry Christmas. Ben

Maria and her children, Cassondra and Aidan, spend several minutes waiting in line and Ben picks out a card for each one of them. "You don't have to give each one of us a message," Maria says. "You might run out."

"I'm all set, Mrs. Delgado," he says, handing both Cassondra and Aidan a card.

"And who's riding with you on top of the carriage in the parade?"

Ben reaches for the remainder of her groceries and puts them inside a bag. "I know who I'm asking but she hasn't been around in a few days."

Maria lifts her eyebrows. "But the parade's tomorrow!" She pats him on the shoulder and says, "If she doesn't show up there are plenty of people who would love to sit with you on that carriage!" She pushes her cart toward the exit doors as Cassondra runs ahead of her.

"Lauren!" Cassondra says, hugging her. "What are you doing here?"

"I kind of like getting a message from Ben and it's been a while so I was grabbing a water and a message before I head home." She smiles at Maria. "Hi, Mrs. Delgado."

"All they can talk about is the sing-a-thon tomorrow! They're very excited."

Lauren squeezes both Cassondra and Aidan to her. "I'm excited, too! It's going to be great!"

"I donated a box to the auction," Cassondra says. "I think it might bring in a thousand dollars."

Lauren grins, listening to her. "I've heard a lot about that box!"

"It's the prettiest box you've ever seen. Trust me."

Lauren laughs. "Oh, I do! I'll see you tomorrow, okay?" She waves good-bye and heads to a refrigerated case near the front for a bottle of water. She is disappointed to see that Ben is not here today. As she steps into the vestibule the opposite set of doors slide open and she smiles as Ben walks through them, zipping up his coat.

"I've been looking for you!" he says, throwing his arms in the air.

"And I was looking for you! I didn't get a message today." He reaches inside his coat pocket and pulls one out, handing it to her. "Wow! Thanks! That's what I call service!"

"Go ahead. Read it."

The vestibule becomes chilly every time the outside doors open so she zips her coat up higher as she reads.

> *The Christmas parade will not be the same without you. Would you ride on the carriage with me and wave at people and wish them a Merry Christmas? I only get to choose one person to help me and I know you'll do a great job! Merry Christmas. Ben*

She looks at him. "Really?"

He looks at the floor and then up at her. "I've been waiting to ask you for a long time. I haven't seen you in a few days."

"Why me?"

He shrugs. "I just thought that since you're new in town, this would be a great way for you to see the town and most everybody who lives here all at once, and that it'd be a great way for them to meet you!"

She laughs. "I'd love to! That's really nice of you, Ben. Do you do this every year?"

He shakes his head. "Nope. First time."

"I don't know what to say. Thank you! What time do I need to show up tomorrow and where do I go?"

They walk into the parking lot and he notices his mom pulling in and turning into the space where she normally parks as she waits for him. He begins to walk toward her. "Nine-thirty in front of the parks department building. We will be in the first carriage. Right in front of the parade."

She smiles, watching him walk away. "I'll be there! Can't wait!" Lauren opens her car door and slips into the seat, smiling.

Stacy's car is warm as Ben gets inside. "Well! I did it! I asked her to ride on the carriage for the parade." He is beaming, so proud of himself.

"Are you serious? So you saw her again? When?"

"Just now. When I got off work. I walked right through the doors and there she was."

Stacy puts the car in reverse. "With not a minute to spare!"

He looks sheepish. "If she hadn't shown up I was going to ask you, Mom. Hope you're not disappointed."

She laughs. "I get to be with you every day. So how did you do it?"

Ben crosses his arms as if he's being interviewed by the local news station. "Well, I walked out the doors and there she was and she said that she had come into the store to get one of my Christmas messages. So I pulled a card right out of my pocket and handed it to her."

Stacy pulls out onto the road, her face wide with surprise. "You put it on a card? What did it say?"

"I asked her if she wanted to sit on the carriage and smile and wave at people and say 'Merry Christmas,' that it would be a good way for her to see the town and for everybody in town to get to know her."

She slaps the steering wheel. "I'm so proud of you! What a great way to welcome someone to town! And you finally know her name! What is it?" Ben's face falls as he turns to look at his mom. "What's wrong?"

"I forgot to ask her her name."

They laugh all the way home.

Twenty-seven

By the time Lauren shows up at nine the next morning, the floats are lined up, and cars and trucks are parked along the road and on the grass of the parks department. She finds a spot farther down the road and hoofs it back to the parks department, looking for Ben. Her breath makes small clouds in the air and she pulls her scarf up over her mouth. Maria Delgado wears a bright red coat with yellow gloves as she directs a tractor pulling a long-bed trailer covered with hay bales. Football players and cheerleaders from the local high school each hold a red sack, no doubt filled with candy for the parade route. She spots Ben in front of a table at the hot chocolate dispenser and runs to catch him.

"Ben!"

"Lauren?" Stacy peers around Ben.

"Hey, Stacy! I thought you'd be at the gazebo."
She notices that Ben is wearing a white sash draped

from shoulder to waist, with red lettering that reads
GRAND MARSHAL.

Ben looks at his mom and Lauren. "You know each other?"

"You know Stacy?" Lauren asks.

"She's my mom!"

Stacy moves from the hot chocolate line, looking at Ben. "How do you know Lauren?"

"I met her at the store and asked her to ride on the carriage with me."

Stacy smacks her forehead. "You are kidding me! How did we not talk about this?"

"You told me your son worked at a grocery store but there are a lot of grocery stores and I just never thought about Ben being your son."

"I never knew you went to Clauson's," Stacy says.

"I went there the first day for something quick to eat and got a message from Ben, so like everybody else, I just kept going back for more. It was so awesome of him to ask me to do this."

Ben smiles and reaches for a hot chocolate, handing it to her. "I have a confession, though," he says, glancing at Stacy. "I never knew your name. Not even last night when I asked you to ride in the carriage for the parade."

Lauren bends over laughing, careful not to spill the hot chocolate. "That makes this even more awesome!"

When all the floats and bands are in place, Maria directs Ben and Lauren to take their places on top of the first carriage. A beautiful brown horse named Major has his own wreath of green around his neck and swags of evergreen decorate the simple red carriage. Ben and Lauren take their seats as Maria places a red wool blanket over their legs. "Remember! Wave and throw candy and wish everyone a Merry Christmas," she says, handing them two large red sacks filled with candy. "Thanks again for leading our parade, Ben!"

Lauren spots Travis standing in front of the parks department building and she waves. "Merry Christmas!" she yells, getting his attention.

Surprised, he waves as the carriage pulls away. "What's going on?" he yells after her.

"I'm riding with the grand marshal!" She is laughing and her face is bright and pink in the cold, which makes Travis smile.

People applaud and cheer as the horse pulling the carriage for Ben and Lauren approaches. She watches his face and remembers from science class in high school that we can't see light itself. We can only see what it lights up: a beaming point in a black sky, a candle's flame in a dark home, or a hand reaching out for us from the shadows on a moon-bright night. God lights up Ben and that light splashes onto everyone he meets. She listens as the crowd calls out to Ben; he isn't just some guy who works at the grocery store. He is part of this family. He turns to her, waving to people on her side of the carriage and his face is electric. He waves his arm in front of her, trying to get someone's attention. "Merry Christmas, Mr. Borroli!" He looks at her. "My old history teacher." He waves and shouts and throws candy as if his life depends on it. "Isn't this great?"

She waves with abandon, using both arms to throw out Christmas cheer for somebody who may be like she was a few weeks ago, looking for a place to belong, a place to call her own, looking for the light that beams from Ben's face onto everyone standing along the parade route. "It is so great, Ben!" she yells. They travel down Oak Street, then Fourth Street before the horse clip-clops its way onto Main Street. They will travel around the entire square, waving at shop-keepers, bankers, restaurant staff, firemen, and the librarians who have left the front desk to watch the parade. She hears her name coming from the crowd and smiles when she sees both Holly and Betty, in front of Betty's Bakery, waving and shouting at her.

She laughs out loud when the carriage approaches the gazebo and she sees the children from Glory's Place holding up makeshift signs made from lyric sheets that spell out W-E L-O-V-E Y-O-U L-A-U-R-E-N! Stacy, Gloria and Marshall, Miriam, Dalton and Heddy shout and wave the bright green scarves in the air as the carriage passes.

"What a great day!" Ben hollers, throwing candy to the kids.

Lauren shouts above the noise of the crowd. "It's the best day of my life!"

She had to park her car several blocks away and is out of breath when she arrives at the gazebo. The area is covered with parade onlookers who are now scoping out the silent auction items for Glory's Place. She smiles when she sees Gloria waving both arms over her head to get her attention. "We had no idea you were going to have such a place of honor in the parade today," she says, standing between two tables. "I always knew that Ben Engler was a brilliant, dis-cerning young man."

"It looked like it was great fun," Miriam says, ad-justing the bright green scarf around her neck.

Lauren smiles. "It was *so* much fun!" Someone squeezes her hand and Lauren looks down. Cassondra is adorable in a white fluffy hat with flaps that cover her ears and tassels that tie beneath her chin.

"I wish I could have ridden on the carriage with you!"

"That would've been great!" Lauren says.

"Look at our beautiful auction!" Gloria says, spreading her arms.

"I'm so sorry I couldn't be here to help you set up," Lauren says, looking over the items.

"Are you kidding?" Gloria says, moving out of the way of potential shoppers. "And have you miss the parade!"

Something catches Lauren's eye on a table, and as she walks toward it she can hear Gloria talking in the background but can't make out the words. She stops in front of the table and gasps. Cassondra opens her arms like a magician's assistant about to present the next bit of magic. "Isn't it beautiful?"

Lauren's face is solemn as her mouth drops open. "It can't be."

"Is something wrong?" Gloria asks, watching her.

Lauren runs her fingers over the lettering on top, muttering the words beneath her breath. "The Lord says, 'I will guide you along the best pathway for your life. I will advise you and watch over you'." Tears pool in her eyes as she reads the words over and over again. She opens the lid and feels a stream of tears sliding down her cheeks when she sees the letter *L* scratched into the wood on the underside.

"What's wrong?" Cassondra asks.

Lauren scoops up the box and kneels in front of Cassondra. "This was my box when I was a little

girl." Her voice begins to tremble. "My aunt gave this
to me when I was younger than you. How did you
get it?"

Cassondra doesn't know what to make of what
Lauren is saying. "It was in my doctor's office and he
gave it to me."

"And Cassondra gave it to me for the auction,"
Gloria says, looking at the box and then at Lauren. "I
knew it had a special purpose for the auction! I just
knew it!" She points to the box. "That verse wasn't
random all those years ago. God has been guiding
you and watching over you all along." Lauren stares
at the words, trying to put the pieces together.

"I kept dreams inside of it and I thought it would
be perfect for the auction," Cassondra says. She studies Lauren's face. "How can it be your box from when
you were little?"

Lauren wipes a tear off her face and begins to
laugh. "I think it's one of those Christmas miracles
that Miss Glory talks about. But I would never have
known about it if you hadn't donated this box to the
auction. You are a huge part of this miracle!" She
looks at Gloria. "You both are!" Cassondra beams
and throws her arms around Lauren's neck.

"And just wait until you hear Miriam's role in this
whole thing," Gloria says, winking. "This box was
meant to be here!"

Miracles occur in the most unlikely places and in
the most unusual ways. Sometimes, we just need to
get out of the way and let them happen.

If it is cold, no one seems to notice. The sounds of
Christmas ring out from the gazebo, echoing off the
clock tower of the courthouse to the steeple of the

church, from the rooftop of Wilson's to the doorway of Betty's Bakery. "Away in a Manger," "Winter Wonderland," "Joy to the World," "Rudolph the Red-Nosed Reindeer," "The First Noel," "Silent Night," and so many other beloved songs and carols fill that magnificent square with the reminder of the joy and promise and peace and miracle that is Christmas.

Lauren holds on to her box, unable to set it down for even a moment, and is surrounded by Gloria and her husband, Marshall; Miriam; Ben and his dad, Jacob, and sister, Lucy; Dalton and Heddy; Cassondra's mom, Maria, and her dad, Craig; and Travis, who is right next to her as they watch Stacy lead the children of Glory's Place through one glorious song after another.

And Lauren smiles in the midst of them.